ALSO BY LUCIA BERLIN

Welcome Home

A Manual for Cleaning Women

Where I Live Now

So Long

Homesick

Safe & Sound

Phantom Pain

Legacy

Angels Laundromat

A Manual for Cleaning Ladies

EVENING IN PARADISE

EVENING IN PARADISE

MORE STORIES

LUCIA BERLIN

FARRAR, STRAUS AND GIROUX NEW YORK

Farrar, Straus and Giroux
175 Varick Street, New York 10014

Printed in the United States of America
First edition, 2018

Most of these stories previously appeared in the collections *Angels Laundromat* (Turtle Island, 1981), *Phantom Pain* (Tombouctou, 1984), *Safe & Sound* (Poltroon, 1988), *Homesick* (Black Sparrow Press, 1991), *So Long* (Black Sparrow Press, 1993), and *Where I Live Now* (Black Sparrow Press, 1999). The foreword, "The Story Is the Thing," previously appeared in the journal *Square One*, no. 3 (Spring 2005).

Library of Congress Cataloging-in-Publication Data
Names: Berlin, Lucia, author. | Berlin, Lucia. Musical vanity boxes. |
Berlin, Lucia. Sometimes in summer.
Title: Evening in paradise : more stories / Lucia Berlin.
Other titles: Musical vanity boxes. | Sometimes in summer.
Description: First edition. | New York : Farrar, Straus and Giroux, 2018.
Identifiers: LCCN 2018002535 | ISBN 9780374279486 (hardcover)
Classification: LCC PS3552.E72485 A6 2018 | DDC 813/.54—dc23
LC record available at https://lccn.loc.gov/2018002535

Designed by Jonathan D. Lippincott

www.fsgbooks.com
www.twitter.com/fsgbooks • www.facebook.com/fsgbooks

10 9 8 7 6 5 4 3 2 1

CONTENTS

FOREWORD: THE STORY IS THE THING

MARK BERLIN

God bless her, Lucia was a rebel and a remarkable craftswoman, and in her day she danced. I wish I could tell all the tales, like when she picked up Smokey Robinson on Central Avenue in Albuquerque, smoking a joint, as they headed to his gig at the Tiki-Kai Lounge. She got home late, a little Chanel left under the scent of sweat and smoke. We went to a sacred dance at Santo Domingo Pueblo in New Mexico on the invite of a minor elder. When a dancer fell, Lucia thought it was her fault. Unfortunately, so did the entire pueblo, us being the only outsiders. For years this was our totem for bad luck. Our whole family learned how to dance on beaches, through museums, into restaurants and clubs as if we owned the places, through detoxes and jails and award ceremonies, with junkies, pimps and princes and innocents. The thing is, if I were to tell Lucia's story, even from my perspective (objective or not), it would be hailed as magical realism. There is no way anyone would believe this shit.

My first memory is of Lucia's voice, reading to my brother Jeff and me. It didn't matter what the story was because each night held a tale in her soft singsong blend of Texas and Santiago, Chile. Songs like "Red River Valley." Cultured, but folksy—

thankfully lacking her mother's El Paso twang. I am perhaps the last person to have talked to her, and she again read to me. I don't remember what (a book review, a bit from the hundreds of manuscripts people asked her to read, a postcard?), just her clear, loving voice, swirls of incense, wisps of sunset, both of us sitting in silence afterward staring at her bookcase. Just knowing the power and beauty of the words on those shelves. Something to savor and ponder.

Along with humor and writing, I inherited her bad back, and we would groan and laugh in unison or harmony as we reached for more Cambozola, a cracker or grape. Griping about medications and side effects. We laughed about the first precept of Buddhism: life is suffering. And the Mexican attitude that life is cheap, but it sure can be fun.

As a young mother she strolled us through the streets of New York: to museums, to meet other writers, to see a letterpress in action and painters at work, to hear jazz. And then we were suddenly in Acapulco, then Albuquerque. First stops on a life that averaged about nine months in any abode. Yet home was always her.

Living in Mexico scared her witless. Scorpions, intestinal worms, falling coconuts, corrupt police, and eager dope dealers; but as we reminisced the day before her birthday, we had somehow survived. She outlived three husbands and God knows how many lovers; doctors had told her at fourteen that she would never have children and wouldn't live past thirty! She bore four sons, of which I'm the oldest and most trouble, and we were all hell to raise. But she did it. And well.

Much has been made of her alcoholism and she had to struggle against the shame it brought her, but in the end she lived nearly twenty years sober, producing her best work and inspiring a chunk of the new generation with her teaching. The latter no surprise, as she had taught off and on since she was twenty. There were tough times, dangerous even. Ma would wonder aloud why no one came and took us kids away when it was really bad for her. I dunno, we came out okay. We all would have withered in suburbia; we were the Berlin Bunch.

Much of our experience is unbelievable. The stories she could have told. Like the time she went skinny dipping in Oaxaca on mushrooms with a painter friend. They freaked out when they emerged from the water, green head-to-toe from copper in the stream. I can only imagine how that looked with her pink rebozo!

I won't even try to describe the junkie recovery colony outside Albuquerque (see her story "Strays"), but imagine Buñuel and Tarantino doing a movie inside a movie involving sixty hardcore ex-cons, Angie Dickinson, Leslie Nielsen, a dozen sci-fi zombies, and the aforementioned Berlin Bunch.

My favorite memory is of a sunset in Yelapa glinting off Buddy Berlin's saxophone, swirls of bebop and wood smoke as Ma cooked dinner on a comal, her face radiant in the coral light, flamingos fishing, legs akimbo, in the lagoon outside, the sound of surf and pinging frogs, our feet crunching on the coarse sand floor. Doing our homework by lamplight and scratchy Billie Holiday.

Ma wrote true stories; not necessarily autobiographical, but close enough for horseshoes. Our family stories and memories have been slowly reshaped, embellished, and edited to the extent that I'm not sure what really happened all the time. Lucia said this didn't matter: the story is the thing.

Mark Berlin, Lucia's first son, was a writer, a chef, an artist, a free spirit, a lover of animals and all things garlic. He passed away in 2005.

EVENING IN PARADISE

THE MUSICAL VANITY BOXES

"Hear the instruction of thy father and mother, for they shall be an ornament of grace unto thy head and chains about thy neck. If sinners entice thee, consent not."

Mamie, my grandmother, read that over twice. I tried to remember what instruction I had had. Don't pick your nose. But I did want a chain, one that rang when I laughed, like Sammy's.

I bought a chain and went to the Greyhound bus depot where a machine printed things on metal discs . . . a star in the center. I wrote LUCHA and hung it around my neck.

It was late in June 1943, when Sammy and Jake cut Hope and me in. They were talking with Ben Padilla and at first made us go away. When Ben left, Sammy called us out from under the porch.

"Sit down, we're going to cut you in on something."

Sixty cards. On the top of each card was a tinted picture of a Musical Vanity Box. Next to it was a red seal that said DON'T OPEN. Under the seal was one of the names on the card. Thirty three-letter names with a line beside them. AMY, MAE, JOE, BEA, etc.

"It costs a nickel to buy a chance on a name. You write the

person's name next to it. When all the names are sold we open the red seal. The person who chose that name wins the Vanity Box."

"Hell of a lot of Vanity Boxes!" Jake giggled.

"Shut up, Jake. I get these cards from Chicago. Each one makes a buck and a half. I send them a dollar for each and they send me the boxes. Got that?"

"Yeah," Hope said. "So?"

"So you two get a quarter for every card you sell, and we get a quarter. That makes us fifty-fifty partners."

"They can't sell all those cards," Jake said.

"Sure we can," I said. I hated Jake. Teenage punk.

"Sure they can," Sammy said. He handed the cards to Hope. "Lucha's in charge of the money. It's eleven thirty . . . get going . . . we'll time you."

"Good luck!" they shouted. They were shoving each other over in the grass, laughing.

"They're laughing at us . . . they think we can't do it!"

We knocked on our first door . . . a lady came and put on her glasses. She bought the first name. ABE. She wrote her name and address next to it, gave us five pennies and her pencil. Precious loves, she called us.

We stopped at every house on that side of Upson. By the time we reached the park we had sold twenty names. We sat down on the wall of the cactus garden, out of breath, triumphant.

The people thought we were darling. We were both very little for our age. Seven. If a woman answered, I sold the chance. My blond hair had grown out twice the size of my head, like a big yellow tumbleweed. "A spun gold halo!" Because my teeth were gone I put my tongue up when I smiled, as if I were shy. The ladies would pat me and bend down to hear . . . "What is it, angel? Why, I'd just love to!"

If it was a man, Hope sold. "Five cents . . . pick a name," she drawled, handing them the card and the pencil before they could shut the door. They said she had spunk and pinched her dark bony cheeks. Her eyes glared at them through her heavy black veil of hair.

We were concerned now only with time. It was hard to tell when people were home or not. Cranking the doorbell handles, waiting. Worst of all was when we were the only visitors in "ever so long." All of these people were very old. Most of them must have died a few years later.

Besides the lonely people and the ones who thought we were darling, there were some . . . two that day . . . who really felt it was an omen to open the door and be offered a chance, a choice. They took up the most time, but we didn't mind . . . waited, breathless too, while they talked to themselves. Tom? That darn Tom. Sal. My sister called me Sal. Tom. Yes, I'll take Tom. What if it wins??

We didn't even go to the houses on the other side of Upson. We sold the rest in the apartments across from the park.

One o'clock. Hope handed the card to Sammy, I poured the money onto his chest. "Christ!" Jake said.

Sammy kissed us. We were flushed, grinning on the lawn.

"Who won?" Sammy sat up. The knees of his Levi's were green and wet, his elbows green from the grass.

"What does it say?" Hope couldn't read. She had flunked first grade.

ZOE.

"Who?" We looked at each other . . . "Which one was that?"

"It's the last one on the card."

"Oh." The man with the ointment on his hands. Psoriasis. We were disappointed, there were two really nice people we had wanted to win.

Sammy said we could keep the cards and money until we

had sold them all. We took them over the fence and under the porch. I found an old breadbox to keep them in.

We took three cards and left through the alley, in back. We didn't want Sammy and Jake to think we were too eager. We crossed the street, ran from house to house, knocking on doors, all the way down the other side of Upson. All down one side of Mundy to the Sunshine Grocery.

We had sold two whole cards . . . sat on the curb drinking grape soda. Mr. Haddad kept bottles for us in the freezer, so it came out slushy . . . like melted popsicles. The buses had to make a narrow turn at the corner, just missing us, honking. Behind us the dust and smoke rose around Cristo Rey Mountain, yellow foam in the Texas afternoon sun.

I read the names aloud—over and over. We put Xs by the ones we hoped would win . . . Os by the bad ones.

The barefoot soldier . . . "I NEED a Musical Vanity Box!" Mrs. Tapia . . . "Well, come in! Good to be seeing you!" A girl sixteen, just married, who had showed us how she painted the kitchen pink, herself. Mr. Raleigh—spooky. He had called off two Great Danes, had called Hope a sexy runt.

"You know . . . we could sell a thousand names a day . . . if we had roller skates."

"Yeah, we need roller skates."

"You know what's wrong?"

"What?"

"We always say . . . 'Do you want to buy a chance?' We should say 'chances.'"

"How about . . . 'Want to buy a whole card?'"

We laughed, happy, sitting on the curb.

"Let's sell the last one."

We went around the corner, the street below Mundy. It was dark, matted with eucalyptus and fig and pomegranate trees, Mexican gardens, ferns and oleander and zinnias. The old women didn't speak English. "*No, gracias,*" shutting the doors.

The priest from Holy Family bought two names. JOE and FAN.

There was a block then of German women, flour on their hands. They slammed the doors. Tsch!

"Let's go home . . . this isn't any good."

"No, up by Vilas School there are lots of soldiers."

She was right. The men were outside in khakis and T-shirts, watering yellow Bermuda grass and drinking beer. Hope sold. Her hair stuck now in strings over her olive Syrian face, like a black bead curtain.

One man gave us a quarter and his wife called him before he got his change. "Give me five!" he yelled through the screen door. I started to write his name.

"No," Hope said. "We can sell them again."

Sammy opened the seals.

Mrs. Tapia had won with SUE, her daughter's name. We had an X by her, she was so nice. Mrs. Overland won the next. Neither of us could remember who she was. The third winner was a man who bought LOU, which really should have gone to the soldier who gave us the quarter.

"We should give it to the soldier," I said.

Hope lifted up her hair to look at me, almost smiling . . . "Okay."

I jumped the fence to our yard. Mamie was watering. My mother was playing bridge, my dinner was in the oven. I read Mamie's lips over the H. V. Kaltenborn news from indoors. Grandpa wasn't deaf, he just turned it up loud.

"Can I water for you, Mamie?" No thanks.

I banged the front door rippling stained glass on the wall. "Git in here!" he yelled over the radio. Surprised, I ran in smiling, started to climb into his lap, but he rustled me away with a clipped-out paper.

"You been with those dirty A-rabs?"

"Syrians," I said. His ashtray glowed red like the stained-glass door.

That night . . . Fibber McGee and Amos and Andy on the radio. I don't know why he liked them so much. He always said he hated colored people.

Mamie and I sat with the Bible in the dining room. We were still on Proverbs.

"Open rebuke is better than secret love."

"Why?"

"Never mind." I fell asleep and she put me to bed.

I woke when my mother got home . . . lay awake beside her while she ate Cheese Tid-Bits and read a mystery. Years later, I figured out that during World War II alone my mother ate over 950 boxes of Cheese Tid-Bits.

I wanted to talk to her, tell her about Mrs. Tapia, the guy with the dogs, how Sammy had cut us in fifty-fifty. I put my head down on her shoulder, Cheese Tid-Bit crumbs, and fell asleep.

The next day Hope and I went first to the apartments on Yandell Avenue. Young army wives in curlers, chenille bathrobes, mad because we woke them. None of them bought a chance. "No, I *don't* have a nickel."

We took a bus to the Plaza, transferred to a Mesa bus to Kern Place. Rich people . . . landscaping, chimes on the doors. This was even better than the old ladies. Texan Junior League, tanned, Bermuda shorts, lipstick and June Allyson pageboys. I don't think they had ever seen children like us, children dressed in their mothers' old crepe blouses.

Children with hair like ours. While Hope's hair ran down her face like thick black tar, mine stood up and out like a tufted yellow beach ball, crackling in the sun.

They always laughed when they found out what we were selling, went to find some "change." We heard one of them talking to her husband . . . "Just come and see them. Actual urchins!" He did come, and he was the only one who bought a chance. The women just gave us money. Their children stared at us, pale, from their swing sets.

"Let's go to the depot."

We used to go there even before the cards . . . to hang around and watch everybody kissing and crying, to pick up dropped change beneath the ledge under the newsstand. As soon as we got in the door we poked each other, giggling. *Why* hadn't this ever occurred to us? Millions of people with nickels and nothing to do but wait. Millions of soldiers and sailors who had a girl or a wife or a child with a three-letter name.

We made out a schedule. In the mornings we went to the train station. Sailors stretched out on the wooden benches, hats folded over their eyes, like parentheses. "Huh? Oh, morning, sweethearts! Sure."

Old men sitting. Paying a nickel to talk about the other war, about some dead person with a three-letter name.

We went into the COLORED waiting room, sold three names before a white conductor pushed us out by our elbows. We spent afternoons at the USO across the street. The soldiers gave us free lunch, stale ham-and-cheese sandwiches wrapped in wax paper, Cokes, Milky Ways. We played ping-pong and pinball machines while the soldiers filled out the cards. Once we made a quarter each punching the little counter that kept track of how many servicemen came in while the woman that did that went somewhere with a sailor.

New soldiers and sailors kept coming in with each train.

The ones who were already there told them to buy our chances. They called me Heaven; and Hope, Hell.

The plan had been to keep all sixty cards until they were sold but we kept getting more and more money and extra tip money and couldn't even count it.

We couldn't wait to see who had won anyway, even though there were only ten cards left. We took the three cigar boxes of money and the cards to Sammy.

"Seventy dollars?" Jesus Christ. They both sat up in the grass. "Crazy damn kids. They did it."

They kissed and hugged us. Jake rolled over and over, holding his stomach, squealing, "Jesus . . . Sammy you are a genius, a mastermind!"

Sammy hugged us. "I knew you could do it."

He looked through all the cards, running his hand through his long hair, so black it always looked wet. He laughed at the names that had won.

PFC Octavius Oliver, Fort Sill, Oklahoma. "Hey, where'd you *find* these cats?" Samuel Henry Throper, Anywhere, USA. He was an old man in the COLORED part who said we could have the Vanity Box if he won.

Jake went to the Sunshine Grocery and brought us drippy banana popsicles. Sammy asked us about all the names, about how we did it. We told him about Kern Place and the pretty housewives in chambray shirtdresses, about the USO, about the pinball machines, the dirty man with the Great Danes.

He gave us seventeen dollars . . . more than fifty-fifty. We didn't even take a bus, just ran downtown to Penney's. Far. We bought skates and skate keys, charm bracelets at Kress and a bag of red salted pistachio nuts. We sat by the alligators in the Plaza . . . Soldiers, Mexicans, winos.

Hope looked around . . . "We could sell here."

"No, nobody's got money here."

"But us!"

"Worst part will be delivering the Musical Vanity Boxes."

"No, because now we have skates."

"Tomorrow let's learn to skate . . . hey we can even skate down the viaduct and watch the slag at the smelter."

"If the people aren't home we can just leave them inside the screen door."

"Hotel lobbies would be a good place to sell."

We bought drippy Coney Islands and root beer floats to go. That was the end of the money. We waited to eat until we got to the vacant lot at the beginning of Upson.

The lot was on top of a walled hill, high above the sidewalk, overgrown with fuzzy gray plants that had purple blossoms. Between the plants all over the lot was broken glass dyed to different shades of lavender by the sun. At that time of day, late afternoon, the sun hit the lot at an angle so that the light seemed to come from beneath, from inside the blossoms, the amethyst stones.

Sammy and Jake were washing a car. A blue jalopy with no roof and no doors. We ran the last block, the skates thumping inside the boxes.

"Whose is it?"

"Ours, want a ride?"

"Where'd you get it?"

They were washing the tires. "From a guy we know," Jake said. "Want a ride?"

"Sammy!"

Hope was standing up on the seat. She looked like she was crazy. I didn't understand yet.

"Sammy—where'd you get the money for this car?"

"Oh, here and there . . ." Sammy grinned at her, drank from the hose and wiped his chin with his shirt.

"Where did you get the money?"

Hope looked like an ancient old pale yellow witch. "You cheating motherfucker!" she screamed.

Then I understood. I followed her over the fence and under the porch.

"Lucha!" Sammy, my first hero, called, but I followed her to where she squatted by the breadbox.

She handed me the stack of filled cards. "Count them." It took a long time.

Over five hundred people. We looked over the ones we had put Xs by, hoping that they would win.

"We could buy Musical Vanity Boxes for some of them . . ."

She sneered. "With what money? There is no such thing as a Musical Vanity Box anyway. You ever hear of a Musical Vanity Box before?"

She opened the breadbox and took out the ten unsold cards. She was crazy, groveling in the dust under the porch like a dying chicken.

"What are you doing, Hope?"

Panting, she crouched in the honeysuckle opening to the yard. She held up the cards, like the fan of a mad queen.

"They're mine now. You can come. Fifty-fifty. Or you can stay. If you come it means you are my partner and you can't ever talk to Sammy again the rest of your life or I'll murder you with a knife."

She left. I lay down in the damp dirt. I was tired. I just wanted to lie there, forever, and never do anything at all.

I lay there a long time and then I climbed over the wooden fence to the alley. Hope was sitting on the curb at the corner, her hair like a black bucket over her head. Bent, like a Pietà.

"Let's go," I said.

We walked up the hill toward Prospect. It was evening . . .

all the families were outside watering the grass, murmuring from porch swings that creaked as rhythmically as the cicadas.

Hope banged a gate behind us. We walked up the wet concrete path toward the family. Iced tea, sitting on the steps, the stoop. She held out a card.

"Pick a name. Ten cents a chance."

We started out early the next morning with the rest of the cards. We said nothing about the new price, about the six we had sold the night before. Most of all we said nothing about our skates . . . for two years we'd been hoping for skates. We hadn't even tried them on yet.

When we got off the bus at the Plaza, Hope repeated that she'd kill me if I ever spoke to Sammy again.

"Never. Want blood?" We were always cutting our wrists and sealing promises.

"No."

I was relieved. I knew I would talk to him someday and without blood it wouldn't be so bad.

The Gateway Hotel, like a jungle movie. Spittoons, clicking punkahs, palm trees, even a man in a white suit, fanning himself like Sydney Greenstreet. They all waved us away, rattled their faces back behind their papers as if they knew about us. People like the anonymity of hotels.

Outside, across the heat-sinking tar of the street to catch a trolley for Juarez. Mexicans in *rebozos*—smelling like American paper bags and Kress candy corn, yellow-orange.

Unfamiliar territory . . . Juarez. I knew only the fountained mirrored bars, the "Cielito Lindo" guitar players of my mother's war-widow nights out with the "Parker girls." Hope only knew the dirty-donkey movies. Mrs. Haddad always sent her along on Darlene's dates with soldiers, so everything would be okay.

We stayed at the Juarez end of the bridge, leaning like the taxi drivers, the wooden snake sellers against the shade of the Follies Bar, padding forward as they did when the clusters of tourists, bobbing boy-soldiers came off the bridge.

Some smiled at us, anxious to be charmed, to be charming. Too hurried and awkward to look at our cards, shoving us pennies, nickels, dimes. "Here!" We hated them, as if we had been Mexicans.

By late afternoon the soldiers and tourists squirted off the ramp, clattering onto the sidewalk into the slow hot wind of black tobacco and Carta Blanca beer, flushed, hopeful . . . what will I see? They gushed past us, pushing pennies nickels into our fists without ever looking at the upheld cards or into our eyes.

We were reeling, giddy from the nervous laughter, from the lurching out, darting out of the way. We laughed, bold now, like the wooden snake and clay pig sellers. Insolent, we stood in their way, tugging at them. "Come on, only a dime . . . Buy a name, ten cents . . . Hey rich lady, a lousy dime!"

Dusk. Tired and sweaty. We leaned against the wall to count the money. The shoeshine boys watched us, mocking, even though we had made six dollars.

"Hope, let's throw the cards into the river."

"What, and just beg like these sick bums?" She was furious. "No, we're going to sell every name."

"We've got to eat sometime."

"Right." She called to one of the street boys . . . "*Oye*, where can we eat?"

"Eat *mierda*, gringa."

We got off the main street of Juarez. You could look back at it, hear it, smell it, like a huge polluted river.

We began to run. Hope was crying. I had never seen her cry.

We ran like goats, like colts, heads lowered clopping clopping over the mud sidewalks, loping then, muffled. Sidewalks hard red dirt.

Down some adobe steps into the Gavilán Café.

In El Paso, those days, 1943, you heard a lot about war. My grandfather pasted Ernie Pyle into scrapbooks all day, Mamie prayed. My mother was a Gray Lady at the hospital, played bridge with the wounded. She brought blind or one-armed soldiers home to dinner. Mamie read to me from Isaiah about how someday everybody would beat their swords into plowshares. But I hadn't thought about it. I had simply missed and glorified my father, who was a lieutenant somewhere overseas . . . Okinawa. A little girl, I first thought about the war when we went into the Gavilán Café. I don't know why, I just remember thinking then about the war.

It seemed everyone in the Gavilán Café was a brother, or a cousin, a relative, even though they sat apart at tables or at the bar. A man and a woman, arguing and touching. Two sisters flirting over their mother's back. Three lean brothers in denim work clothes, stooped with the same falling brother lock of hair over their tequilas.

It was dark cool and quiet although everyone was talking and someone was singing. The laughter was unstrained, private, intimate.

We sat on stools at the bar. A waitress came over, carrying a tray with a blue-and-purple peacock on it. Her black-rooted hennaed hair was piled into wavy mounds, caught with combs of gold and carved silver and broken mirrors. Fuchsia enlarged mouth. Green eyelids . . . a crucifix of blue-and-green butterfly wings sparkled between her conic yellow satin breasts. "*¡Hola!*" She smiled. Brilliance of gold-capped teeth, red gums. Dazzling Bird of Paradise!

"*¿Qué quieren, lindas?*"

"Tortillas," Hope said.

The lady-bird waitress leaned forward, dusting crumbs away with blood-red nails, murmuring to us still in her green Spanish.

Hope shook her head . . . "*No sé.*"

"*¿Son gringas?*"

"No." Hope pointed to herself. Syrian. She spoke then in Syrian and the waitress listened, her fuchsia mouth moving with the words. "Eh!"

"*She's* a *gringa*," Hope said about me. They laughed. I envied their dark languages, their dark eyes.

"*¡Son gringas!*" the waitress told the people in the café.

An old man came over to us, carrying his glass and a Corona beer bottle. Straight . . . standing, walking straight and Spanish in a white suit. His son followed in a black zoot suit, dark glasses, watch chain. This was bebop time, *pachuco* time . . . The son's shoulders were stooped, in fashion, head lowered to the level of his father's pride.

"What's your name?"

Hope gave him her Syrian name . . . Sha-a-hala. I gave him the name the Syrians called me . . . Luchaha. Not Lucía or Lucha but Lu-cha-a. He told everybody our names.

The waitress was named Chata, because her nose turned up like a rain pipe. Literally, it means "squat." Or "bedpan." The old man was Fernando Velasquez and he shook hands with us.

Having greeted us, the people in the café ignored us as before, accepting us with their easy indifference. We could have leaned against any of them and fallen asleep.

Velasquez took our bowls of green chili over to a table. Chata brought us lime sodas.

He had learned English in El Paso where he worked. His son worked there too in construction.

"*Oye, Raúl . . . diles algo* . . . He speaks good English."

The son remained standing, elegant behind his father. His cheekbones shone amber above a bebop beard.

"What are you kids doing over here?" the father asked.

"Selling."

Hope held up the stack of cards. Fernando looked at them, turned each of them over. Hope went into her sales pitch about the Vanity Boxes . . . "The name that wins gets a Musical Vanity Box."

"*Válgame Dios* . . ." He took the card over to the next table, explained it, gesturing, banging on the table. They all looked at the card and at us, uncertainly.

A woman in a bandana turban beckoned to me. "*Oye*, somebody wins the boxes, no?"

"*Sí*."

Raúl had moved over, silent, to pick up one of the cards, looked down at me. His eyes were white through his dark glasses.

"Where are the *boxes*?"

I looked at Hope.

"Raúl . . ." I said. "Of *course* there are no Musical Vanity Boxes. The person that wins the name wins all of the *money*."

He bowed to me, with the grace of a matador. Hope bowed her wet head and cussed in Syrian. In English she said, "Why did we never think of that?" She smiled at me.

"Okay, *chulita* . . . give me two names."

Velasquez was explaining the game to people at the tables, Chata to a group of men at the bar with strong wet backs. They shoved two tables into ours. Hope and I sat at each end. Raúl stood in back of me. Chata poured beer for everyone seated around the table, like at a banquet.

"*¿Cuánto es?*"

"Un quarter."

"*No tengo . . . ¿un peso?*"

"Okay."

Hope stacked the money in a pile in front of her. "Hey . . . *we* still get our quarter cut." Raúl said that was fair. Her eyes glittered under eyeshade bangs. Raúl and I wrote down the names.

The names themselves were more fun in Spanish, nobody could say them right and kept laughing. BOB. Spilt beer. It took only three minutes to fill one card. Raúl opened the seal. Ignacio Sanchez won with TED. *Bravo!* Raúl said he'd made just about the same amount working all day. With a flourish, Ignacio scattered the coins and crumpled bills onto Chata's peacock tray. *¡Cerveza!*

"Wait a minute . . ." Hope took out our quarter cut.

Two peddlers had come in, pulled chairs up to the table.

"*¿Qué pasa?*"

They sat with straw baskets in their laps. "*¿Cuánto es?*"

"*Un peso* . . . un quarter."

"Let's make it two," Raúl said. "*Dos pesos*, fifty cents." The new men with the baskets couldn't afford it, so everyone decided they could go for one this time since they were new. They each put in a peso on the pile. Raúl won. The men got up and left without even having a beer.

By the time we had sold out four cards everyone was drunk. None of the winners had kept their money, just bought more chances, more food, tequila now.

Most of the losers left. We all ate tamales. Chata carried the tamales in a washtub, a casserole of beans we dipped into with hot tortillas.

Hope and I went to the outhouse behind the café. Stumbling, shielding the candle Chata had lent us.

Yawn . . . it makes you pensive, reflexive, to pee, like New Year's.

"Hey, what time is it?"

"Oh."

It was almost midnight. Everyone in the Gavilán Café kissed us good-bye. Raúl took us to the bridge, holding each of our tiny hands. Gentle, like the pull of a dowser's branch, drawing our bony bodies into the *pachuco* beat of his walk, so light, slow, swinging.

Under the bridge, on the El Paso side, were the shoeshine hustlers we had seen that afternoon, standing in the muddy Rio Grande, holding up cones to catch money in, digging in the mud for it if it fell. Soldiers were throwing pennies, gum wrappers. Hope went over to the rail. "*¡Hola, pendejos!*" she hollered and threw them all our quarters. Fingers back. Laughter.

Raúl put us in a taxi and paid the driver. We waved to him out the back window, watched him walk, swinging toward the bridge. Spring onto the ramp like a deer.

Hope's father started beating her the minute she got out of the taxi, whipped her up the stairs with a belt, screaming in Syrian.

No one was home but Mamie, kneeling for my safe return. The taxi upset her more than Juarez. She never went anywhere in a taxi without a bag of black pepper in case of attack.

In bed. Pillows behind me. She brought me custard and cocoa, the food she served to the sick or the damned. Custard melted like a communion wafer in my mouth. The blood of her forgiving love I drank while she stood there, praying in a pink angel gown, at the foot of my bed. Matthew and Mark, Luke and John.

SOMETIMES IN SUMMER

Hope and I were both seven. I don't think we knew what month it was or even what day it was unless it was Sunday. Summer had already been so hot and long with every day just like the other that we didn't remember that it had rained the year before. We asked Uncle John to fry an egg on the sidewalk again, so at least we remembered that.

Hope's family had come over from Syria. It wasn't likely that they would sit around and talk about weather in Texas in the summertime. Or explain how the days are longer in summer, but then they start getting shorter. My family didn't talk to each other at all. Uncle John and I ate together sometimes. My grandma Mamie ate in the kitchen with my little sister Sally. My mother and Grandpa, if they ever ate, ate in their own rooms, or out somewhere.

Sometimes everybody would be in the living room. To listen to Jack Benny or Bob Hope or Fibber McGee and Molly. But even then nobody talked. Each laughed alone and stared at the green eye on the radio the way people stare at the television now.

What I mean is there was no way Hope or I would have heard about summer solstice, or how it always rained in El Paso in the summer. No one at my house ever talked about stars, probably didn't even know that in summer there were sometimes meteor showers in the northern sky.

Heavy rains overflowed the arroyos and the drainage ditches, destroyed houses in Smeltertown and carried away chickens and cars.

When the lightning and thunder came we reacted in primitive terror. Crouched on Hope's front porch, covered in blankets, listening to the cracks and rumbles with awe and fatalism. We couldn't not watch, though, huddled shivering, and made each other look when the arrows lit up all along the Rio Grande and cracked into the cross of Mount Cristo Rey, zigzagged into the smelter smokestack crack crack. Boom. At the same time the trolley on Mundy Street shorted out in a cascade of sparks and all the passengers came running out just as it began to rain.

It rained and rained. It rained all night. The phones went out and the lights went out. My mother didn't come home and Uncle John didn't come home. Mamie started a fire in the woodstove and when Grandpa got home he called her an idiot. The electricity is out, fool, not the gas, but she shook her head. We understood perfectly. Nothing was to be trusted.

We slept on cots on Hope's porch. We did sleep although we both swore we were up all night watching the sheets of rain come down like a big glass-brick window.

We had breakfast in both houses. Mamie made biscuits and gravy; at Hope's house we had *kibbe* and Syrian bread. Her grandma braided our hair into tight French braids so that the rest of the morning our eyes slanted back as if we were Asian. We spent the morning spinning around in the rain and then shivering drying off and going back out. Both of our grandmothers came to watch as their gardens washed completely away, down the walls, out into the street. Red caliche clay water quickly rose above the sidewalks and up to the fifth step of the concrete stairways of our houses. We jumped into the water, which was warm and thick like cocoa and carried us along for blocks, fast, our pigtails floating. We'd get out, run back in the cold rain, back past our houses all the way up the block and then jump back into the river of the street and become swept away some more, over and over.

The silence gave this flood a particularly eerie magic. The trolleys couldn't run and for days there were no cars. Hope and I were the only children on the block. She had six brothers and sisters, but they were bigger, either had to help in the furniture store or were just gone somewhere always. Upson Avenue was mostly retired smelter workers or Mexican widows who spoke little English, went to Mass at Holy Family in the morning and the evening.

Hope and I had the street all to ourselves. For skating and hopscotch and jacks. Early in the morning or in the evening the old women would water their plants but the rest of the time they all stayed inside with the windows and blinds shut tight to keep out the terrible Texan heat, but most of all the caliche red dust and the smoke from the smelter.

Every night they burned at the smelter. We would sit outside where the stars would be shining and then the flames would shoot out of the stack, followed by massive sick convulsions of black smoke that darkened the sky and veiled everything around us. It was quite lovely really, the billows and undulations in the sky, but it would sting our eyes and the smell of sulfur was so strong we would even gag. Hope always did but she was just pretending. To give you an idea of how scary it was every night, when the newsreel of the first atom bomb was shown at the Plaza Theater some Mexican joker hollered, "*Mira*, the *esmelter*!"

There was a break in the rains and that's when the second thing happened. Our grandmothers shoveled the sand away and swept their sidewalks. Mamie was a terrible housekeeper. "She always used to have colored help, that's why," my mother said.

"And you had Daddy!"

She didn't think that was funny. "I'm not going to waste my time cleaning this roach-infested dump."

But Mamie took trouble with the yard, sweeping the steps and sidewalk, watering her little garden. Sometimes she'd be right on the other side of the fence from Mrs. Abraham but they ignored one another completely. Mamie did not trust foreigners and Hope's grandmother hated Americans. She liked me because I made her laugh. One day all the children were lined up at the stove and she was giving them *kibbe* on fresh hot bread. I just got in line and she served me before she realized it. That's how I got my hair brushed and braided every morning too. The first time she pretended she didn't notice, told me in Syrian to hold still, hit me on the head with the brush.

There was a vacant lot next to the Haddad house. In summer it was overgrown with weeds, bad thistles so you wouldn't even want to walk through it. In fall and winter you could see that the lot was carpeted with broken glass. Blue, brown, green. Mostly from Hope's brother and his friends shooting BB guns at bottles but also just throwaways. Hope and I looked for bottles to turn in for refunds, and the old women took bottles to the Sunshine Market in their faded Mexican baskets. But in those days most people would drink a soda and then just toss the bottle anywhere. Beer bottles would fly out from cars all the time making little explosions.

I understand now that it had to do with the sun setting so late, after we had both eaten dinner. We were back outside, squatting on the sidewalk playing jacks. For only a few days, from our position low on the ground, we could see beneath the weeds on the lot at the very moment when the sun lit the mosaic carpet of glass. At an angle, shining through the glass like a cathedral window. This magical display only lasted a few minutes, only happened for two days. "Look!" she said the first time. We sat there, frozen. I had the jacks clasped tightly in a sweaty palm. She held the golf ball up in the air, like the Statue of Liberty. We watched the kaleidoscope of color spread out before us dazzling, then soft and blurry, then it vanished. The next day it happened again, but the day after that the sun just quietly turned to dusk.

Sometime soon after the glass or maybe it was before, they burned early at the smelter. Of course they burned at the same time. Nine p.m. but we didn't realize that.

In the afternoon we had been sitting on my steps, taking off our skates when the big car pulled up. A shiny black Lincoln. A man sat in the driver's seat wearing a hat. He made the window near us go down. "Electric windows," Hope said. He asked who lived in the house. "Don't tell him," Hope said, but I told him, "Dr. Moynahan."

"Is he home?"

"No. Nobody's home but my mother."

"Is that Mary Moynahan?"

"Mary Smith. My father is a lieutenant in the war. We're here for the duration," I said.

The man got out of the car. He wore a suit with a vest and a watch chain, had a stiff white shirt. He gave each of us a silver dollar. We had no idea what they were. He told us they were dollars.

"Will they take them for money in a store?" Hope asked.

He said yes. He went up the stairs and knocked on the door. When there was no answer he turned the metal crank that rang a raspy bell. After a while the door opened. My mother said angry things that we couldn't hear and then she slammed the door.

When he came back down he gave each of us two more silver dollars.

"I apologize. I should have introduced myself. I'm F. B. Moynahan, your uncle."

"I'm Lu. This is Hope."

He asked then where Mamie was. I told him she was at First Texan Baptist, across from the library downtown. "Thank you," he said and drove off. We both put our dollars in our socks. Just in time, because my mother was running down the steps, her hair in pin curls.

"That was your uncle Fortunatus, the snake. Don't you dare tell a soul he came. Do you hear me?" I nodded. She whacked me on the shoulder and the back. "Don't say a single word to Mamie. He broke her heart when he left. Left them all to starve. She'll get all upset. Not a word. Understand?" I nodded again.

"Answer me!"

"I won't say a word."

She gave me another whack for good measure and went back upstairs.

Later everyone was at home, in their own rooms as usual. The house had four bedrooms to the left of a long hall, a bathroom at the end, with the kitchen dining and living room on the other side. The hall was always dark. Pitch black at night, blood red from the stained-glass transom during the day. I used to be terrified of going to the bathroom until Uncle John taught me to start at the front door, whisper over and over to myself, "God will take care of me. God will take care of me," and run like hell. That day I tiptoed because in the front bedroom my mother was telling Uncle John that Fortie had come. Uncle John said he wished he'd been there so he could have shot him. I stopped then outside the door to Mamie's room. She was singing Sally to sleep. So sweet. "Way down in Missoura when my mammy sung to me." When I came out of the bathroom

Uncle John was in Grandpa's room. I listened there as Grandpa told Uncle John that Fortunatus had tried to come inside the Elks' club. Grandpa had sent word for him to leave or else he'd call the police. They talked some more but I couldn't hear. Just bourbon gurgling into glasses.

Finally Uncle John came into the kitchen. I had iced tea while he drank. He put mint in his glass so Mamie would think he was drinking tea too. He told me that Uncle Fortunatus had left home years and years before, just when they really needed him. Both John and Grandpa were drinking badly and couldn't work. Uncle Tyler and Fortunatus were supporting the family until Fortunatus went to California in the middle of the night. Left a note that said he'd had enough of Moynahan trash. He didn't ever send any money or even a letter, didn't come home when Mamie almost died. Now he was president of some railroad. "Best not to mention seeing him," Uncle John told me.

Everybody was in the living room for Jack Benny. Sally was still asleep. Mamie sat on her little chair, with the Bible open as usual. But she wasn't reading it. She was looking down at it and there was a look of happiness on her old face. I understood that Uncle Fortunatus had found her and had talked with her. When she looked up, I smiled. She smiled back at me and looked back down. My mother was standing in the doorway, smoking. This smiling made her nervous and she began to make all these Shh! signs and faces at me behind Mamie's back. I just looked at her with a blank stare like I had no idea what she was talking about. Grandpa was listening to the radio and laughing at Jack Benny. He was already drunk. Rocking hard in his leather rocking chair and tearing the newspaper into little strips, burning it up in the big red ashtray. Uncle John was drinking and smoking in the dining room doorway, taking it all in. He was ignoring my mother's signs to him to get me out of there. I figured he could see that Mamie was smiling too. My mother was making Shoo! signs at me to leave. I acted like I didn't notice and sang along with the Fitch commercial. "If your head scratches, don't itch it! Fitch it! Use your head! Save your hair! Use Fitch shampoo!" She was looking at me so mean I couldn't stand it, so I took one of the silver dollars out of my sock.

"Hey, look what I got, Grandpa!"

He stopped rocking. "Where'd you get that? You and them A-rabs steal that money?"

"No. It was a present!"

My mother was slapping me. "Rotten little brat!" She dragged me out of the room and threw me out the front door. I remember it as her carrying me by the neck like a cat, but I was very big already so that can't be true.

The minute I was outside, Hope hollered to come quick. "They're burning early!" That's what I mean about us thinking it was early. It just hadn't gotten dark.

Massive billows and swirls of black smoke were rising from the smokestack high into the air tumbling and cascading with a terrible speed unfurling in billows over our neighborhood as if it were night now with foggy wisps creeping over the roofs and down alleys. The smoke thinned and danced and spread farther over the whole downtown. Neither of us could move. Tears flowed from our eyes because of the foul sting and stink of the sulfur fumes. But as the smoke dissipated over the rest of the town it too was backlit like the glass had been by the sun and now even smoke turned into colors. Lovely blues and greens and the iridescent violet and acid green of gasoline in puddles. A flare of yellow and a rusty red but then mostly a soft mossy green that reflected in our faces. Hope said, "Yucko, your eyes turned all those colors." I lied and said hers did too but her eyes were black as ever. My pale eyes do change color so they probably did turn in the spirals of the smoke.

We never chattered like most little girls. We didn't even talk much. I know we didn't say a word about the terrible beauty of the smoke or of the glowing glass.

Suddenly it was dark and late. We both went inside. Uncle John was asleep on the porch swing. Our house was hot and smelled of cigarettes and sulfur and bourbon. I crawled into bed next to my mother and fell asleep. It seemed like the middle of the night when Uncle John shook me awake and took me outside. "Wake your pal Hope," he whispered. I threw a rock at her screen and in seconds she was outside with us. He led us to the grass and told us to lie down. "Close your eyes. Closed?"

"Yes."

"Yes."

"Okay, open your eyes and look toward Randolph Street up in the sky."

We opened our eyes to the clear Texas sky. Stars. The sky was filled with stars and it was as if there were so many that some were just jumping off the edge of it, tumbling and spilling into the night. Dozens, hundreds, millions of shooting stars until finally a wisp of cloud covered them and softly more clouds covered the sky above us.

"Sweet dreams," he whispered when he sent us back to bed.

By morning it was raining again. It rained and flooded all week until finally we got tired of getting cold and muddy and we ended up spending our dollars going to movies. The day Hope and I got home from *The Spanish Main* my father had come back safe from the war. Very soon we went to live in Arizona so I don't know what happened in Texas the summer after that one.

ANDADO

A GOTHIC ROMANCE

It was just flowering. In other countries the tree is called mimosa or acacia, but in Chile it is called aromo. The word has the softness of the fallen yellow blossoms that carpeted the courtyards. It was last period; the girls in fourth form were dreamy, inattentive by that hour, the white aprons that covered their school uniforms grubby and wrinkled. The girls filled pens from inkwells on each desk and the nibs made rasping sleepy scratches in their copybooks. The rain-wet branches of yellow aromo echoed the sound against the windows.

Señora Fuenzalida droned. The students called her "Fiat." She looked like a car. Short, squat, almost black, with mirrored headlight sunglasses. Where did she get those sunglasses, in Santiago, in 1949? American glasses, nylons, and Zippo lighters were luxury items then.

She would have seen everything even without them. She heard Laura in the back row, behind Quena and Conchi. The faintest hiss of pages being slit with a penknife, pages Laura should have cut and read the night before. The teacher called Laura "Suspiros" as her page cutting made the sound of sighs.

"*¡Suspiros!*"

"*Mande, señora.*" Laura stood at attention, hands clasped in front of her stained apron.

"Who said, '*Lloveré cuando se me antoje*'?"

Laura smiled. She had just seen it. I'll rain whenever I feel like it.

"You haven't read it!"

"I have. It was the crazy man, in the asylum."

"*Siéntese.*" Señora Fuenzalida nodded.

The bell finally rang. The pupils stood by their desks until Señora Fuenzalida left the room, then gathered their books and filed out into the hall. They hung their aprons in lockers, buttoned on clean white collars and cuffs. They buttoned their gray gloves, put on broad-brimmed hats with long ribbons. Book bags heavy with homework, even though there was a four-day holiday.

Laura walked with Quena and Conchi up Las Lilas toward Hernando de Aguirre. The sky had cleared; the sun was setting coral pink on the immense snow-covered Andes. Their shoes crushed aromo blossoms as they walked and the smell enveloped them. The yellow flowers carpeting the sidewalks muffled their footsteps.

It would have been hard to tell that Laura was an American. The daughter of a mining engineer, she had the quality of adaptation common to army brats and children of diplomats. They learn quickly, not just the language or the jargon, but what is done, who is to be known. The problem for such children is not being isolated or always new, but that they adapt so quickly and so well.

The girls stood at the corner of El Bosque and Las Lilas, discussing plans for the long weekend. The French Olympic team was spending its summer at the Chilean resort. Quena would take lessons from Emile Allais himself. It had snowed in the mountains all week, but look, now it's clear. The sky was almost dark. Two caped carabineros passed, rifles over their shoulders, boots black against the aromo.

Conchi's plans were the same every weekend. Dressmaker, hairdresser, ballet lesson, tennis lesson. Lunch at the Crillon. Rugby or polo in the afternoon. Tea at El Golf. She was having cocktails with Lautaro Donoso at the Charles. What if he should want to dance cheek to cheek?

Laura mentioned that she would be spending the four days at the Ibañez-Grey fundo. Conchi and Quena were impressed. Andrés Ibañez-Grey was senator of mines, had been ambassador to France. One of the wealthiest men in Chile, his estate in the south spanned the entire width of the country, from the Andes to the Pacific. "Chile is a narrow country . . . but still . . . !" Quena said. What neither girl knew, and Laura didn't care about, was that both Ibañez-Grey and her father worked with the CIA. Her friends also didn't know that Laura's parents weren't going. They had backed out that morning, her mother ill again. Laura knew they would say it was improper for her to go, even though Don Andrés's sister would be chaperone. It would be a small party. He was a widower. Two of his sons were going, and the fiancée of one of his sons.

They parted then, agreeing to meet on Monday evening to study chemistry. At home Laura hung up her hat and blazer, changed from her school uniform. Her parents were having a reception that night. Her father was.

Laura checked on her mother, Helen, who was asleep. The room reeked of Joy perfume and gin. In the hall outside her mother's room old Damián was shuffling around, rags tied to his feet, polishing, polishing the parquet floors. He was always there, upstairs and downstairs, day in and day out, just as his small grandson was always in the garden. His sole task was to pluck dead petals off azaleas. Two *mozos* and Domingo, the butler, moved most of the garish "French" furniture into the garage.

Domingo helped Laura arrange masses of cineraria and ranunculus from the florist, daffodils from the garden, hundreds of candles. There were mirrors everywhere . . . Helen never could decide about paintings. At night, with the candles lit, it would look better, Laura said. She went over lists with Domingo and the maids, checked the meatballs, the empanadas. María and Rosa were excited; their hair was in curlers.

Laura put on a cocktail dress and makeup that she would never have worn around her own friends. She looked at least twenty-one, pretty, and a little cheap. Her father, in a tuxedo, knocked on her door and they went downstairs. They greeted military and mining people, diplomats, Chilean and Peruvian dignitaries, the British and American ambassadors. One of Laura's functions was to translate; few of the Americans spoke Spanish. Helen, in three years, had learned only "*Traiga hielo.*" "*Traiga café.*" Laura circulated, making introductions, conversation. She was cornered by a Señor Soto, a seedy Bolivian official. His remarks were insinuating, offensive. Laura signaled to her father, who came over, but just grinned at Señor Soto and said "Isn't she a honey?" and left. Laura shook her arm away.

Andrés Ibañez-Grey was in the foyer. His hair was silver, his eyes so pale gray they seemed like the sightless eyes of a statue. Domingo took his hat and coat. Laura went to greet him.

"I'm Laura. It was nice of you to invite me to the fundo, even if my parents can't go." Don Andrés kept her hand in his.

"Ted said his child would be coming, not a lovely woman."

"I'm fourteen. I'm just all dressed up for this party. Please come in." The American ambassador was right there. The two men embraced. Laura fled, embarrassed.

She took a tray of food and coffee up to her mother, propped her up in bed. Laura described the food and flowers to her, told her what everyone was wearing, who had sent regards.

She told Helen about Andrés Ibañez-Grey. "Mama, he's a hundred times more impressive than in photographs." An imperious Jefferson.

"He's worth more than any old twenty-dollar bill, that's for sure," Helen said.

"I wish you were coming tomorrow. Can't you change your mind? I don't want to go."

"Don't be silly. It's supposed to be fabulous. Besides, your daddy really needs to get in good with the guy. I wish I could handle these things."

"What things?"

Helen sighed. "Oh. Christ. Anything."

She hadn't eaten any food. "My back is killing me. I'm going to try and get some sleep." She had that look that meant she wanted a drink. Laura never actually saw her mother drink.

"Good night, Mama."

Laura checked on things in the kitchen again but didn't go back to the party. Her father had been looking for her, María said, but Laura ignored her. In her room she phoned Conchi before she went to bed. They talked about Quena, how bossy and *metete* she was. Laura knew that probably only minutes before Quena and Conchi had been gossiping about her. If she wasn't so sleepy she would call Quena to talk about how foolish Conchi was, going out with Lautaro Donoso. He was much too old, had racehorses. He stayed out all night, then went to the steam baths, and then, still wearing his *smoking*, went to Mass without having been to bed.

The girls all dated men much older than themselves. It was understood that these men had other, entirely separate, social lives. With the young virgin girls from Santiago College or the French schools they went to rugby and cricket games, played golf and tennis. They took the girls to the opera, to chaperoned dances and to nightclubs before dinner. But late at night the men had another world of nightclubs and casinos and parties, with mistresses or women of *medio pelo*. This would go on for the rest of their lives, had begun really, when they were children. Their mothers, in furs, came in to kiss them good night. But it was the maids who fed them, who rocked them to sleep. María packed Laura's clothes while Laura talked and when she finished packing she began to brush Laura's hair. Laura put her hand over the mouthpiece. No, María, you're too tired. *Hasta mañana*. To Conchi she said she was going to bed before it got cold. María had put a hot brick in the foot of it.

Laura was about to turn off the light when María returned with cocoa. She kissed Laura on the forehead. *Buenas noches, mi doña*. From the empty streets outside echoed the chant of the watchman calling . . . *Medianoche y andado*. Midnight and "walked." *Andado y sereno* . . . Safe and sound.

Rain beat down on the glass roof of the dark Mapocho railway station. Sleek trains glistened black outside. Black umbrellas, black uniformed porters vanished into white steam that hissed billowing from the trains. There were photographers, not from the society pages, as Conchi had hoped, but from the leftist papers. The senator of mines and the Yanqui imperialist who are raping our country confer together at Mapocho Station.

The two men were saying hello and good-bye. Laura stood apart, awkward, next to Don Andrés's son Pepe. He was young, wore a black seminary uniform. He rocked, blushing, staring at his feet. Xavier, the eldest son, was just the opposite. Dashing, disdainful in English tweed. Laura disliked him already. Why is it sophisticated to be bored? Elegant travelers and theatergoers affect the same pained look of ennui. Why not say "A trip? Exciting! Wonderful play!"?

Xavier and his fiancée, Teresa, were arguing with her

mother. The mother was very upset. Don Andrés's sister, Doña Isabel, was ill, unable to come. Teresa's mother felt there was not an appropriate chaperone. Don Andrés convinced her that his housekeeper, Pilar, would be in attendance, watching over Teresa and Laura. Mollified, the woman left with Laura's father.

Don Andrés sat next to the window against red velvet. The conductor and several porters stood talking and laughing with him, hats clasped in their hands. Across the aisle, Xavier and Teresa faced Laura and Pepe. Teresa spoke baby talk to Xavier in a high voice that jarred with her matronly figure. Pepe began reading a text in Latin even before the train left the station.

Xavier told Laura that in two weeks Pepe would be entering the priesthood. Lost to us, forever. But, of course found. You are Catholic? Xavier was tall, his hair jet black, otherwise he was much like his father, patrician, sardonic. With utmost tact he "placed" Laura. Good school. Ostentatious neighborhood. No, she didn't know Europe. She played tennis at the Prince of Wales. Didn't belong to El Golf. Summer at Viña del Mar. She knew Marisol Edwards but not the Dusaillants. Her French was good. You haven't read Sartre?

"I've read very little. Most of my life was spent in mining camps in the States. I'm like Jemmy Buttons," Laura said. At least she had read Subercaseaux, if not Darwin.

"A prettier noble savage," Don Andrés said from across the aisle. "Laura, come sit by me. I'll tell you where we are."

She moved with relief to the seat opposite him, pressed her forehead to the window, cold. The outside of the glass was splattered with soot from the engine. Yellow aromo reflected in the Bío-Bío River, in lakes, in pools of water. Don Andrés named the towns they passed, the rivers they crossed; named the fruit trees, told her what would be planted in the fields. When the porter came by, playing a gong for luncheon, Don Andrés said for the others to go ahead. It was as simple as that, the pairing of Don Andrés and Laura for the holiday.

In the dining car there were more waiters and busboys than patrons, an inordinate amount of china and silver and wine-glasses for each course, endless courses that proceeded from a galley scarcely three feet square.

Don Andrés asked her about the mountains in Idaho and Montana, the silver and zinc mines. How did the miners live? Where were the smelters? She was glad to talk about these places, was homesick for them. Laura had not forgiven her father for leaving the mines, for becoming an executive and a politician. He hadn't wanted to. It was Helen who had so much wanted glamour and romance and money. But now, just as in the Rocky Mountains, she still rarely left her room.

Laura told Don Andrés about the desert in New Mexico and Arizona. Yes, it was like Antofagasta. She told him how she used to climb in the mountains with her father, pan for gold in the creeks. He had taken her down into the mines ever since she was a little girl. Sometimes in a regular lift down the mine-shaft; in small mines on a big barrel attached to a rope, holding on to the rope, her head level with the rough denim of the miners' knees. The smell of the mines. Dank, dark. How it felt to go into the earth itself. The shock when she saw her first open-pit mine at Rancagua, the Anaconda copper pit. The vast gash of it, the rape of it.

She blushed at the word. She had been talking on and on, giddy with wine and attention. How embarrassing, please forgive me. Not at all. Enchanted. She and Don Andrés were the only people left in the dining car. There were so many waiters that she hadn't noticed.

She hadn't noticed his arm on the back of her chair, how his hair brushed her shoulder when he filled her glass. Without any self-consciousness, without any consciousness at all, she had eased into the man's presence. In the vestibules between cars he took her arm to steady her, drew her in to him when a *mozo* passed with luggage. She didn't react to such intimacies, as she would have with any other man. She was simply enveloped.

This would never happen to her again. When she grew older she would always be in control, even when being submissive. This would be the first and last time anyone took over herself.

Pepe was asleep, across the aisle from Xavier and Teresa. His face was pale, dark lashes shadowed his cheekbones; his hands held a rosary, the Latin book. Xavier and Teresa were playing canasta.

"Good. We'll join you."

"Papá, you don't play canasta."

"Teresa, you and I will play Xavier and Laura."

Pleasant, the rest of the journey. It grew dark outside. Joking and laughter. Soothing sound of shuffled cards. Tap tap tap as they were dealt. The whistle of the train, the steady rain on the metal roof. Click and flare of Don Andrés's gold cigarette lighter. His gray eyes squinting through smoke.

Tea was brought by four tuxedoed *mozos*. A samovar of tea, pewter coffee urn, sandwiches, *cuchuflís* with caramel. Teresa poured. She and Laura were friendly now, chatting about shops. New York. Saks. Bergdorf's.

It was dark, raining still, when the train stopped in Santa Bárbara. They were met by Gabriel, the mayordomo of the fundo. A saffron-colored huaso in a heavy poncho, wide-brim hat, boots with spurs. Laura and Don Andrés rode in the cab; the others climbed into the back of the covered truck. Gabriel and two other men loaded the luggage, boxes and boxes of food.

The truck was the only vehicle at the station or on the muddy streets. There were two gas lamps in the town square; black-shawled women hurried to vespers in a candlelit church.

Once beyond the square there was no one to be seen. Hours then, in open country, over the bad road, never once a house or a light or another car. Not a windmill or a telephone pole. Deer and fox, rabbits and other field animals ran before the headlights. The rain was the only sound. Don Andrés and Gabriel talked about plowing, planting, horses, and sheep. Who had died, which men had left for the city. Santiago was the city. At last they came upon faint flickering lights, a cluster of huts in a grove of eucalyptus trees. The truck slowed and Don Andrés lowered his window. Blast of aromo and pine, the smell of oak fires. His peons lived here. Don Andrés didn't use the Chilean word for peasant, *roto*, which means broken.

They drove on then, up a rise, stopped at high iron gates. A caped figure opened the gates, waved them on, past miles of poplar, orchards bare except for a faint pink flurry of plum blossoms. At the top of the hill Don Andrés had Gabriel stop the truck. They got down in the rain. Far down in the valley stood a stone gabled house, yellow lights reflecting in a lake beneath it. There was no other light anywhere, for miles and miles around, but everywhere in the darkness pulsated the yellow groves of aromo. Laura was moved by the majestic view, the silence, but she laughed.

"In an American movie this is where you would say, 'All this is mine.'"

"But it's a black-and-white movie. I can only say that all this will soon be gone."

Back in the truck she asked him if there would be a revolution, if the Communists would ever have power.

"*Claro que sí.* It will be soon."

"My father says it can never happen."

"Your father is very naïve. But, of course, that is his charm."

•

Dogs barked in the cobblestone courtyard. A dozen servants were silhouetted in the lamp and candlelight from the open door. Inside, the parquet floors glowed beneath richly colored Persian rugs. Dark Spanish paintings, pale faces dreamy in the candlelight. An old woman, Pilar, shook hands with them all. Don Andrés told her that she was to be Teresa's chaperone, to get Teresa settled and unpacked. Where is Dolores?

Aquí, señor. A beautiful green-eyed girl, no more than Laura's age, with black braids to her waist. She was to take care of Laura, he said. Laura followed the girl up the curving staircase. The two skipped lightly up the stairs, like children. Laura was trying to imagine how the house had been built, how the materials or the laborers themselves were brought to such a remote place at all . . . like building the Sphinx. She kept stopping to look at tapestries, carvings. Dolores laughed. "Wait until you see your room!"

A curtained brocade bed, a blue-tiled fireplace, an oval mirror above an antique chest. The bathroom was marble; a dozen candles reflected in the mirrors. The water was tepid but next to the tub were copper buckets of boiling water.

The windows with wavering old glass and the yellow blurred mirrors added to the illusion of a dream. Dolores disappeared in the mirror but her voice was still there, soft, the singsong of the huaso. "*E' una hora, ma' o meno',*" she said when asked what time dinner would be ready. She unpacked Laura's things and added another log to the fire. She stood, waiting, until Laura nodded. *Gracias.* Alone, in the mirror, Laura's reflection trembled, an old sepia photograph that floated in flickerings of light.

The others were already in the huge living room. A fire blazed. Teresa was at the grand piano, playing Chopin's "Gota de Agua." She played it over and over during the holiday. The tune played over and over in Laura's head whenever she was to remember Junquillos. Don Andrés handed her a glass of sherry.

"I'm in love with this house, like an English governess!"

"Don't go to the east wing!" Xavier smiled. Laura liked him a little better, smiled back.

"I built this from my dreams," Don Andrés said, "from French and Russian novels. The country itself is pure Turgenev."

". . . The serfs are," Xavier said.

"No politics, Xavier. Laura, my son is a socialist, a would-be revolutionary. A typical Chilean anarchist, discussing the plight of the masses while a valet brushes his coat." Xavier said nothing, drank. Pepe turned pages at the piano.

"Laura, you will really fall in love with my carriages. I collect them. You can play Becky Sharpe, Emma, Madame Bovary."

"I don't know any of them."

"You will one day. This way, when you do meet them, you'll put down the book and think of my barouche landau, and of me."

(Oh. True.)

There were fireplaces in the dining room too. Two *mozos* served them, appearing from wherever they stood, back in the shadows of the room.

Pepe was animated and gay. His mare had foaled; there were dozens of new lambs. He and his father talked about different events on the estate . . . the animals, births and deaths of peons.

After dinner Xavier and Teresa played backgammon in the living room; Pepe and Laura had brandy and coffee with Don Andrés in his study. A smaller fire, tended by a *mozo* who came in from the hall whenever it began to smolder or when a log fell with a shatter of sparks.

The three of them read out loud. Neruda. Rubén Darío's "*La princesa está triste. La princesa está pálida.*"

"Let's read Turgenev's *First Love*. You begin, Pepe, but with more feeling. You'll make a perfect priest, the way you drone."

When it was Laura's turn to read she traded places with Pepe to be by the light. As she read she glanced up from time to time at the two men across from her. Pepe's gray eyes were closed, but Don Andrés's eyes looked into hers as she read, as Zoraida wound a skein of wool around poor Vladimir's hands.

> *Oh gentle feelings, soft sounds, the goodness and growing calm of a heart that is deeply moved, the melting gladness of the first tender raptures of love. Where are you? Where are you?*

"Pepe's asleep. He missed the best part."

"You're falling asleep too. I'll show you to your room."

He adjusted the wick to the lantern by her bed, kissed her brow. Cool lips. "*Buenas noches, mi princesa.*"

You silly fool, Laura told herself. He almost made you swoon! Just like someone in Mama's romances.

Laura lay in bed, unable to fall asleep. Dolores tiptoed in and raised the window a few inches. She put a log on the fire, turned out the lantern. After Dolores had left, Laura got out of bed and went to the window. She opened it wide to the fragrance of pine and yellow aromo. It had stopped raining. The sky had cleared to a dazzle of stars that lit the fields and the courtyard. Laura saw Dolores cross the cobblestones of the courtyard and enter a door next to the kitchen. Minutes later Xavier crossed the yard and tapped on the door. Dolores opened it, smiling, and drew him in, to her.

Laura heard Teresa's window slam softly shut. Laura went back to bed. She tried to stay awake then, to think, but she fell asleep.

Days are brighter when the nights have no electricity. The

sun burst warm into the room, caught in a pearl-handled letter opener, the brass firedogs, the cut-glass marmalade jar on the breakfast tray. Outside the window the three white peaks of Las Malqueridas glistened against a clear blue sky.

"They're riding already," Dolores said. "Don Pepe says for you to hurry; he wants you to see the colt. I brought you these riding clothes."

"I was just going to wear these pants . . ."

"But these will look much nicer."

In riding clothes, with her hair up, Laura looked, in the dark mirrors, like a painting of someone in another age. Dolores was removing the breakfast tray, stepped back to let Teresa enter the room. Laura searched their faces for some expression—of rivalry, scorn, embarrassment—but both were impassive.

"My bedclothes are musty," Teresa said. "Please change them, or air them."

"I'll tell your maid." Dolores walked out, her head high. Teresa pouted, flung herself onto the chaise by the window.

"I wish Tía Isabel were here. She'd have me walk with her by the lake. I hate horses. Don't you?"

"No. I love horses. But I've never ridden English saddle."

Pepe was calling from the courtyard. He rode a chestnut mare, led a graceful black one. Laura called down to Pepe that she would be right there. But Teresa kept talking. She wanted to marry soon. Marriage would cure Xavier of his rash politics, would settle him down. How long had they been engaged? Since they were born, Teresa said. Their fathers had decided it. Fortunately they had fallen in love.

"Let's go. It's a perfect day," Laura said, but Teresa was taking off her coat. "No. I'm going to stay and knit. I'm ill. Tell Xavier to come keep me company."

"If I see him. Look, he and Don Andrés are far away, near the foothills."

Pepe helped her to mount the fine mare, Electra. They went first to see the foal, then rode in the potrero by the stable. Pepe watched as she jumped logs, small hurdles. They both laughed out loud, because of the splendid day, the vibrant horses. Xavier and Don Andrés were cantering toward them.

"Let's meet them. Can you take the fence?" But they were at the fence before she could answer.

"Not a bad jump," Don Andrés said.

"Not bad? It was great. My first jump!"

"Do it again."

Before she rode off Laura gave Xavier Teresa's message.

"*Que regio.* She's a bore to ride with. Let's go to the river, Pepe!" The brothers cantered away, shouting to one another. Laura took the jump again, but badly.

"Once more," he said and whipped Electra's rump; the horse raced off. Startled, Laura pulled on the reins so sharply that the horse reared and she fell to the ground. Don Andrés didn't dismount, laughed down at her.

"The two of you are well matched."

"I'm not skittish."

"Neither is she. But she doesn't do anything she doesn't want to do."

"I want to jump. I'll do it. Don't touch my horse."

"*Ándale.*"

Nice soar of a jump. They raced then to catch up with Pepe and Xavier, galloping through aspen groves, over meadows, through furrowed fields. The four of them rode all morning, not talking except for an occasional shout to point out baby lambs, trillium, violets, masses of jonquils that gave the fundo its name. Deer drank from the same stream their horses did. They crossed the river that raged high with melted snow. Snorting horses, icy water. From the foothills they looked far down into the valley. It seemed to Laura exactly as it must have been when the Spaniards first came. Even in the Rocky Mountains of her childhood there had always been a reminder of civilization . . . a distant rattle of ore cars, a buzz saw, an airplane. On the way home they did see a huaso tending sheep, another was plowing a field, oxen tied to his plow.

The dining room that had been so dark the night before was bright with sunshine, looked out onto the lake and the white Andes. The riders were tired, sunburnt, hungry. Xavier had lost all affectation, Pepe and Laura all shyness. What a morning! Teresa was gay too, or pretended to be. Or maybe she doesn't mind about Dolores and Xavier at all, Laura wondered. No, she must be jealous. She couldn't show it though, or even let on that she knew. It would spoil her role, the innocent fiancée. Did Xavier really love her? Surely he was in love with Dolores. This was romance. Laura couldn't wait to tell Quena and Conchi.

"I'm having a wonderful time!" Laura said.

"*¡Yo también!*" everyone else said. They ate trout and lentil soup, roast lamb, just-baked bread. After lunch Teresa and Xavier went rowing on the lake. Pepe went to take a nap.

There were eight different carriages. An ornate gilded coach, upholstered in pink brocade, with mirrors, gold flowerpots, elaborately carved stands for footmen. American stagecoaches, landaus, sulkies. Laura climbed into each one, chose a black two-seated Tilbury with gleaming mahogany, black leather.

Don Andrés harnessed his stallion, Lautaro, to the carriage. They rode past the lake and the yellow aromo. Wave to Teresa and Xavier. Spinning on and on then to the crisp clop clop of Lautaro's hooves. It grew dark. Don Andrés lit the lanterns.

"Do you want to go back for tea?"

"No."

"Good."

They crossed a wooden bridge above the river, were sprayed

by the high water, rode on in the darkness as he talked to her then of his childhood. Like hers, he said, because he was lonely, an only child, never a child. His mother had died when he was born; his father had been cold, autocratic. French and English boarding schools. Alone with books when he was at home. He had been educated at Harvard, Oxford, the Sorbonne, had met his wife in Paris. No, she was a Spaniard. She died, years ago.

It was time to go home. He turned the carriage around, gave Laura the reins. Wait. Don Andrés got down from the carriage. His hair silver against the yellow aromo trees. He returned with violets that he arranged in the neck of her cape.

Laura wished they weren't reading *First Love*. She could feel her cheeks burning. "Pepe, you have a turn." She handed him the book. When Don Andrés read she couldn't take her eyes off his mouth, the white gleam of his teeth.

Later, in bed, she thought that she was in love. She went over every moment she had spent with him, every word he had said. What did she wish? Her dreams didn't go beyond a kiss.

Dolores woke her with a breakfast tray. A fine day. Don Pepe wanted to ride with her. Xavier and Don Andrés had gone hunting. Teresa and Pilar were on the terrace, embroidering for her trousseau. Pillowslips. Dolores had packed a lunch for Pepe and Laura.

"Thank you. Do you ride, Dolores?"

"All the time. But not when the family is here." Laura wanted to ask Dolores about her and Xavier, about love.

"How old are you?" was all she could ask.

"Fifteen."

"Were you born here?"

"Yes, in the kitchen! My mother was always the cook here."

"So you've known Xavier long?"

Dolores laughed. "Of course. Since I was born. He taught me to ride, and to shoot."

Laura sighed, dressing. Dolores didn't act like she was in love. She had looked it, though, when she opened the door to Xavier. Had Helen, Laura's mother, ever been in love? There was no one she could talk to. Especially not Quena or Conchi, although love was all they ever talked about. The three of them practiced kissing by kissing the medicine cabinet. But when you kissed the cabinet your nose went to the side of the mirrored door. Where did noses go? That's how much they knew about love. The desire Laura felt . . . she would not have been able to match the feeling with the word.

She and Pepe rode to a lower pasture to see the new lambs and kid goats, then rode to Gabriel's house to visit his wife. The old woman was delighted to see Pepe. She put water on for tea, called the neighbor women over to greet him. Our Pepino to be a priest! They stood around him as he drank, in the smoky dirt-floored hut, smiling at him with deep affection. He knew all their names, their animals' and their children's names. No, it would be years before he could return. He'd think of them. Pray for them. The women embraced him, shook Laura's hand as they left. Pepe was solemn as he and Laura ate their lunch under a huge aromo tree.

"Are you nervous about becoming a priest?"

"Scared. It's a big step."

"Why are you doing it? Do you have a calling?"

"No. I want to make . . . changes, gestures. I'm too cynical to be a revolutionary. Many reasons. To justify myself, to make a difference in the world, to get away from my father. My confessor says not to worry about reasons if my commitment is firm."

"Seems like Xavier wants the same things."

"Yes. I don't know how he'll find them."

"He says the *reforma* is the only answer. To give the land to the people."

"It will take so long. And it won't be the leaders who will ruin it, but the people themselves. Their nature and their religion demand a patriarchy. They will turn their liberators into new *patrones*."

"You sound like my grandpa, talking about how negroes were happier when they were slaves."

They finished the bota of wine and ate the two pears. Aromo petals stuck to them as they leaned back in the yellow softness.

"I wonder if I'll ever justify myself," she said.

"That's easy for women."

"What do you mean . . . the lilies of the field?"

"No. You don't have to do, to be true to who you are."

"How will I learn who that is?" She sighed as they stood up, brushed off yellow blossoms. They mounted their horses.

"Race you home!"

From the stables they could see Don Andrés and Xavier at the kitchen door. Pheasant feathers shone iridescent purple green in the sunlight. Dolores smiled; she held the dazzling birds. Xavier stroked her black hair. Behind them, Teresa came into the kitchen, stood transfixed in the darkened room. Her pearls glinted; the teapot was white on the waiting tray. Teresa smashed the pot on the brick floor and left the room. Xavier's hand remained frozen on Dolores's black hair.

Tea by the large fireplace. A new pot. Teresa wasn't there.

"Where is your fiancée?" Don Andrés asked.

"She is no longer my fiancée."

"Nonsense. Go reassure her, Xavier."

"I broke the engagement. I'm not going to marry her."

"Don't be a fool. You can't do that."

"But I can, Papá. No, Laura, no sugar, thank you."

Don Andrés was pale, furious. "Laura, let's go for a ride."

"It's raining."

"Very lightly."

He rose to leave and Laura followed him. Xavier looked at his father's back with hatred, triumph.

Lautaro flew over the rain-slick road. The lanterns flickered in the wind; pink blossoms, yellow aromo blurred past them in the dark. The sky began to clear, but the stars had not yet brightened the night. Laura and Don Andrés didn't speak.

They heard the river before they saw it, and then the clatter of Lautaro's hooves on the wooden bridge. His ghastly screech as the bridge gave way. They were both thrown from the Tilbury into the icy churning water. The lanterns went out, hissing. They flailed in the water, tearing off their capes, jackets. Don Andrés yelled at her to grab on to the carriage, to help unfasten the horse. Spinning spinning in the river. Lautaro neighed hysterically, kicking and biting at them as they worked on the harnesses. His hooves, rocks, the carriage banged into Laura and Don Andrés as they plunged downstream.

The horse was free, thrashing, bleating. He lunged again and again onto the bank until finally he clambered up and was gone. The Tilbury spun and tumbled down the river in the foam, silver now in starlight.

Trembling, panting under an aromo tree, Don Andrés tore his shirt up to bandage gashes in his leg, her arms. A fire, he said, but his gold lighter didn't work.

"Gabriel will come looking for us when Lautaro gets back, but we're miles downstream from where he'll start. Pray that he doesn't try to cross the bridge. We'd better start walking, get to the rise above the river. Take your clothes off and wring them out."

"I'm fine."

"Don't be foolish. Wring out your clothes."

They were shuddering; their teeth were chattering.

Aromo stuck to their bare bodies like yellow fur. Laura was cold and afraid. She felt desire and didn't know what to do, how to do what they were doing. She held his silver head as he kissed her breasts. Fringe of yellow aromo rocking against the sky. An astonishment of pain. "What have I done?" he whispered into her throat. Warm, his breath and body. Sperm glistened, steaming, on her legs as she dressed herself.

It was as bright as day, with shooting stars and the Andes neon-white. Blood soaked their bandages. They limped along, exhausted and sore.

"Lautaro wasn't lame, was he?"

"No."

What about me? she thought. Wounded, with blisters from her wet boots, her chest aching from walking so fast. He had not even glanced at her.

"What about me?" she said out loud. "Why are you angry with me?"

He turned to her, but still didn't look at her. Pale gray eyes.

"I'm not angry with you, *mi vida.* I have ruined you and have nearly killed my best horse."

He called out for Gabriel. His voice echoed into the vast valley and then there was silence. They walked on.

Ruined? Am I ruined? For such a quick confusing moment? Will everyone know, looking at me? Is Dolores ruined?

Laura's blisters hurt so badly that she took off her boots. He told her not to but she ignored him, pretended not to feel the rocks and twigs beneath her feet.

And if so many women risk being ruined maybe there is something wrong with me, that I scarcely noticed what was going on.

She had to urinate. "Go on. I'll catch up with you." Her underpants glittered red, soaked with blood. She took off her wet wool pants, threw the underpants away so Dolores wouldn't see them.

"*Apúrate.*"

"Go on. I said I'd catch up with you."

She climbed the hill behind him, scattering rocks.

"If you're angry because you think I'll tell somebody, you needn't worry." There was no one to tell, to ask.

He stopped then and held her to him, kissed her hair, her forehead, her eyelids.

"No. I hadn't thought of that. I'm trying to think about what I have done. What I can possibly do about it."

"Please kiss me," she said. "I've never been kissed before."

He turned away from her but she caught his head and put her mouth on his. His tongue opened her lips then and they kissed until, dizzy, they sat down on the hill.

Galloping. They listened, called out. An answering cry. It was Gabriel on his horse, leading horses behind him. Ponchos and brandy. Cigarettes for Don Andrés. Home then, the two men far ahead of her, shouting to each other, cantering up and down the rolling hills in the fluorescent silver night.

Xavier was in the kitchen with Dolores. Two mauve spots on his cheekbones showed that he was drunk. Don Andrés and Laura drank brandy too while Dolores bandaged Don Andrés's legs. Both he and Laura were scraped and bruised, from the carriage, the rocks, Lautaro's hooves. Don Andrés described the accident as a glorious adventure, with Laura rescuing his prize Thoroughbred. Laura was stunned when she learned the value of the horse.

"There must have been a moment when you hated yourself for tying that stallion to a Tilbury," Xavier said.

"More than a moment. It was utterly senseless of me."

Xavier smiled. "Papá, that's the first time you ever admitted a mistake."

•

Laura undressed and climbed into the candlelit tub. Dolores gathered up her clothes. "Your pants are bloody. *¿Llegó la tía?*" Did your "aunt," your period, arrive? Laura shook her head. The eyes of the two girls met in the mirror.

Laura woke, frightened because she could barely move, but then she remembered and opened her eyes. It was almost noon, dark and raining outside. A fire burned in the grate. Dolores brought her breakfast. "You are to stay in bed. Don Andrés hopes that you don't feel too bad."

"Where is he?"

"He rode to Santa Bárbara early this morning. He won't be back until tonight."

"Where is everybody else?"

"Pilar is in bed, ill. Teresa is in bed, ill. Pepe is in his room, reading. Xavier's in the dining room. *Está tomado.*" Drunken, taken. Laura noticed that Dolores was sitting on the foot of her bed. It's because we are the same now, ruined, she thought. Dolores must have sensed the thought; she jumped up with an apology.

"*Perdóname*, Doña Laura. I'm very tired. The morning has been confusing."

Laura was ashamed then, reached out to hold Dolores's hand.

"Forgive me. It sure is a confusing morning. It's afternoon for one thing. I'm so sore. Oh! Look at my face!" In the dark mirror one cheek was scraped raw, an eye was green and black. Laura burst into sobs of self-pity. Dolores too began to cry. The girls held each other, rocking, and then Dolores left the room.

The house was still. The one hunting dog that was allowed indoors paced the shining floors, his toenails clicking. A lonely sound, like a telephone ringing in an empty house.

Xavier was asleep in his father's study. He woke when Laura walked past him to get the Turgenev book.

"It's our noble savage! Atalanta, who plunged into the icy torrents to save the perishing beast!"

"Shut up."

"Sorry, *gringuita*. You must feel rotten. Come sit by me."

Pepe appeared in the doorway. He had just shaved, was pale.

"Laura! *¡Pobrecita!* What a frightening accident. Are you all right? And Xavier, what's wrong? What is going on?"

"Come in, Pepito. You look as bad as we do. Are you scared? Changing your mind?" Xavier got up, poured three glasses of sherry, put a log on the fire.

"It must be time for sherry. What time is it?" On cue, a *mozo* came in to ask if they would care for lunch. "God, no."

"I mean, we don't want to eat, do we? Really, Pepe, are you all right?"

Pepe nodded. "Yes. I'm just saying good-bye. But it is as if I had already left."

"That's how I feel. But at least you know where you're going. I'm just saying good-bye."

"To what?"

"Everything. Teresa. Law. Papá. Everything up to now."

"You're not joking. What will you do?"

"I haven't got that far yet. It is the last time I'll ever come to Junquillos, that I know."

"*Ai*, Xavier." The brothers stood, embraced, and then the three sat silent. The fire. Rain against the windows. Blur of yellow aromo by the lake.

"*¿Y tu, gringa?* You'll be back, most certainly," Xavier said.

"No. I won't be back."

"Of course you will," Pepe said. "Papá is so fond of you."

Xavier laughed. "And Laura, what are you saying good-bye to? Your innocence?"

"Yes, Xavier, I am," Laura said.

"Xavier, how rude!" Pepe was shocked. "You are drunk!"

Don Andrés arrived just before dinner, on Electra. Staccato of hooves on the cobblestones. Two men came then, by truck, and were shown into the living room. Don Andrés had gone to change.

At dinner Xavier was very drunk, splashing wine. Pepe was ashen, silent. Neither Laura nor Teresa pretended not to be miserable. Don Andrés talked about drainage, crops, timber. It was Pepe who first realized what was going on.

"Papá! You're not selling Junquillos?"

"Everything but the house and stables."

Tears shone in two thin lines down Pepe's face. Teresa left the table, sobbing. If I were kind I would go to her, Laura thought, but she didn't go. Xavier laughed bitterly.

"Bloody shrewd, as always. You know that all of this land will be given to the people. Why not the precious house, too? It will go soon enough. A school, perhaps."

The men talked until after midnight in the study. Laura finished *First Love* by lamplight in her room. She lay awake. Aromo and pine. She didn't think, was simply awake, alone.

The train ride was long, delayed by rain, flooding. Don Andrés worked on papers. Laura sat facing him. Across the aisle Pepe read and Xavier slept, or pretended to sleep, while Teresa knitted something voluminous and burnt orange. She seemed to have settled into an affronted spinsterhood, wearing glasses that she had not put on before. No baby talk now. And then she and Pepe both fell asleep too. Don Andrés was looking at Laura.

"Junquillos was lovely," she said.

"You are lovely. Please forgive me, Laura."

He looked back down at the papers in his lap. Laura stared

out the soot-spattered window. Rain dripped from the sodden aromo trees. Well, Laura thought . . . a weekend in the country.

At the station Teresa's mother rushed her away as if there had been an accident. Laura's father had sent a Chinese driver.

Good-bye, thank you for a marvelous time.

The house was silent when she got home, cold. María came in, fastening her bathrobe. They embraced.

"We missed you! May I fix some cocoa? What happened to your poor face?"

"An accident. An adventure, really, but I'm too tired to talk about it. Where are my parents?"

"Your mother is in the hospital. She took too many drugs; she turned blue and wouldn't wake up. She'll be home tomorrow."

"Was she upset? Did something happen?"

María shrugged. "*¿Quién sabe?* Your father said she was just too overtired."

"*Overtired!*" The two of them giggled.

"Is he with her now?"

"No. He's at a dinner party. Doña, you look very bad."

"I'm . . . I'm overtired! It was beautiful, María. I'll tell you all about it tomorrow. I'm going to bed. No bath, no cocoa. But wake me at five tomorrow. I have to study chemistry."

"Quena called. She got home too late to study. And Conchi called, said she was in love and didn't ever want to study."

Cram for chemistry in the morning. As much time inking symbols on their wrists under their white cuffs. But the test wasn't so bad. Physics then. Dry, dry Señor Ortega. Algebra. History. Laura's hand ached from taking notes.

Lunch finally. Grace was always said in English. God bless this food for our use and our lives for Thy service. During the meal only French could be spoken; not much was said. A stroll through the rose garden. Just enough time to hear that Conchi was in love again. He called her *tú*, held her hand at the film.

Quena had skied all day, every day. The snow had been fine. Emile Allais had given her lessons without charging. Laura was brief but dramatic about the carriage accident. She raved about Electra, the house, the Marie Antoinette coach. More about Electra. Yes, she had worn a riding habit after all. "Oh, thank God," Conchi sighed.

The bell rang. English. Flower in a crannied wall. French then with Madame Perea dozing over knitting. *Le passé simple.* Spanish, at last. Where were we? "*¡Suspiros!*"

Laura stood. "I haven't read the lesson."

Señora Fuenzalida laughed. "That never seemed to present a problem before. Your first black mark."

Quena and Conchi were surprised too when Laura didn't go with them to the Golf for tea. "Mama's ill again."

Helen was asleep. Laura studied until dinner, ate alone.

She stood at the foot of her mother's bed. "Hi. Are you okay?"

"I'm fine. Have a good time?"

"Yes. I wish you had come. It was beautiful, like a novel."

"Were the people nice?"

"Real nice. Just family. I rode a Thoroughbred." Helen was looking at a sty on her eyelid in a hand mirror. Laura sat down on the bed across from her mother. Am I in love, Mama? she asked herself. Could I be pregnant? Have I been ruined? Mama, help me.

Out loud she said, "I'm sorry you went to the hospital, Mama. You need to get out more. Let's go to a movie this weekend, or to lunch at the Prince of Wales."

"Get me that magnifying mirror from the bathroom, will you, sweetheart?"

Laura was asleep when her father flicked on the light in her room. He was flushed, red-eyed, was pulling off his tie.

"Sure did miss you, baby. Have a good time?"

"Wonderful."

"How'd you like Andy? Classy guy, no?"

"Classy. Daddy, what about Mama?"

"She got hold of some sleeping pills, that's all. She'll be fine. Just wanted a little attention."

Laura could hear the *velador* as he walked the streets. Loud at first, echoing. *Son las once, andado y sereno.*

Block by block he chanted to the neighborhood that the streets were patrolled and safe. He sang to the night that the moon was full. *¡Son las once, luna llena!* Until at last it trailed into a faraway falsetto . . . *Andado y sereno.*

DUST TO DUST

Michael Templeton was a hero, an Adonis, a star. Truly a hero, a much-decorated bombardier in the RAF. When he returned to Chile after the war he had been a star rugby and cricket player for the Prince of Wales team. He raced his BSA for the British motorcycle team and had been the champion for three years. Never lost a race. He even won the last one before he spun out and hit the wall.

He had arranged for Johnny and me to have seats in the press box. Johnny was Michael's little brother and my best friend. He idolized Michael as much as I did. Johnny and I felt disdain for everything then and a contempt for most people, especially our teachers and parents. We even conceded, with some scorn, that Michael was a cad. But he had style, cachet. All the girls and women, even old women, were in love with him. A slow, slow low voice. He gave Johnny and me rides on the beach in Algarrobo. Flying over hard wet sand, scattering flocks of gulls, their wing beats louder than the motor, than the ocean. Johnny never made fun of me for being in love with Michael, gave me snapshots and clippings in addition to the ones we helped his mum paste in scrapbooks.

His parents didn't go to the race. They were at the dining

room table having tea and bickies. Mr. Templeton's tea was rum, really, in the blue cup. Michael's mum was crying, sick with worry about the race. He'll be the death of me, she said. Mr. Templeton said he hoped Mike would break his bloody fool neck. It wasn't just the race . . . this was pretty much their daily conversation. Even though he was a hero, Michael still had no job after three years back from the war. He drank and gambled and got into serious troubles with women. Whispered phone calls and late-night visits from fathers or husbands, slamming doors. But women just became even more fascinated with him and people actually insisted upon loaning him money.

The stadium was crowded and festive. The racers and pit crews were glamorous, dashing Italians, Germans, Australians. The main contenders were the British team and the Argentines. The English rode BSAs and Nortons; the Argentines Moto Guzzis. None of the racers had Michael's panache, his nonchalance or white scarf. What I am saying is that even with the shock of his death, even with the bike in flames, with Michael's blood on the concrete wall, his body, the shrieking and the sirens, it all had his particular throwaway insouciance. That it was the last race, and he had won it. Johnny and I didn't speak, not about the terror, nor about the drama of it.

The dining room at home was buzzing and crowded. Mrs. Templeton had frizzed her hair and powdered her face. She was saying that it would be the death of her but in fact she was very lively, making tea and passing scones and answering the telephone. Mr. Templeton kept on saying, "I told him he would break his bloody neck! I told him!" Johnny reminded him that he had said he wished Michael would.

It was exciting. Nobody but me had visited the Templetons for years, and now the house was full. There were reporters from the *Mercurio* and the *Pacific Mail*. Our "Michael album" was open on the table. People were saying hero and prince and tragic waste all over the house. Groups of beautiful girls were upstairs and downstairs. One of the girls would be sobbing while two or three others patted her and brought her tissues.

Johnny and I kept up our usual stance of mirthful scorn. We had not actually realized that Michael was dead, didn't until the Saturday night after the funeral. That was when we used to sit on the rim of the tub while he shaved, humming "Saturday night is the loneliest night in the week." He'd tell us all about his "birds," listing their attributes and inevitable, very funny, flaws. The Saturday after he died we just sat in the tub. We didn't cry, just sat in the tub, talking about him.

We had fun, though, watching the flurry before the funeral, the rivalries between the mourning girlfriends. Most amazing of all was the way the entire British colony of Santiago decided that Michael had died for the King. Glory to the Empire, the *Pacific Mail* said. Mrs. Templeton was peppy, had us and the maids beating rugs and oiling bannisters and baking more scones. Mr. Templeton just sat with his blue cup muttering how Mike never could take direction, had been hell-bent.

I was allowed to leave school for the burial. I wouldn't have gone at all but there was a chemistry test second period. After that I took off my school apron and went to my locker. I was very solemn and brave.

There are things people just don't talk about. I don't mean the hard things, like love, but the awkward ones, like how funerals are fun sometimes or how it's exciting to watch buildings burning. Michael's funeral was wonderful.

In those days there were still horse-drawn hearses. Massive creaking wagons drawn by four or six black horses. The horses wore blinders and were covered in thick black net, with tassels that dragged dusty in the streets. The drivers wore tails and top hats and carried whips. Because of Michael's hero status many organizations had contributed to the funeral, so that there were six hearses. One was for his body, the others for flowers. Mourners followed the hearses to the cemetery in black cars.

During the service at Saint Andrew's (high) Anglican church many of the sad girls fainted or had to be led away because they were so overcome. Outside the gaunt and jaunty drivers smoked on the curb in their top hats. Some people always associate the heady smell of flowers with funerals. For me it needs to be mixed with the scent of horse manure. Parked outside too were over a hundred motorcycles which would follow the cortege to the cemetery. Gunnings of engines, splutters, smoke, backfires. The drivers in black leather, with black helmets, their team colors on their sleeves. It would have been in poor taste for me to tell the girls at school just how many unbelievably handsome men had been at that funeral. I did anyway.

I rode in the car with the Templetons. All the way to the cemetery Mr. Templeton fought with Johnny about Michael's helmet. Johnny held it on his lap, planned to place it in the grave with Michael. Mr. Templeton argued, reasonably, that helmets were hard to come by and very dear. You had to get someone to bring them from England or America, and pay a stiff duty for them too. "Sell it to some other sod to race in," he insisted. Johnny and I exchanged glances. Wouldn't you know he'd only care about the cost?

More glances and grins between us in the cemetery itself with all the tombs and crypts and angels. We decided to be buried at sea and promised to attend to that, for each other.

The Canon, in white lace over a purple cassock, stood at the head of the grave, surrounded by the British racing team, their helmets crooked in their arms. Noble and solemn, like knights. As Michael's body was lowered into the ground the Canon said, "Man, that is born of woman, hath but a short time to live, and is full of misery. He cometh up, and is cut down, like a flower." While he was saying that Odette tossed in a red rose and then so did Conchi and then Raquel. Defiantly, Millie stalked up and threw in a whole bouquet.

It was lovely then what the Canon said over the grave. He said, "Thou shalt show me the path of life. In Thy presence is the fullness of joy, and at Thy right hand there is pleasure for ever more." Johnny smiled. I could tell he thought that was just what to say for Michael. Johnny looked around, to be sure it was the end of the roses, stepped to the rim of the grave, and tossed in Michael's helmet. Ian Frazier, closest to the grave, cried out with grief and impulsively threw his own helmet on top of Michael's. Pop pop pop then, as if mesmerized, each member of the British racing team tossed his helmet upon the casket. Not just filling the grave but mounding it up with black domes like a pile of olives. Most merciful Father, the Canon was saying as the two grave diggers piled earth upon the mound and covered it with wreaths of flowers. The mourners sang "God Save the King." Upon the faces of the race drivers were expressions of sorrow and loss. Everyone filed sadly away and then there was a clatter and roar of motorcycles and an echoing and clatter of hooves as the hearses galloped off, careening dangerously, whips cracking, the tails of the drivers' black coats flapping in the wind.

ITINERARY

Were there any jet airplanes then? DC-6 from Santiago to Lima. Lima to Panama. A long night from Panama to Miami, ocean glittering. We had always made the trip by boat before, from Valparaiso to New York. The voyage took over a month. It wasn't just the beauty of it but the crossing of oceans and continents and seasons . . . a comprehension of vastness.

This was my first plane trip, my first trip anywhere alone. I was leaving Chile for college in New Mexico. It was the going alone that was so glamorous. Dark glasses and high heels. Pigskin luggage from Bariloche, a graduation present. Everyone was at the airport. Well, not my father, he couldn't get away, but even my mother and all my friends. Everyone was talking and laughing except Conchi and Quena and me, crying. We had made time capsules. Letters to be opened in thirty years, with avowals of friendship and predictions about our futures. They came out pretty right. Both of them married who they thought they would and gave their four or five children the names they said they would. Boris María, Xavier Antonio. But both Quena and Conchi died in the revolution, years before it was time to open the letter. The predictions for me were all wrong. I married and had children too, when I was supposed to be single, a journalist, in a walk-up apartment in Manhattan. I do live alone in a walk-up now.

It was exciting, boarding the plane, everybody waving from the observation deck. We buckled in and listened to the steward. The plane taxied down the runway and then stopped, for a very long time. Hot. It's summer in Chile in December. There was some problem; the plane turned back to the airport for an hour wait.

Everyone had gone; the lobby was deserted. An old man was pushing a rag with a stick, mopping. I could see my mother in the bar with some Americans from the plane. I went to the door and she saw me, looked surprised and then looked away, as if I weren't there. She's like that, doesn't see what she doesn't want to, but actually sees everything that's going on, more than most people. She once confided to me something "downright rotten and mean" she had done. It had been at the Sunshine Mine in Idaho, when I was little. She hated the Sunshine Mine, all of the dozens of mining camps we lived in, hated the "common" women and their tacky houses. We lived in tar-paper cabins with woodstoves too, but she didn't notice that. She wore a wool coat with a fur collar, glassy-eyed foxes. Hats with blue feathers. None of the women could play bridge well at all. But they were playing that day and the room was hot. There were ridiculous Halloween decorations. Orange and black crepe paper, jack-o'-lanterns. The women talked about cooking and recipes. "The last two things I would ever want to hear about." My mother glanced up from her cards and saw that a lantern had caught fire to a curtain. Flames blazed. She just looked back down at her hand and said, "I bid four no trump." Finally the fire got totally out of hand and the women fled to stand outside in the rain until the fire truck came from the mine. "I can't tell you how desperately bored I was."

Taking off above Santiago was splendid. The Cordillera was

at the wingtips, you could see the sparkle of the snow. Blue sky. We circled back over Santiago toward the Pacific. I saw Santiago College and the rose garden. Santa Lucía Hill. It had never occurred to me that I would want to go back home.

Ingeborg, my father's secretary in Lima, was supposed to meet me at the airport. I wished he hadn't done that. He was always planning, making lists. Goals and priorities. Timetables and itineraries. In my purse was a list of all the people who were to meet me, their numbers if I should get lost, embassy phone numbers, etc. I dreaded this secretary, spending three hours with her. His secretary in Santiago wore her hair in a net, had a blind mother and a retarded son she went home to every night, on two buses, standing, probably, after she got off work at six thirty. But when Ingeborg wasn't at the airport I felt scared, not a glamorous traveler at all. I called the number on my list and a woman with a European Spanish accent said to take a cab to 22 Cairo. Ciao.

In Lima the slums were as foul and desolate as in Santiago. Miles and miles of shacks made of cardboard and tin drums, roofs shingled with flattened tin cans. But in Chile the Andes are there and the blue sky and you just naturally look up, above the stench and misery. In Peru the clouds hang low, grim and wet. Drizzle mixes with wispy fires. A long bleak ride into town.

One thing I still like in the U.S. is windows. How people leave their window curtains open. Walking through neighborhoods. Inside people are eating, watching TV. A cat on the back of a chair. In South America there are high walls with broken glass on them. Crumbling old walls with small beat-up doors. The door to 22 Cairo had a frayed and knotted bell pull. An old Quechuan hag opened it. Her legs were bound in urine-soaked rags for chilblains. She stood back to let me in, into a brick patio with a tiled fountain. Cages with finches and canaries. Roses. Banks of cineraria, anemones, nemesia. It was as if the sun were shining. Bougainvillea cascaded from every wall and up the stone staircase into the *sala*. Pale wood floors with rich Peruvian rugs. Pre-Incan *huacos*, masks. Masses of tuberoses and bowls of gardenias, narcotic, cloying. Had my father ever been there? He hated smells.

The "Doña" was in the shower. The maid brought me an *aguita* in a demitasse. I sat politely but it seemed as if this Ingeborg was never coming so I got up and looked around. A blue Chinese vase, a harpsichord. An antique wooden desk. On top of it was a photograph of an old couple in black, both with black canes. Snow against bare trees. A faded framed snapshot of a blond child with a borzoi. There was a large color photograph of my father in a silver frame. In his Oaxacan poncho, a big hat. He was wearing an open shirt, a rose-colored shirt that I had never seen before. He was smiling. Laughing. Behind him were ruins, the Andes, clear blue sky. I sat back down in the chair. The little demitasse spoon clattered.

Ingeborg came in wearing a white robe, loose, showing long tan legs. Her blond hair was in a single braid down her back. A waft of what I now know to be L'Interdit. She was lovely.

"God, I'm glad your plane was late, never could have made it. I guess I still didn't, did I? But I'll feed you a nice lunch anyway and pay for a cab back. You don't look at all like him. Do you resemble your mother?"

"Yes."

"She's pretty? She's sick?"

"Yes."

"Are you hungry? Lunch will be on time at least. Forgive me for not driving you to the airport. But most of all Eduardo (Eduardo? My father, Ed?) wanted me to feed you and to see that you weren't lonely. But I don't think you are a lonely type. That is a wonderful suit. The way he spoke about you I expected a little girl, a child who would want to color, or tease my birds."

I laughed. "I expected an old woman. With cats and *National Geographics*. Are you Swedish?"

"German. You know nothing about me? But that is typical of him. I hate cats. I think there is a *National Geographic* around here somewhere. You only need one, they're all exactly the same."

"When was that picture taken? The one on the desk?" My voice sounded stern, judgmental, just like his.

She squinted, looking at it. "Oh, years ago, at Machu Picchu. Divine day. Doesn't he look . . . happy?"

"Yes."

Lunch was on a terrace above the garden. Ceviche. Sorrel soup, a purple clematis in the center. Empanadas and chayote. She only had the soup, drank gin and tonic while I ate, asking me questions. Do you have a *novio*? What does Eduardo do on Saturdays? Are those Italian shoes? That's the worst about Lima . . . no decent shoes and no sunshine. What will you study? What do your parents talk about together? Coffee?

She buzzed for the maid to go get me a cab. The phone rang. She said *¿Bueno?* and then put her hand over the mouthpiece.

"If you want to *maquillarte* the bath is down the hall."

"Sorry, love," she said to the phone. The doorbell rang, the cab was there. She put her hand over the phone again and to me she said, "Sorry, dear, but I have to talk to this person. Come give me a kiss. Good luck! Ciao!"

On the plane from Lima to Panama I sat next to a Jesuit priest. The type of choice I often make. One that appears safe and sensible. He had had a nervous breakdown after working in the wilds for three years. The steward finally took me back to sit in his little kitchen.

Mrs. Kirby met me in Panama. Her husband was vice president of Moore Shipping, the boats that my father's company used to ship copper, tin, and silver. I could tell that she didn't want to do this at all. I didn't either. We shook gloved hands. It was hot. We were driving, in a Rolls, in the Canal Zone, in a faded photograph. Everything was off-white, the houses, the clothes, the people. The lawns were manicured, beige grass. Long shadows. An occasional palm tree. Hot. I asked her if it was summer or winter. She got on the tube to her chauffeur and asked him. He said he thought it was spring.

"So what would you care to see?" she asked me. I said I'd enjoy seeing Panama City. In minutes the silent car had passed a magic invisible barrier and we were in Panama. It was as if the sound had been turned on. *¡Mambo! ¡Que rico el mambo!* Car radios blared; music came from every shop. Street vendors sold food, parrots, toys, bright fabrics. Black women laughed in flowered dresses. Flowers everywhere. Beggars, children, dogs, cripples, bicycles. "This has been an adequate tour," she said to the tube and we slid quickly back into the pale silence of the American sector.

Mrs. Kirby and a lady called Miss Tuttle and I played canasta all day. Maybe just all afternoon, until teatime, finally. They scarcely spoke to me. Inquired after my poor mother's health. Did my father just travel around telling people how sick my mother was? Was she sick? Maybe he had told her she was sick, so she was. Mr. Kirby arrived, in Bermuda shorts, a damp guayabera. He had been playing golf.

"So you're old Ed's daughter. Apple of his eye, I expect." A black servant brought mint juleps. We were on a veranda now, looking out on the ecru grass, drooping birds-of-paradise.

"So Ed thinks shipping ore on Chilean tankers will placate them, eh? That his game?"

"John!" Mrs. Kirby whispered. I saw that he was drunk.

"If the Reds nationalize the mines only way we'll keep our control is to boycott shipping. He's playing right into their hands.

Biting off the hand that feeds him, for sure. Pigheaded man, your father."

"John!" she whispered again. "Mercy. How are we doing for time?"

I insisted that they not come to the airport, that I needed to study for an entrance exam. Turned out there really was such an exam and I should have studied for it.

The best part about the Panama stopover was talking to the chauffeur on the tube. The airport was a low, ramshackle building, hidden by banana trees, fragrant vines, hibiscus. Another old man mopping the floor with a rag and a stick. Night fell. Blue runway lights. Black jungle ticking with insects and birds. What had Mr. Kirby meant about Chilean tankers? Was my father pigheaded?

In Miami it was morning and winter. In the airport women wore fur coats and their dogs wore fur coats. I was terrified by so many dogs. Little dogs with hair dyed peach to match the women's hair. Painted toenails. Plaid bootees. Rhinestone or maybe diamond collars. The whole airport was yapping. No towels in the bathroom but a machine you pressed for hot air. I waited at the Panagra desk for my aunt Martha. I dreaded her too, hadn't seen her since I was five. My mother said she was a hick. My parents fought about the money my father sent her and Grandma Proctor, my great-grandmother, who was ninety-nine. She and Aunt Martha lived in a tract house in Miami.

I cringed when I saw her, with all the snobbishness of a vain teenager. She was grotesquely fat, with a goiter, an immense goiter on her neck almost like another Siamese head. Doctors must have found a cure for goiters. When I was little there were hundreds of people running around with goiters. Aunt Martha had blue permanented hair and big round rouge spots on her cheeks.

She wore a red flowered muumuu and she crushed me to her, rocking me, hugging me. I was enfolded into the vast poinsettias on her breasts. In spite of myself I clung to her, sank into her and her smell of Jergens lotion, Johnson's baby powder. I stifled a sob.

"You sweet darling! I'm so glad to see you! Poor thing, you must be worn to a frazzle. Going off to college . . . your folks must be just busting with pride!" She swept up my bag. "No, no, you let me take care of you for a little while. Thought we'd have some lunch. Grandma and I, we come here a lot, to watch the planes. Good hot turkey sandwiches too."

We sat in a booth by the tinted plate glass overlooking the runways. Lay really, as she sort of lounged and I found myself lying into her, like on a chaise. We ate hot turkey sandwiches and then cherry pie à la mode. I was sleepy, leaned into her and listened, like to bedtime stories, while she told me about how my grandmother got TB so they moved to Texas from Maine. Then both my grandmother and grandfather died and Grandma Proctor came to care for Martha and Eddie, my father.

"So poor Eddie had to go out and work when he was twelve years old . . . picking cotton and cantaloupe. He'd be so tired he used to fall asleep eating dinner late at night, barely get off to school in the morning. But he's been working and providing for us ever since. He worked in the mines then, at Madrid and Silver City, put himself through Texas School of Mines. That's where he met your mother."

How was it that I had not known any of this?

"He bought us our place in Miami. Course it was hard for us to leave Marfa, our friends and all, but he said it would be for the best. Land sakes, I've been talking on and on. Best we be getting to the boarding gate."

She gave me a basket that had MIAMI BEACH embroidered on it. Inside was a little satin diary with a lock and key. Brownies wrapped in wax paper. She hugged me again.

"Eat well, now. Always eat breakfast and get plenty of sleep." I clung to her, didn't want to leave her.

A long flight from Miami to Albuquerque. I was blasé now about oxygen masks and life preservers. I didn't get off the plane in Houston. I was trying to think. What did my parents talk about? My father and Ingeborg. It's hard for anybody to imagine their parents making love. It wasn't that. I couldn't imagine him wearing a rose-colored shirt. Laughing that way.

It was sunset as we circled Albuquerque. The Sandias and the miles of rocky desert were a deep coral pink. I felt old. Not grown up, but the way I do now. That there was so much I did not see or understand, and now it is too late. The air was clean and cold in New Mexico. No one met me.

LEAD STREET, ALBUQUERQUE

"I get it . . . you look at it one way and it's two people kissing, another way and it's an urn."

Rex grinned down at my husband, Bernie. Bernie just stood there, grinning too. They were looking at a large black-and-white acrylic that Bernie had worked on for months, part of his Master's Exhibit. That night we were having a preview and party at our apartment on Lead Street.

There was a keg of beer and everybody was pretty high. I wanted to say something to Rex about that crack. He was so blasted arrogant and cruel. And I wanted to kill Bernie for just smirking. But I just stood there, letting Rex stroke my behind while he insulted my husband.

I freshened up the onion dips and chips and guacamole and went out on the steps. No one else was outside, and I was too depressed to call anybody to come see the unbelievable sunset. Is there a word opposite of *déjà vu*? Or a word to describe how I saw my whole future flash before my eyes? I saw that I'd stay at the Albuquerque National Bank and Bernie would get his doctorate and keep on painting bad paintings and making muddy pottery and would get tenure. We would have two daughters and one would be a dentist and the other a cocaine addict. Well, of course I didn't know all that, but I saw how things would be hard. And I knew that years and years from then Bernie would probably leave me for one of his students and I'd be devastated but then would go back to school and when I was fifty I'd finally do things I wanted to do, but I would be tired.

I went back inside. Marjorie waved to me. She and Ralph lived upstairs. He was an art student too. Our place on Lead Street was in an old, old brick building, with high ceilings and windows, wood floors and fireplaces. Just a few blocks from the Art Department, on a huge lot with wild sunflowers and purple weeds. Ralph and Bernie are still good friends. Marjorie and I got along okay. She was good, simple. She was a bagger at Piggly Wiggly, cooked things like Beenie-Weenie Wonder. Came over one morning ecstatic because she figured out that she could just lie in bed and pull all the sheets and blankets tight, then just slide out carefully and tuck everything in. A real time-saver! She saved butter wrappers to oil cake pans with. Why am I being so petty? I loved her.

"Guess what, Shirley! *Rex* is moving in to the vacant apartment! And he's getting married!"

"Damn. Well, that will pep things up around here."

It was exciting news. He was an exciting man. Young, only twenty-two, but his talent and skill were incredible even then. We all accepted the fact that he was destined for fame. He is pretty famous now, here and in Europe. He works in bronze and marble, simple classic pieces, not at all the wild stuff he was doing in Albuquerque. His sculpture is pure, the conception of it filled with respect and care. It catches your breath.

He wasn't handsome. Big. Red-haired with sort of buckteeth and a weak chin, a jutting brow over piercing beady eyes. Thick glasses, potbelly, beautiful hands. He was the sexiest man I ever knew. Women fell for him in a second; he'd slept with the entire Art Department. It was power and energy and vision. Not like a forward-looking vision, although he had that too. He saw everything. Details, light on a bottle. He loved seeing things, looking. And he made you look, made you go see a painting, read a book. Made you touch the eggplant, warm in the sun. Well, of course I had a wild crush on him too, who didn't?

"So who is she? Who could it be?" I sat beside Marjorie on our sagging sofa bed.

"She's seventeen. American, but grew up in South America, acts foreign, shy. English major. Maria is her name. That's the scoop so far."

The men were talking about the Korean War, as usual. Everybody was afraid of the draft, as school was no longer a deferment. Rex was talking.

"You have to have a baby. It came out last week. Fathers are now exempt from service. Can you think of any other reason for me to get married, for chrissake?"

That's how it started. I mean I don't think we all just went to bed that night and conceived babies. But maybe we did, since exactly nine and a half months later Maria, Marjorie, and I all gave birth, and our husbands didn't get drafted. Not the same day. Maria had Ben, a week later I had Andrea, and a week after that Marjorie had Steven.

Rex and Maria were married by a justice of the peace and then they moved in. But not like other people. You know, you clean the place up, borrow a pickup truck, put up bookshelves, drink beer, unpack and collapse. They painted for weeks. Everything was white and beige and black, except the kitchen was a burnt ochre. Rex built most of the furniture. It was stark and modern, set off by his huge black metal and stained-glass sculptures, black-and-white prints. A fine Acoma pot. The only other color was on the ruby throats of the Javanese temple birds in a hanging white cage. It was impressive, straight from *Architectural Digest.*

He even redid her. We went over, with stuff to eat, while they were unpacking. She was sweet and fresh. Lovely, with curly brown hair and blue eyes, wearing jeans and a pink T-shirt. But after they moved in her hair got dyed black and actually ironed straight. She wore black makeup and only black and white clothes. No lipstick. Wild heavy jewelry that he had made. She stopped smoking.

She talked more when he wasn't around, was funny in a Lucille Ball way. She joked about the makeover, told us that the first time he had seen her naked he had said, "You are asymmetrical!" He made her sleep on her stomach, nose flat against the pillow; her turned-up nose was a slight imperfection. He was always arranging her, the way she sat, stood. He moved her arms around as if they were clay, tilted her head. He photographed her endlessly. As she grew more and more pregnant he drew charcoal after charcoal study. One of the finest things he ever did is a bronze of a pregnant woman. It's on the grounds in front of General Motors, in Detroit.

We couldn't tell how he felt about her though. Whether he had just married her for the baby. She must have had some money; he bought a rare MG-TD the day after the wedding. I can understand him marrying her just for the way she looked. He wasn't affectionate. He mocked her and ordered her around, but maybe he just couldn't show how he felt.

Maria worshipped Rex. She deferred to him in everything, was almost speechless around him, although with us she joked and chatted. It was scary, or pitiful, however you want to look at it. Every night she went to the studio with him. "I can't say anything, but he lets me watch him. It is so magnificent to watch him at work!"

Little things. One winter morning I went to borrow some

coffee and she was actually ironing his jockey shorts so they would be warm when he got out of the shower.

It wasn't just that she was young. She had moved around all her life. Her father was a mining engineer; her mother had been ill, or crazy. She didn't speak about them, except to say they had disowned her when she got married, wouldn't answer her letters. You got the feeling no one had ever told her or shown her about growing up, about being part of a family or being a wife. That one reason she was so quiet was that she was watching, to see how it was all done.

Unfortunately she studied Marjorie's cooking. I was there one night when Rex got home. She proudly presented him a casserole made out of hamburger and Frito chips. He dumped it in her lap. Hot. "How tacky can you get?" But she learned. Next thing I knew I saw her with Alice B. Toklas, making Shrimp Aurore.

Every day she changed the bottom of the birdcage. *The New Yorker* just fit. She deliberated for hours about what picture to put. No, Rex hates those Steuben glass ads! She hated the birds and would ask me to clip their nails for them, or take their dishes out to clean them.

Maria was scared to death about having a baby. Not the physical part. But what do you do with it?

"What will I teach it? How will I keep it from harm?" she asked.

Those months were happy, with the three of us pregnant. We all learned to knit. Marjorie made everything pink, which was too bad, because it came out Steven. I made everything yellow. I'm practical. Of course, under Rex's direction, Maria made clothes and blankets in reds and blacks and umber. A khaki baby sweater! We spent hours at Sears and Penney's buying receiving blankets and nightgowns and shirts. We'd pack everything carefully away in plastic and then take turns going to each other's houses and taking out every single item. We drank iced tea and ate Wheat Thins and grape jelly while we read to each other from Dr. Spock. Maria always had to reread the part about rinsing out the diaper in the toilet. She liked how he reminded you to take out the diaper before you flushed the toilet.

Rashes. We were all terrified of rashes. They could be nothing. Just heat. Or they could be measles or chicken pox or spinal meningitis. Rocky Mountain fever.

When the babies started to move we'd sit there close on the couch together and feel each other's babies moving and kicking. We'd cry and hug each other, with joy.

The babies would be born in September. Maria got the idea that they needed flowers to be blooming then, so there we were out in the blazing New Mexico sun with our fat selves, hoeing and planting zinnias and hollyhocks and giant sunflowers. Maria even sent away for exactly two hundred poplar trees from the Department of Agriculture. She insisted on planting them all herself. They were only two inches high but she planted them three feet apart, like it said to. All around the house, almost all around the whole block! She had to buy more hose that she lugged home on the bus from Sears. The poplars grew though, were at least two feet tall when the babies came.

I've long since remarried. To Will, a banker, a kind, strong man. I have a doctorate in history and teach at UNM. The Civil War. Sometimes, going home, I go out of my way to drive past Lead Street and the old apartment. The neighborhood is a slum now, the building a ruin, covered in graffiti, the windows boarded up. But the poplars! Higher than the tall house, shading the whole dusty desolate block. A good thing she planted them so far apart, they are a close lush wall of green.

None of our husbands were around much during our pregnancies. They were either working or teaching or in seminars.

Rex was having an affair with Bonnie, a model, but I don't think Maria knew. With another friend I would tell her, give her advice, butt the hell in, but with Maria you just wanted to protect her, keep her safe. Not that she was stupid. She saw things, but she always had that hesitancy of a blind person on a curb. You had to stop yourself from reaching out to her. Or you reached out, with whatever it was she needed. And she'd smile, Gosh, thanks.

The babies were born. Rex was at a show in Taos when Ben came, so Bernie and I took Maria to the hospital. It was a hard labor. Maria had something the matter with her spine and the coccyx had to be broken before the head could come out. But it did, with hair as bright red as Rex's. Bawling and lusty. It really seemed that he was born with that passion and zest his father had.

When I got to the hospital room the next day I was surprised to see Maria out of bed, and standing at the window. Tears streamed down her face.

"Oh, are you sad Rex isn't here? We finally found him. He'll arrive any minute!" (We had found him at last, at the La Fonda in Santa Fe, with Bonnie.)

"No, that's not it. I'm happy. I'm so happy. Shirley, look at all those people down there. Walking around and sitting in the cars and bringing flowers. They were all once conceived. Two people conceived them and then each of them was born into the world. Born. How come nobody ever talks about this? About dying or being born?"

Rex seemed more interested than pleased about the baby. He was fascinated by the fontanelle. At first he took a lot of photographs, then he stopped. "It's too malleable." Rex became more and more irritated by the baby's crying, spent even more time at the studio. He was working on a series of bas-reliefs. Big, brave ancient things. I've seen them several times at a museum in Washington. I like to remember how we all used to go watch him work on them in the sweltering studio.

He hated the baby's smells. Maria washed every day, by hand, kept changing sheets and diapers. She got even thinner but her breasts were full, her face radiant. "Incandescent!" Rex said, and he did drawing after drawing in warm pastels.

Our Andrea was born, and then Steven. Both dear serene fat babies. Bernie and Ralph were as thrilled as Marjorie and I were, even dropped their seminars to be at home more. Maria and Ben would come over in the evening. We'd all watch Ernie Kovacs and Ed Sullivan, *Gunsmoke.* Sometimes we played Monopoly and Scrabble. Mostly, shamelessly, we just played with the babies, kissed them and nursed them and burped and changed them. A smile! That's just gas. No, it was a definite smile.

We got used to not seeing much of Rex. He even worked all weekend, when we barbecued out by the zinnias and poplars. Maria never complained, but she looked tired. Ben was colicky, didn't sleep. She was always anxious. How can I please him? Soothe him? How can I sleep?

Rex received a grant to study in Cranbrook in the fall. A good art school in Michigan. It happened quickly, he got the news and started packing up his tools. He was at the studio the night before he left. I went over to see Maria. Ben was asleep. Maria was quiet, asked me for a cigarette, but I said no, Rex would kill me.

"Would you take the birds?" she asked.

"Sure. I think they're great. I'll get them tomorrow." That's all we said, even though I sat there for a long time. Horrible time, one of those when you know you should speak, or listen, and the silence echoes.

At six the next morning Rex was packing up the car and trailer, then he drove away. Minutes later Maria appeared at my door with the birdcage and a bag of seed. Thanks! While I got dressed for work I could hear noises from their apartment, hammering and music and thumping.

I got over there just a few minutes before Rex did.

She had taken down all the modern paintings and prints, tacked up college dorm posters. Van Gogh sunflowers. A Renoir nude. A rodeo ad with a bucking cowboy. Elvis Presley.

Covering the ecru couch was a Mexican blanket. Not a Oaxacan blanket but orange green yellow blue red purple with tangled dirty fringe. From the radio that usually played Vivaldi and Bach, Buddy Holly rocked away.

Her hair was in pigtails, tied with yellow ribbon. She wore pink lipstick and turquoise eyeshadow, was back in jeans and the pink T-shirt. Her feet, in cowboy boots, were up on the kitchen table. She was smoking, drinking coffee. Ben crawled around on the black kitchen tile, wearing only a soaking diaper, making wet serpentine swirls. He had zwieback in one hand, all over his face. With the other hand he was swooping pots and pans out of the cupboards and onto the floor.

I stood there. Rex came walking up and into the living room. He hadn't been gone over half an hour.

"Fucking axle broke. Have to wait." He looked around.

"Where are the temple birds?" he asked.

"At my house."

They stared at each other. She sat there, in terror, didn't move, didn't even pick up the baby, who was fussing now, zwieback everywhere. Rex was furious. He lunged toward her. Then he stepped back, and just stood there, utterly stricken.

"Hey, you guys . . . excuse me for butting in, but, please, don't get upset. This is funny. Someday you'll look back and it will seem very funny."

They ignored me. The room was limp, soggy with anger. Rex turned off the radio. Perez Prado. Cherry Pink!

"I'll wait on the steps for the garage to call," Rex said. "No. I might as well just leave," and he left.

Maria hadn't moved.

Missed moments. One word, one gesture, can change your entire life, can break everything or make it whole. But neither of them made it. He left, she lit another cigarette, I went to work.

Both Maria and I were pregnant again. I was really happy, and so was Bernie. Maria didn't want to talk about it. No, of course she hadn't told Rex. So it was different this time; I waited, hoping, for her to get enthused about it.

We had a great autumn though. On weekends we went to the hot springs in the Jemez, had picnics by the river. On hot nights we all piled into our car and went to double features at the Cactus Drive-in. Maria was calmer, happier. She had a translating job, spent hours working while Ben slept. She took a poetry class at UNM, sat in the sun, reading Walt Whitman, smoking, drinking coffee. She always wore a red bandana, because her roots were growing out. She grew more relaxed with Ben, enjoying him. The rest of us went over to her house more, ate chili and spaghetti, played charades with the babies crawling around us.

Thanksgiving. Rex was coming home. God, I couldn't imagine what she was feeling. I was a nervous wreck. I helped her get the house back into pristine condition, lent her some Miltown to get her back off cigarettes. She said she'd rather not be alone with Rex at first, so planned a welcome-back dinner. She put a WELCOME HOME! sign up on the front door but figured he'd think it was corny and took it down.

We were all there, nervous. Several other couples from the department. The apartment looked great. White chrysanthemums in a black Santo Domingo pot. Maria was deeply tanned, wore white linen, a flash of turquoise. Her hair was long, straight, and jet black.

He burst into the room. Dirty and lean and alive, boxes and art folios sliding onto the floor. I had never seen him kiss her before. I ached for them to be okay.

It was a celebration. She had made curry from scratch, there was tons of wine. But it was Rex, really, that brought news and jokes and an eddy of excitement that lit us all. Little Ben careened around the room in his rubber walker, drooling and laughing. Rex held him, swooped him up, gazed at him.

Over coffee, Rex showed us slides of work that he had done that summer, mostly the sculptures of the pregnant woman, but countless other things, drawings, pottery, marble carvings. He crackled with excitement, possibility.

"Now for the *news*. You'll never believe this. I still can't believe it. I have a patron. Patroness. A rich old lady from Detroit. She is *paying* me to go to Italy for at least a year. To a villa outside of Florence. But forget the villa. There is a foundry. A foundry for bronze! I'll leave next month!"

"Ben and me too?" Maria whispered.

"Ben and I. Sure. Although I'll go first and get things together."

Everybody was clapping and hugging until Rex stood up and said, "Wait, that's not all. Get this! I also got a Guggenheim!"

My first thought was for Bernie. I knew he'd be glad for Rex but could understand him being jealous. He was thirty, Rex only twenty-three and his future was there already, on a silver platter. But Bernie meant it when he shook Rex's hand. "No one deserves it more."

Everyone left but Bernie and me. Bernie went home and brought back a bottle of Drambuie. The men drank and talked about Cranbrook, looked through the slides again. Maria and I washed dishes and threw out garbage.

"About time we went home," I said to Bernie and gathered

up Andrea. Maria and Rex had gone in to check on Ben. We waited to say good-bye, heard them whispering in the bedroom.

She must have told him she was pregnant again. Rex came out of the bedroom, pale. “Good night,” he said.

He left the next morning, before she or Ben woke up. He took the paintings and sculptures and pottery, the radio and the Acoma pot. None of us ever saw him again.

NOËL. TEXAS. 1956

"Tiny's on the roof! Tiny's on the roof!"

That's all they can talk about down there. So what, I'm on the roof. What they don't know is I may just never get off.

I didn't mean to be so dramatic. Would have simply gone to my room and slammed the door, but my mother was in my room. So I slammed out the kitchen door. And there was a ladder, to the roof.

I flung myself down, still in a tizzy, and took some sips from my flask of Jack Daniel's. Well, I declare, I thought, it's right nice up here. Sheltered, but with a view of the pastures and the Rio Grande and Mount Cristo Rey. Real pleasant. Especially now that Esther has me all set up with an extension cord. A radio, electric blanket, crossword puzzles. She empties my chamber pot and brings me food and bourbon. For sure I'll be up here until after Christmas.

Christmas.

Tyler knows how I hate and despise Christmas. He and Rex Kipp run plumb amok every year . . . donating to charities, toys to crippled children, food to old folks. I heard them plotting to drop toys and food on Juarez shantytown Christmas Eve. Any excuse to show off, spend money, and act like a couple of royal assholes.

This year Tyler said I was in for a big surprise. A surprise for *me*? I'm embarrassed to admit this. You know I actually imagined that he was taking me to Bermuda or Hawaii. Never in my wildest dreams did I figure on a family reunion.

He finally admitted he was really doing it for Bella Lynn. Bella Lynn is our spoiled rotten daughter who's back home now that her husband, Cletis, left her. "She's so blue," Tyler says. "She needs a sense of roots." Roots? I'd rather see Gila monsters in my hatbox.

First off he invites my mother. Up and takes her out of the Bluebonnet nursing home. Where they keep her tied up, where she belongs. Then he asks his one-eyed alcoholic brother, John, and his alcoholic sister, Mary. Now, I drink. Jack Daniel's is my *friend*. But I still have my sense of humor, not mean like her. Besides she has incestuous feelings for Tyler, always has. Plus he asks her boring boring husband, who didn't come, praise the Lord. Their daughter Lou is here, with a baby. Her husband left her too. She's about as empty-headed as my Bella Lynn. Oh well, in no time they'll both be running off with some new illiterate misfits.

Tyler went and invited eighty people to a party Christmas Eve. That's tomorrow. This is when our new maid Lupe went and stole our ivory-handled carving knives. She hid them in her girdle, bent over for some fool reason crossing the bridge to Juarez. Stabbed herself, almost bled to death and it all ended up Tyler's fault. He had to pay for the ambulance and the hospital and a huge old fine because she was a wetback. And of course they found out about the wetback gardeners and the wash woman. So now there's no help at all. Just poor Esther and some part-time strangers. Thieves.

But the worst worst top of everything is he invited my relatives from Longview and Sweetwater. Terrible people. They are all very thin or grotesquely fat, and all they do is eat. They all look as if they have seen hard times. Drought. Tornadoes. Point is these are people I don't even know, don't ever want to know. People I married him for so I'd never have to see again.

Not that I need any more reasons to stay up here, but there is another one. Once in a while, clear as a bell, I can hear every single word Tyler and Rex are saying down in the shop.

I'm ashamed to admit this, but, what the hell, it's the truth. I'm jealous of Rex Kipp. Now I know Tyler's been sleeping with that tacky little secretary of his, Kate. Well, I.C.C.L. Which means I couldn't care less. Keeps him from huffin and puffin top of me.

But Rex. Now Rex is year in, year out. We spent half of our honeymoon at Cloudcroft, other half on Rex's ranch. Those two fish and hunt and gamble together and fly all around Lord knows where in Rex's plane. What galls me the most is how they talk together, out in the shop, for hours and hours. I mean to say this has nagged me to death. What in Sam Hill are those old farts talking about out there?

Well, now I know.

Rex: You know, Ty, this is a damn good whiskey.

Tyler: Yep. *Damn* good.

Rex: Goes down like mother's milk.

Tyler: Smooth as silk.

(They've only been swilling that rotgut for forty-some years.)

Rex: Look at them old clouds . . . billowing and tumbling.

Tyler: Yep.

Rex: I expect that's my favorite kind of cloud. Cumulus. Full of rain for my cattle and just as pretty as can be.

Tyler: Not me. Not my favorite.

Rex: How come?

Tyler: Too much commotion.

Rex: That's what's fine, Ty, the commotion, It's majestic as all git out.

Tyler: God *damn*, this is a nice mellow hooch.

Rex: That is just one hell of a beautiful sky.

(Long silence.)

Tyler: My kind of sky is a cirrus sky.

Rex: What? Them wispy no-count little clouds?

Tyler: Yep. Now up in Ruidoso, that sky is blue. With those light cirrus clouds skipping along so light and easy.

Rex: I know that very sky you're talking about. Day I shot me two buck antelope.

(That's it. The entire conversation. Here's one more:)

Rex: But do Mexkin kids like the same toys white kids do?

Tyler: Course they do.

Rex: Seems to me they play with things like sardine cans for boats.

Tyler: That's the whole point of our Juarez operation. Real toys. But, what kind? How bout guns?

Rex: Give Mexkins guns? No way.

Tyler: They're all crazy about cars. And the women about babies.

Rex: That's it! Cars and dolls!

Tyler: Tinker toys and erector sets!

Rex: Balls. Real baseballs and footballs!

Tyler: We've got everything figured out just fine, Rex.

Rex: Perfect.

(I mean, what existential dilemma these dickheads got figured out beats all hell out of me.)

Tyler: How you going to find it, flying in the dark?

Rex: I can find anyplace. Anyhow, we'll have the star.

Tyler: What star?

Rex: The star of Bethlehem!

I watched the whole party from up here. Boy was I a relaxed hostess, lying under the starry sky, my little radio playing "Away in a Manger" and "White Christmas."

Esther was up at four, cooking and cleaning. Have to admit Bella and Lou helped her out. The florist arrived and the caterers with more food and booze, bartenders in tuxedos. A truck came to deliver a giant bubble machine Tyler had set up inside the front door. I can't think about my carpet. Loudspeakers started blaring Roy Rogers and Dale Evans singing "Jingle Bells" and "I Saw Momma Kissing Santa Claus." Then cars and more cars kept on coming with even more people I never want to see again in my life. Esther, bless her heart, brought me up a tray of food and pitcher of eggnog, a fresh bottle of old Jack. She was all dressed up in black, with a white lace apron, her white hair coiled in braids around her head. She looked like a queen. She's the only person I like in this whole wide world or maybe it's that she's the only one who likes me.

"What's my slut of a sister-in-law up to?" I asked her.

"Playing cards. Some men started up a poker game in the library and she asks real sweet, 'Ooh, can I play?'"

"That'll teach them."

"That's the very thing I says to myself minute she started to shuffle. Zip zip zip."

"And my mama?"

"She's running around telling folks Jesus is our blessit redeemer."

I didn't have to ask her about Bella Lynn, who was on the back porch swing with old Jed Ralston. His wife, mongoose Martha, we call her, probably too loaded down with diamonds to walk, find out what he's up to. Then Lou comes out with Orel, Willa's boy, an overgrown mutant who plays tight end for the Texas Aggies. The four of them start strolling around the garden, giggling and squealing, ice cubes rattling. Strolling? Those girls were half-lit, their skirts so tight and their spike heels so high they could barely walk. I yelled down at them,

"Tar-paper floozies! White trash!"

"What's that?" Jed asks.

"It's just Mama. Up on the roof."

"Tiny's on the roof?"

So I lay me back down, went back to looking up at the stars. Turned my Christmas music high to drown out the party. I sang, too, to myself. It came upon a midnight clear. Fog came from my mouth and I sounded like a child, singing. I just lay there and sang and sang.

It was around ten when Tyler and Rex and the two girls came sneaking out, whispering and stumbling in the dark. They loaded our Lincoln with two big sacks, drove in two cars down the back pasture to the field by the ditch where Rex lands the Piper Cub. The four of them tied the bags onto the outside of the plane and then Tyler and Rex climbed in. Bella Lynn and Lou turned on the car's headlights to light Rex up a runway. Although seems like it was such a clear night he could have seen by stars.

The plane was so loaded down it barely got off the ground. When it finally did it took a god-awful time to get any altitude. Just missed the wires and then the cottonwoods at the river. The wings dipped a few times, and he wasn't showing off. At last he was headed for Juarez and the tiny red taillight disappeared. I breathed and said thank God and drank.

I lay back down, shaking. I couldn't bear it if Tyler were to crash. Just then the radio played "Silent Night," which always gets me. I cried, just plain bawled my eyes out. It's not true, what I said about him and Kate. I mind it a lot.

The girls were waiting in the dark by the tamarisk bushes. Fifteen, twenty minutes, seemed like hours. I didn't see the plane, but they must have, because they turned the car lights on and it landed.

I couldn't hear a word because of the racket from the party and they had the shop door and windows shut, but I could see the four of them in front of the fireplace. It looked so sweet just like *A Christmas Carol* with them toasting champagne, their faces all glowing and happy.

That's about when the news came on my radio. "A short while ago a mystery Santa dropped toys and much needed food onto Juarez shantytown. But marring this Christmas surprise is the tragic news that an elderly shepherd has been killed, allegedly struck by a falling can of ham. More details at midnight."

"Tyler! Tyler!" I hollered.

Rex opened the shop door and came out.

"What is it? Who's there?"

"It's me. Tiny."

"Tiny? Tiny's still on the roof!"

"Get Tyler, dick-face."

Tyler came out and I told him about the bulletin, said how Rex better hightail it on out to Silver City.

They drove back down to light him out. By the time they got back the house was quiet, except for Esther, cleaning up. The girls went inside. Tyler came over, underneath where I was. I held my breath, listening to him whisper Tiny? Tiny? for a while and then I leaned over the ledge.

"What do you want?"

"Come down off that roof now, Tiny. Please."

THE ADOBE HOUSE WITH A TIN ROOF

The house was a hundred years old, rounded and wind-softened, the same rich brown as the hard earth around it. There were other buildings on the land, a corral, an outhouse, a chicken pen. A small adobe squatted near the south wall of the main house. It didn't have a tin roof like the big house. Smooth and symmetrical, it seemed to have sprung up like a dusty mushroom out of the dirt.

There were four acres of run-down land. Twenty apple trees about to bloom. Dried corn stalks, a rusted hand plow. A thrasher with a curved beak sat under a bare cottonwood by the red pump. Water gushed from the pump when Paul tried it.

Most of the windows were broken, the doors ajar. Inside it was cool and dark and smelled of piñon, cedar. Another pungent scent came from a curtain made of eucalyptus berries and red beads.

Echoes. A faded envelope on the dusty pine floor. Goldenrod FOR COLIC in a yellow glass jar. Paul held Max, the baby, and sat in one of the deep windowsills.

"These walls are three feet thick! This is a great house. I could play the piano as loud as I wanted. The kids could play outside with no worry about cars. Great view! Look at the Sandias from here!"

"It is beautiful," Maya said, "but there's no running water, no electricity."

"We could get plumbing put in . . . easy. We never had electricity at our cabin in Truro when I was a kid."

"But I'd cook on that old woodstove?"

That was the extent of Maya's objections. Gratitude was still a big part of her feeling toward Paul. Her first husband had left her when Sammy was nine months old and she was pregnant with Max. It had seemed like a miracle when Paul came along and loved Sammy and Max as well as her. She was determined to have a good marriage, to be a good wife. Still only nineteen, she had no idea what being a good wife meant. She did things like hold the hot part of the cup when she passed him coffee, offering him the handle.

Paul had just gotten a job in an Albuquerque nightclub. He was a jazz musician, a piano player. They were looking for a place where he could practice and sleep during the day, where the children could play outside.

"Listen!" Maya said. "What's that sound, mourning doves?" They were walking now in the apple orchard.

"Quail. Look, over there." Sammy had spotted them. He ran, chasing them into tamarisk bushes. Way off in the field a roadrunner streaked by and disappeared. They laughed, it was just like the cartoon, only he was black and white, startling against the dull brown dirt.

They drove down to Corrales Road to their friends' house, Betty and Bob Fowler, the only people they knew yet. Bob was a poet, taught English in a private school. He and Paul had gone to Harvard together, were old friends. Betty and Maya got along okay. Maya thought Betty was bossy and officious; Betty found Maya insufferably passive and naïve. Betty and Bob had four daughters, all under five.

The Fowlers were one of the few Anglo families that lived out here, in Alameda. It was farmland and orchards for miles and miles with cottonwoods and Russian olive trees lining the fields. Alfalfa, corn, beans, chili. Holsteins and quarter horses in dusty pastures. Alameda itself consisted of a church, a feed store, a grocery store, and Dela's Bella Della Beauty Parlor.

They all got in the Fowlers' van and went back to look at the house. The Fowlers' four little girls played outside with Sammy and Max while the adults looked around. Bob and Paul talked about putting in plumbing, where to get wood. Betty and Maya talked about the practicalities of washing and cooking. Betty said it would be impossible to live there with two children in diapers. No electricity? A woodstove, no running water, no bathroom? Flatly impossible. Partly as a reaction, Maya insisted that it would be no trouble at all, that women had done it for centuries. It would be fun, in fact.

Betty always knew everything, so she knew that Dela Ramirez had inherited the house from her father. She even knew that the town thought the place should have gone to Pete or Frances García, Dela's brother and sister. Even though they were good-for-nothings, they were older, and besides Dela and her husband had a house.

Dela, at the Bella Della Salon, talked to Betty over a woman's wet head, opening metal clamps with her teeth. Betty had dropped her acting-school voice for a drawl. She chatted on with Dela about the Tafoya brothers, about leasing the alfalfa field, about Head Start and about Head and Shoulders. Maya didn't say anything, read *National Enquirers*, combed her hair. She was new to the local social rituals. Now the two women were talking about dividing canna lilies and painting the bottoms of fruit trees.

"*Oye*, Dela," Betty finally said. "You know of a house for rent around here?"

Dela shook her head. "Nobody rents houses out here." She put paper cones over the woman's ears, wound a net over the pins and clamps. "No, can't think of a thing."

"My friends are looking for a place with some land. Some place with low rent, or no rent maybe in exchange for painting, putting in plumbing, things like that. Clearing the land, fixing the windows. You know . . . improving the property."

"How much rent?" Dela asked, her back to them. She pulled a dryer down over the woman's head, flicked the switch to low, medium, hot, very hot.

"Fifty at the most, I figure . . . since they'll be fixing it up. Can you think of anything?"

"Well, there's my folks' place. Back down off Corrales Road. My brother Pete goes there sometimes. To the little house, not the big one. But it's all my property now."

"Might be good to have somebody taking care of it."

Dela was silent, snapped the switch to hot, medium, low. The woman let the magazine fall on her lap so that she could hear.

"They could rent my folks'. Seventy, though. That's a big place."

"Seventy!" Betty scoffed. Maya leaned forward then and said to Dela, "We'll pay that. But for the whole place, not with your brother there."

"Oh, he wouldn't come, somebody living there. He's a good-for-nothing."

"When can we move in?"

Dela shrugged. Anytime.

"We'll start cleaning it up, putting in windows. When we move in, I'll come pay the rent."

"No," Betty said. "A lease. They'll need a lease if they're going to be doing all those improvements."

Paul and Maya worked hard for the next few weeks, putting in windowpanes, sanding floors, plastering, and painting. The Fowlers helped too, and the two families had picnics outside as the sun set on the Sandias.

The last thing they did was paint the trim on the windows. Santa Fe blue. They made up a song. "Got the Santa Fe Blues." Dipping their brushes in the paint can Paul and Maya would stop and kiss each other, happy about their new house. Sammy and Max ran in the fields, played with trucks and blocks, in the mud by the pump.

The last day they came to paint there were three dogs curled up on the back stone steps. An old bulldog with pink testicles, a mangy bitch with a black tongue, and a furry black puppy. Their owner wasn't in sight. Although the dogs barked at first, they settled back down. The puppy was gentle and let Max carry him upside down around the yard.

Maya made coffee. She and Paul sat in the kitchen. She hadn't tried cooking on the woodstove yet, had used a Coleman stove to make tea and coffee so far.

"You've got paint in your hair," she said. "I wish you didn't have to go back to work." Paul had had Willie Tate sub on piano for five days at the club.

"Me too . . . except that we've really got the group together. Ernie Jones is the best bass player I ever played with. I'm sure Prince Bobby Jack will renew our contract. The club is packed for both sets every night."

•

"Godawmighty what a pretty pretty house!" The woman had walked right in the kitchen door. In her fifties, grotesquely fat, wearing overalls and men's boots. Long matted hair grew out from under a cowboy hat.

"Pretty house! Used to be my house. I got my own house, see, over there cross Corrales Road." She pointed, grinning, toothless, to a shack in the woods beyond the road. "Somebody burnt it up. Jealous. I got a boyfriend, Romulo. You seen him? It was on the TV with the fire engines, you seen it?"

She was quiet for a minute. A stain and then drops on the floor as she wet her pants. "You seen Pete? You see him, you tell him, here's his dogs. Too many dogs. I got my own dogs. Pete was born right where you're sitting. I watched it."

"We live here now," Paul said. "You go home now, to your own house."

"I got my own house. Over there, cross the road. Bottles!"

She had spotted some empty Orange Crush bottles in a pile of trash, went outside and began putting them and other things into a grocery cart. She left, clattering down the rocky road with her cart, throwing rocks back at the dogs when they tried to follow her.

"Take the dogs with you!" Paul called.

"Pete's dogs. They live here. I got my own dogs! My name is Frances."

The Fowlers helped them move into the house. They drank champagne in front of a piñon fire and Maya cooked fried chicken and corn on the cob on the woodstove. The cornbread was burnt on the bottom, but it wouldn't take long to figure out the oven.

Washing dishes was a pain, carrying in the water, heating it up. No, maybe that night it was fun, after that it became a pain.

Maya and Paul couldn't sleep the first night they moved in. They made love on the Navajo rug in front of the fire, drank cocoa, sat in the windowsills and looked at the moonlight in the apple trees. The next morning the trees had begun to bloom! Overnight! They sat outside with their backs against the warm wall in the sun while the boys played nearby with the dogs. Smells of apple blossoms and coffee and piñon smoke.

The door to the little house next to theirs banged open. Paul and Maya jumped, startled; they hadn't heard anyone drive in the night before. Coffee with cream splattered through the torn screen door. The door slammed shut.

Pete came out of the house. A massive swarthy man with long black hair, gold front teeth, green eyes. He was about forty-five, but he walked with the insolent beat of a teenage Chicano. He grinned at them, ducked his head under the spout of the pump, jerked up and down on the handle. Water gushed over his hair and face; his huge back shuddered. He blew and snorted, rinsed out his mouth and spat. He stood up, grinning at them, water streaming from his hair down his dirty undershirt. He spat again and wiped his mouth with the bottom of his shirt.

"I'm Pete Garcia. I was born here."

"I'm Paul Newton, this is my wife, Maya. We live here now. We've leased all the buildings."

"Dela said you wouldn't be coming here now," Maya said.

"Dela! I mind my own business. You mind your own business. I got my own house in town. Sometimes I come here to get a rest from my wife." The dogs were leaping around him to be petted. "This old dog is Bolo. The dumb bitch is Lady, and the baby is Sebache, that means 'very black rock' in Spanish." He grinned.

Paul and Maya were silent as he introduced himself and the dogs to the kids. He went back into the house. When he came back out, he was wearing an army jacket and a cowboy hat. He was carrying a jug of Garden DeLuxe Tokay and a pan of cornmeal mush he put down for the dogs.

He backed his car around the house to where they were sitting. It was an old Hudson with no back doors or windows. He sat there, revving the engine, drinking from his jug. Then he lit a cigarette, gave them a gold grin and a wave, and tore off down the road. The dogs followed the car to Corrales Road, then returned, panting, to settle themselves down in the middle of where the children were playing.

"You'd better go talk to Dela," Paul said.

"Why me? Why not *you* just talk with *him*?"

"It might not be so bad, Maya. I'm actually glad about the dogs. You are stranded out here when I'm at work. No car and no phone. I mean, if something happened to one of the boys . . . at least he could give you a ride somewhere."

"Terrific. Stranded out here with Pete. But it's a blessing, really."

"Sarcasm doesn't become you, Maya."

They didn't discuss it any more. Paul left early to rehearse with the band. Maya and the boys walked in the orchard and by the ditch before she put them down for their naps. She sat on the back step, reading, gazing up at the mountains.

Pete drove up about five o'clock. He parked right beside her and took a bare-root rosebush out of his backseat.

"It's called Angel Face. Pretty, pretty pink rose. Plant it here, north side, so it don't get too hot. I work at Yamamoto's nursery. They ain't gonna miss one rose. This soil is just bad old caliche, so you have to dig a deep deep hole and then put in good dirt and peat moss."

He unloaded sacks of soil and peat moss from his car, got in the car, and drove over to his little house. Maya looked around, finally found a shovel, started to dig a hole. She couldn't even dent the clay earth. She was muttering to herself when he came around the corner with a pick. He let her do the work though, as he sat on the steps drinking beer. He told her how to drape the roots over the cone of good dirt, filling in dirt and watering, then more dirt and peat, packing it gently down, leaving the knob just above the ground. He watched while she carried four buckets of water from the pump.

"Pete! *¡Órale, mano!*" Romulo and Frances were coming up the road. Frances was pushing her grocery cart filled with beer and bags of groceries. Romulo was a tiny wizened man, wearing paratrooper leggings and boots and an aviator hat with its fur flaps down over his ears. He circled round and round Frances, riding a tiny child's bicycle. Frances's four hound dogs and Bolo, Lady, and Sebache barked and cavorted around them. The three of them went into Pete's house. They drank and argued and laughed. They played gin rummy and drank. When they finished a quart of beer, often, they would bang open the door and toss the empty bottles into Frances's shopping cart. When they had to pee, they just peed outside the door, then banged it shut again. Frances squatted outside and splashed, singing, "Pretty little fellow, everybody knows . . . Don't know what to call him but he's mighty lak a rose!" There was nowhere in the house Maya could go and not hear them.

Paul didn't understand when she said they were driving her crazy. That the plants were driving her crazy. Paul thought it was just great, how Pete kept bringing plants, almost every day.

"Ever think that maybe you're prejudiced against Mexicans?" Paul asked.

"Prejudiced? Oh, for Christ's sake. Well, I'm sick of these particular greasers."

"Maya! That's foul. Truly beneath you." He was deeply shocked and left early for work without saying good-bye.

She built two trellises for the climbing American Beauties. Two lilac bushes, a forsythia next to the pump. A trumpet vine against the outhouse. Honeysuckle climbed up the clothesline pole. A Peace rose, a Joseph's Coat, a Just Joey. Abe Lincoln.

Maya planted every bush. Every day she carried bucket after bucket of water. Pete leaned against the wall, drinking beer, watching her. "More fertilizer!" he said. He had dumped a pickup load of horse manure for her to spread.

Bathing the kids was fun, now that it was warmer, in the washtub by the pump. Paul showered and changed into his tuxedo every night at work. At first Maya took baths in the washtub on the kitchen floor, but it made too big a mess, took too many buckets. She showered at the Fowlers' and after her shower watched Betty's kids while Betty went grocery shopping. Twice a week the two women went to Angel's Laundromat on North Fourth Street. The couples had dinner together a few times a month. Over dinner and later over coffee or wine it was the two men who talked about poetry, jazz, painting. The women cleared the table, washed dishes, got the kids to sleep, listened to their husbands.

Spring windstorms began, whipping sand against the windows, whipping the blossoms off the trees. Maya and the children stayed inside. The children were cranky, whiney. She wished they had a radio or a television set. She got tired of squatting for hours on the floor, playing games, reading, singing songs. Paul slept late, practiced long hours every day. Scales, never ending.

The wind howled, the heat from the woodstove blasted into the kitchen. Her hair stuck damp to her forehead. It was horrible to pump water with sand pelting her face. The water got full of sand. Coffee had sand in it, beans had sand in them. Butter crunched with sand. Sand beat against the outhouse and filled her hair and eyes as she ran back to the house.

"When in God's name are we going to get the plumbing put in?" she asked.

"Look, get off my back. I'm working on new tunes. We're working out new arrangements. The band is really coming together. You know how important this is to me."

Paul went to work. She spent the afternoon making a devil's food cake. She was taking it out of the oven when Pete banged on her door.

"You got to water more. Those plants are crying for water."

"It's too hard in these windstorms, Pete."

"Well, they need more water. Here, I brought you a lantana bush and a flat of zinnias. Don't wet the zinnia leaves when you water. They'll get rot."

"Oh . . . Thanks, Pete."

The wind wasn't blowing so hard after all. She went outside. Sammy and Max helped her plant the lantana and zinnias beside the steps. She watered the new plants, hauled buckets of water to all the rosebushes, the tomatoes. She'd do the rest tomorrow.

That night Maya and Paul had cake and milk in front of the fireplace. Outside the wind blew sand against the windows. Paul had bad news, he said. He had talked to a plumber in town before he went to work. It would cost a fortune to have a bathroom and kitchen put in by a licensed plumber.

"Maybe there's someone out there who can do it. Why don't you go ask one of the Romeros?"

The next day, after he went to work, she and the children crossed the alfalfa field to Eleuterio Romero's. Eleuterio met her at the fence. "Yes?" he said.

"I'm Maya Newton," she said, offering her hand. He didn't take it, just stared insolently at her with his brown eyes.

"We wanted to have some plumbing put in," she said. "Do you know of anyone around here who could do it?"

"Why didn't you live in town if you wanted plumbing?"

"We like it out here."

"Why don't your husband put it in?"

"He doesn't have time. He's a musician."

"I know him. Plays with Prince Bobby Jack? Out at the Skyline Club? He's a good piano player."

"Isn't he?" She smiled, pleased. "Anyway, he works hard, and sleeps days and we really need some plumbing."

"Ask my brother Tony. He lives in the last house."

Romero land began with Eleuterio's, at the edge of their road, ran all the way down Corrales Road to North Fourth Street. The land was divided into four three-acre tracts, one for each brother. The next two farms were Ignacio's and Eliseo's, much like Eleuterio's. Flat adobe houses in the center of corn and chili and alfalfa fields. Children, pickup trucks, wrecked rusted cars in the back fields. Horses, cows, chickens, dogs. Red chili hung in *ristras* outside the kitchen doors in the sun. There was always a huge cauldron in the yard, for making *chicharrónes* out of pig skin, menudo, posole. The last farm was Tony's, on the other side of the irrigation ditch. He was the youngest brother. He only raised alfalfa for his horses; during the day he worked as a butcher. He had a big stucco house, painted green, with a fiberglass awning. Tony and Eliseo were building a filling station between their houses. Concrete block, with plate glass windows. On Sundays all the brothers would park their cars in Eleuterio's field. Their children would play with the other small children in the pasture. Eleuterio's older children would sit on the front porch: boys with comb-wet pompadours, girls with crinolines, self-conscious lipstick. They would sit and drink Cokes, watching their cars cruise on Corrales Road. The women stayed inside, sometimes coming out to check on the black pot, filled with posole. Smoke poured from the kitchen chimney. The Romero brothers sat drinking beer on benches against the wall of the house, facing the mountains, in the shade if it was hot, against the south wall in the sun if it was cold.

The next morning, while Paul slept, Maya drove to Tony's house. Tony wasn't home. Rosie, his wife, asked Maya to come into the kitchen, to sit down, please. She sat down too, smiling. She was sure Tony could do their plumbing, she said. Proudly, she showed Maya the kitchen sink and the washing machine, the bathroom. She turned on the water in the tub and flushed the toilet. Sammy and Max were fascinated. "It's wonderful," Maya sighed. She and Rosie drank coffee, chatted, talked about their children, their husbands. Rosie invited her to watch *Ryan's Hope* with her, but Maya said they'd better be going; it was about time for Paul to wake up.

Tony came the next afternoon. He and Paul sat in the orchard on a bench, smoking, drinking beer. Tony drew figures in the dirt with a stick; Paul nodded. They shook hands and Tony drove off in his pickup with half the money for the job, all the money Paul and Maya had saved. But still, Paul said, it was less than a third what a licensed plumber would cost.

The next day Tony came with a truckload of pipe. He and

Eleuterio unloaded it by the pump. That afternoon he drilled holes in the kitchen wall and floor and in the room where the bathroom was going to go. The next day the two brothers spent hours digging a cesspool near the Russian olive trees. A wide deep hole. Max and Sammy jumped down into it. They climbed and made roads for trucks in the mounds of clay.

Tony didn't come back. They saw him at the store. It was time to plow, he said. In the mornings Paul and Maya watched the brothers in the fields, burning weeds, fixing fences, taking turns behind a horse-drawn plow. Several weeks passed, and then it was time for them to plant. But by then it was warm and the wind had gone. It was nice to wash outside. Maya and the boys were brown and strong. They helped her weed and water. The tomato and corn plants were growing, the lilac and forsythia bushes in bloom!

Paul bought a Mexican hammock that he hung between two apple trees. Before he left for work the four of them would lie in it, swaying softly, watching meadowlarks and red-winged blackbirds, a white-breasted shrike. Beyond them, above them, were the Sandia Mountains and the blue sky. All day long the color of the mountains changed and shifted. Browns and greens and deep blues until at sunset they blazed pink, then magenta, melting into velvety purple under a mauve sky.

Before she put the boys to sleep inside, she would lie with them in the hammock and read stories. That's where they were the night Pete moved in, pulling a blue trailer behind the Hudson. There was a bed and table and woodstove, boxes of dishes and food. The dogs, who had been riding in the trailer, leapt out to come greet the boys.

"Pete, we leased *all* these buildings. You have no right to move in here."

"No right? I was fuckin' born here! Dela has her own house. I'll live where I feel like."

"Pete. We have a lease. *We* live here now."

"You mind your own business. I mind my own business."

Ordinarily, after the boys were asleep, Maya would water the plants, then drink coffee and read in the hammock until it grew too dark to see. But she couldn't read with him just a few yards away, banging the door, singing, chopping wood, hollering at the dogs. Fuming, she went inside and lit a lantern by the red chair in the living room. She tried to read *Middlemarch* and to ignore the rattle of Frances's cart, the howling of all the dogs, Romulo's laughter. Anywhere she went in the house and even in the outhouse she could hear their drunken arguments and taunts and joking. Fuckin' A, *mano*! Or: Chees, *¡a la morí, ese pendejo! Pinche jodido*, this chili's too salty, *compadre*. Yelps as one of them would kick a dog. *¡Vayase, pinche perra!*

Maya woke when Paul got home. She lit the candle by the bed. Even by candlelight he looked pale and tired. He smelled of cigarette smoke, stale beer, nightclub. He took off his tuxedo and bow tie, the ruby studs from his shirt.

"God, I'm bushed. Saturday night. Every drunk and redneck in town was at the club." He got into bed and put on the black mask that helped him sleep in the morning. Before he could put in his earplugs, she said, quickly, "Pete moved in. Really moved in, a stove, all his furniture."

"For crissake. I'm sick of hearing about Pete. You and Dela will have to straighten it out. We'll talk about it tomorrow. I'm exhausted." He put his earplugs in.

In the morning she realized she had forgotten to fill the water jug. When she went to get a bucketful from the pump, it wouldn't work. It had lost its prime. She went and banged on Pete's door. He had been asleep, was in stained jockey shorts.

"Morning, sunshine!" He grinned.

"Hi, Pete. Do you have any water? I'm completely out and the pump's lost its prime."

"How come you don't have no water? My mama, she always had a big *olla* of water. Ooh that water tasted so cold, and so sweet. Maya, is our water the best water you ever tasted or no?"

She laughed. "You know, it is pretty good water. Pete, do you have any? To prime the pump?"

"I'll be back in a minute."

She waited. Sammy and Max came outside, hungry for breakfast. Pete returned, barefoot, in Levi's and no shirt. He had a jug of water. He poured it slowly into the back of the pump.

"*Pinche*, no good, and that's all the water I had."

"I'll go see if I have a pitcher or something with some water in it." Maya went inside. When she came back out, empty-handed, Pete was slowly pouring a quart of Hamm's beer into the pump. It caught; water gushed into the tub.

"Hamm's will fix just about any problem you got," he said.

"Yeah. Well, thanks."

After she fed and dressed the kids, she put them and the laundry in the car. On her way to the Fowlers' she passed Tony's. He and his brother were installing the new gasoline pumps. She pulled into the gravel in front of them.

"Hi, Tony. How are things looking, you know, about our plumbing?"

"Lookin' good! Me and Eliseo, we want to get the concrete laid here before the rains start. Another coupla weeks I'll be by and you'll be in business!"

•

After Paul left for work, she bathed the boys in water that had been warming in the sun and put them to bed. She took the tub inside, heated water on the stove, hauled in more buckets, and took a bath herself. She put on clean clothes and went out to read in the hammock, balancing her book and a cup of coffee. It was early evening and smelled of apple trees and alfalfa and horse manure. Nighthawks circled above the orchard.

Pete drove up and lurched to a stop outside his door. A woman was with him, a henna-haired sleazy tart. Both of them staggered into the little house. Sounds of fighting, bottles breaking, angry sex came from the house. Maya tried to read. *¡Puta desgraciada!* Pete hit the woman then, again and again. She was screaming, sobbing. A chair broke a window. Max woke up, crying and frightened, and then Sammy woke up. She took them into the big bed and sang to them for a while until they went back to sleep.

In the morning the woman was gone. Pete was washing at the pump, hungover and puffy-eyed. Maya went out in her bathrobe.

"Pete, don't ever do that again. You terrified my kids. It was disgusting. I'll go for the police next time."

"You mind your business; I'll mind my business. I'm late for work."

The dogs barked as usual while he revved the engine. He put the car in reverse, backed up, by mistake, and ran over Sebache. The dog screeched. Sammy and Max screamed from the bedroom window. Blood oozed from under the tire.

The dog was dead.

"Fuckin' A. Poor little puppy. I'm late for work. Maya, you bury him for me?"

Maya sat in the hammock with the boys, comforting them. They had never seen death, were upset, fascinated. She dug a grave by the cesspool hole, wrapped the puppy in an old towel, let Sammy and Max cover it with dirt.

"Now do we water it?" Sammy asked. She laughed, was laughing and crying. That really confused them. They had never seen her cry before. The three of them sat in the hammock and cried. Then they ate breakfast.

Pete drove up, not in his car, but a Yamamoto's truck. He dropped a weeping willow in the dirt by the kitchen door. For Sebache.

Paul got up later and they had lunch. She was about to bring up Pete when Ernie Jones came in the door carrying his bass.

"Ernie and I are going to jam out here before we go to work. Buzz Cohen might come sit in. He's a sax player I used to play with in college, hasn't played in a long time. He used to be great."

"It'll be good to hear you. Shall I make some coffee?"

"I brought some sodas," Ernie said.

The boys were thrilled. Sebache was forgotten as they listened to the music. Maya listened too, humming. Then she planted the willow tree and carried water to the plants. She was stumbling along with two full buckets to the trumpet vine when Buzz Cohen pulled up in a red Porsche.

"Quick, let me take you away from all this!" He smiled. He was dark, handsome, sexy. Undoubtedly a cad, she thought, but she smiled back.

"You Buzz? I'm Maya, Paul's wife. Go on in."

They played every afternoon. Buzz found excuses to come into the kitchen, for a beer or a drink of water, or outside, to ask about staking tomato plants. She enjoyed it, the attention. She was sorry when the music stopped and the men left. Then Pete would get home, and then Romulo and Frances and the dogs.

It was July and hot. Field mice came into the house through

all the holes Tony had drilled for the plumbing. Brazen mice, running all over the house all day. At night there were scurryings and rattlings and even crashes and bangs as they knocked over brooms, pots and pans. She put mousetraps down, behind the stove and the piano. What was horrible was that they worked right away. A few minutes after she'd put them down there would be a snap and a tiny wailing and a dead mouse. Crack crack crack. So she stopped doing it.

One night a mouse ran across her face when she was in bed. The next day she put poison in safe places in the kitchen and bedroom.

That night some noise woke her up. She lit a candle and went into the kitchen for a drink of water. Dozens of dying mice were reeling around the kitchen floor, crying in little voices. She screamed, terrified. The children woke up. They were scared too by all the mice staggering around the kitchen, like drunken windup toys. She was trying to sweep them out the door when Pete showed up.

"*¡Hijola!* What's the matter with the mice?"

"They're dying. I put poison down today." Pete lit another candle and sat down at the kitchen table. She put the boys to bed. When she came back to the kitchen, Pete was gathering the mice into a bag. It was the first time he had been inside her house.

"Poison. Maya, you crazy or something? Those meeses go outside, Bolo and Lady'll eat them and die. Your kids will find them and get sick and die. What did they do to you, them meeses? They don't hurt nobody. Besides they'll go back out when it rains. All they want is water."

"Water!"

"That was bad, Maya. They don't hurt you none."

"They're driving me crazy. And so are you guys, hollering and arguing every night, and the dogs barking. Crazy."

"We're driving you crazy? We're your friends. Your neighbors. I'm your best neighbor. You come here! Come on, come here!" He stepped out on the back porch.

"Smell our American Beauties! Just smell them!"

In the cool night air the perfume of the roses was sweet and strong. Just underneath their heavy scent was sultry summer honeysuckle.

Paul drove up, got hurriedly out of the car.

"What's wrong?" He glared at Pete, who stood there in jockey shorts.

"She put rat poison down. I was telling her she could up and kill her own kids, putting poison down. Am I right or no?"

"Right. Good Lord, Maya, that was stupid."

I'm losing my mind, she thought. She left them both and went in to bed.

One evening it was so hot Pete and Romulo moved their table out under the trees. They played dominoes and drank beer. Frances was cleaning Pete's kitchen. All of the furniture was outside and she was pouring buckets of water onto the floor, sweeping it out, singing "Mighty lak a rose." Sammy and Max were in the tub by the pump. Maya sat by the tub, holding her book in one hand, trailing the other in the water. Nighthawks sailed above the orchard. Eleuterio had irrigated; there was a wet sweet smell of alfalfa.

Buzz drove up in his Porsche. He got out, but left the motor on so music played loud. Stan Getz, bossa nova. Buzz had brought a large pitcher of frozen daiquiris. He and Maya sat on the steps, drinking from wineglasses. Frances danced under the cottonwoods to "The Girl from Ipanema." Pete scowled; dominoes clicked. The daiquiris were strong. Cold, cold, delicious! "Sure!" Maya said when Buzz suggested that she and the boys pile into the car. They'd drive down by the Rio Grande where it was cool, go to a drive-in for hamburgers and root beer.

It was fun. A pretty summer night. When they got home, Buzz waited in the kitchen while she put the boys to bed.

"I had a good time," Maya said.

"Me too," Buzz said. "Damn, what a cheap date. Give her an ice cube and she'll follow you anywhere." They laughed and he kissed her. It thrilled her. He kissed her again. "You need some loving, someone to take care of you." She pulled him to her, thirsty for him.

Pete was banging on the door.

"What is it?"

She stood inside the kitchen, behind the door. She had only lit one candle.

"What are you doing, in the dark?" Pete asked. "Sugar. I need to borrow some sugar. I can't drink my coffee with no sugar."

She poured sugar into a cup. Mice scattered behind the canisters.

"Here." She handed the cup out the door.

"Thanks."

After Pete had left, Buzz drew her to him again, but Maya had come to her senses. She moved away. "Good night," she said. "Don't come back when Paul's not here."

In August the thunderstorms came. It was wonderful, the sound of the rain on the tin roof, the lightning and thunder. There were tomatoes and squash and corn. Maya and the boys swam and fished in the clear ditch every day.

But the mice never did go away. The plumbing never got put in. Buzz came back often when Paul wasn't home.

In the autumn Paul got a job in New York. He and Maya

packed everything into the van and a U-Haul trailer. Pete and Frances and Romulo moved into the big house that same day. They stood waving and waving as the car and the U-Haul drove away. Maya waved too and she wept. The plants, the red-winged blackbirds, her friends. She knew she'd never be back. She knew this wasn't a good marriage either. Frances died a few years later, but Pete and Romulo still live in the house. They are both old now. They sit under the trees and play dominoes and drink beer. You can see the place from Corrales Road. A fine old adobe, well over a hundred years old. It's the house with the blazing red trumpet vine, the house with roses, everywhere.

A FOGGY DAY

Downtown the Washington Market is deserted until midnight Sunday when suddenly the fruit and vegetable markets open out onto the streets, wild banners of lemons, plums, tangerines. Farther down, toward Fulton Street, subtle reds and browns of potatoes, squash and yellow onions.

The buying and loading go on staccato until dawn when the last delivery truck is gone and the Greek and Syrian merchants speed off in black cars. By sunrise the market is as empty and dingy as it was before, except for the smell of apples.

Lisa and Paul walked in the rain, in deserted downtown Manhattan. She talked. "It's like living in the country down here. Corn and watermelon in the summer . . . Seasons. This is where they bring the Christmas trees for all New York. They're stacked for blocks and blocks. Forests! One night it snowed and three dogs were running wild like wolves in *Doctor Zhivago.* You couldn't smell cars or factories, just pine trees . . ." She babbled on as she always did when she talked with him, or with dentists.

She wanted him to see it as beautiful, the city, her city. She knew he didn't. He was looking at the men eating raw yams and stolen grapefruit, or burning orange crates in rusty incinerators. Bronze K Ration SIX FOR A DOLLAR cans, green Gallo Port bottles glistened in the light of the fires, shimmered in the rain. An old man vomited into the gutter where purple fruit wrappers blurred indigo at the grate like crushed anemones.

He would find no beauty at night, during the time when fires dotted the landscape for blocks around, silhouetting the gestures of the men into drunken ritual dances. Or from her window at dawn, looking down upon a half-naked black boy, asleep on a dazzling truck bed of limes.

It started to rain hard. They waited in the doorway of Sahini and Sons, Artichokes, until it lessened into a drizzle, then they walked on again, wet. Slow and lanky, like they used to walk in Santa Fe, like old friends.

In Santa Fe Lisa's husband, Benjamin, had worked at George's restaurant, with Paul. George was a mean lesbian who dressed like a cowboy, imagined herself Gertrude Stein, and served Toklas-type food. Escargots, marrons glacés. Benjamin played subdued jazz piano and Paul was headwaiter. They wore tuxedos. Neither of them said anything. The witty talkative patrons all dressed like Indians . . . velvet, silver, turquoise.

The men got home around two thirty in the morning, smelling like Shrimp Aurore and cigarette smoke. Lisa cooked breakfast while they counted their tips out upon the round wooden table in the kitchen. Once Benjamin made ten dollars for playing "Shine on Harvest Moon" five times for a politician. The men laughed, telling her about the customers and George.

Eventually they were both fired. Paul had an actual showdown with George on dusty Canyon Road, just like in *High Noon*. He did look a bit like Gary Cooper. She looked like Charles Laughton in cowboy drag and Bette Davis black lipstick. She won.

In Benjamin's case he showed up to work one night and there was a Mexican with maracas singing "*Nosotros, que nos quisimos tanto . . .*" Benjamin rolled his Yamaha piano out, and, with difficulty, up into the VW van.

It was a good year though. Piñon smoke, laughter. The three of them listened and listened. Miles, Coltrane, Monk. They also listened to scratchy tapes of Charles Olson, Robert Duncan, Lenny Bruce.

Paul was a poet. It seemed he didn't sleep at all. He wrote, somewhere, all morning. Benjamin slept late, practiced, played most of the afternoon, and listened to music, earphones on, with the seriousness of a student in a language lab.

Benjamin was a large quiet man, a kind man with a firm sense of Right and Wrong. He was fatherly and patient to Lisa, except when she exaggerated (often) which he said was tantamount to lying. He never spoke in the past or future tense.

Every night she was surprised when he made love to her. He was tender, playful and passionate, kissing her everywhere, her eyes, her breasts, her toes. She loved his strong hands on her breasts and how he would make her come with his tongue. She loved the nakedness in his hazel eyes as he entered her.

Each night she thought that it would be different in the morning between them, after what had happened, as she had felt the first time she ever had sex . . . she wouldn't look the same the next day.

After they made love he would put Vaseline and white gloves on his hands and then put on a Lone Ranger sleep shade and earplugs. Lisa would sit up in bed, smoking, remembering silly things that had happened that day and wishing she could wake him.

During the day she spent most of her time with Paul, reading, talking, arguing at the kitchen table. Later she imagined that it rained that whole time, because for months she and Paul read Darwin and W. H. Hudson and Thomas Hardy, by a piñon fire that also existed only in her mind.

•

Then there was Tony. An old Harvard friend of Benjamin's, rich and darkly handsome. He drove Lisa home from Albuquerque to Santa Fe in twenty minutes, in a Maserati, in the rain. If other cars didn't dim their lights he would turn his completely off.

He used to take Lisa to dinner at George's, to hear Benjamin play. Benjamin played fine for his old bebop friend. "Round Midnight," "Scrapple from the Apple," "Confirmation."

Tony wore Italian suits with leather lapels. Paul handed them menus, silent. Tony was breaking up with his wife. He sighed, "Man . . . I hate endings . . . I only dig beginnings."

"Far out," Lisa said. "I dig endings myself."

Their eyes met over crystal glasses of cabernet sauvignon. ". . . and there will never, ever be another you . . ." Benjamin played. A Chet Baker tune . . .

The love affair between Lisa and Tony was inevitable, or so Tony said. Cheaply predictable, Paul said. Benjamin said nothing at all.

She was nineteen years old. Not to excuse her, just that she was at an age that needs a good talking to. She loved it when Tony said things like "We were meant for each other. Our eyebrows both grow together in the middle . . ."

One night when Benjamin came home she said, "Ben. I want words! I want words! I want a word with you!"

He looked at her. He took off his bow tie and the nine ruby studs from his tuxedo shirt. He took off his jacket and his shoes and sat down next to her on the rollaway bed.

"Babs," he said. (He used to call her Babs.)

He was silent then, taking off his pants and shorts and socks. He sat naked on the bed, tired, and she knew what a good man he was.

"I'm a man of few words," he said. He held her head in his piano-playing hands.

"I love you," he said. "I love you with all my heart. Don't you know that?"

"Yes," she said and she turned over and cried herself to sleep.

It all got very passionate and painful and yes cheaply predictable. Lisa left Benjamin, taking only "Far Away and Long Ago" by W. H. Hudson. She left for Tony and romance, but Tony was "going through a lot of changes right now" so she went to live alone in a stone house in Tijeras Canyon.

Benjamin drove up to the house. She had sighed, watching him come from the window. Paul walked behind him, pale.

"Hey, Babs . . . it's time to move on. We're going to New York. Go get in the van," Benjamin said.

She stood there, trying to think. Benjamin had already climbed into the VW. Paul waited in the doorway while she gathered together her few things. She lit a cigarette and sat down.

"Christ. Go get in, will you?"

Stumbling, she followed Paul.

When they got to the house, after a silent ride, Benjamin changed into a tuxedo and went to work. He was playing with Prince Bobby Jack, at the Skyline Club. "She brings me coffee in my favrit cup . . ." Good blues.

Lisa and Paul packed everything into boxes from M and B Liquors. An uncanny moon toppled fluorescent over the Sandia Mountains. Ordinarily she and Paul would have rejoiced at such an event. They just witnessed it, shivering outside.

"Be a good wife to him, Lisa. He loves you, with all his heart."

Benjamin and Lisa left for New York the next morning. Paul waved good-bye and walked away toward the apple trees.

Lisa drove most of the way to New York, even through Chicago. Benjamin slept most of the way, with his eyeshade on, except when they crossed the Mississippi River. That was really beautiful, the Mississippi River.

They drove through the little town where Paul was born and saw the house and the barn. At least Lisa insisted that that must be the place . . . She could imagine him in the green field. Towhead kid. Red-winged blackbirds. She missed Paul a lot.

"Well, Paul," Lisa said to him on the second day of his visit to New York, in the Varick Street drizzle . . . "What did you want to talk to me about?"

"Nothing, really . . . I just didn't want to wake Benjamin." (Benjamin had played a Bronx wedding the night before.)

"New York was a good move," he went on to say. "I can't believe how he is playing."

"Really! Man . . . he has worked . . . six months just to get in the union . . . then strip joints, one-nighters, Grossinger's . . . but he's been jamming with some great musicians."

"He's had some good jazz gigs though."

"I wish you had heard him play with Buddy Tate, with all those old, old-time Count Basie cats. He was really swinging."

"He's always swinging . . . he is a fine musician."

She knew that.

"I saw Red Garland last week, at Birdland. He was standing at the bar. I said hello and he said hello back."

She was thinking about Red Garland, humming how he played "You're My Everything," when her arm brushed Paul's on Varick Street. She got so dizzy with desire for Paul she stumbled, then skipped, to get back in step. I am wicked, she said to herself and concentrated on the sidewalk. Step on a crack. Break your mother's back.

"Let's ride the Hoboken ferry!" she said, as pleasant as ever.

They crossed to the old ferry station. It was empty. So clearly a Saturday morning. A newsman asleep, whiskery, a *Time* paperweight clutched in his hand. A cat stretched awake on the magazine rack. Silly kittens, all gray.

It was very dark. Rain swirled soot into cracked diamond skylights. Paul and Lisa's footsteps echoed loud, nostalgic, like in an old empty gym, or a train station in Montana late at night during some family crisis.

The ferry was barely visible in the fog, an elegant heavy Victorian lady, skirting tugs and obtusely slow garbage barges. The ferry creaked slowly, carefully, into the landing. Paul and Lisa's footsteps echoed loud again on the wooden deck. Pigeons moaned above them on the rotting roof, their iridescent oil-feathers the only color of the morning.

The two of them were alone on the boat. They laughed, changing seats a dozen times, promenading the decks. Fog surrounded the boat.

"Paul! There's no New York! No New Jersey! Maybe we're in the English Channel!"

They stared and stared out into the fog until eerily then there were yellow boxcars, red cabooses from the Jersey shore. A dream about a freight yard in North Dakota.

The ferry banged into the pilings. Gulls fluttered, then balanced again on the swaying logs.

"Come on, let's get off," he said.

"If we stay we don't have to pay."

"Lisa, why don't you ever do things right? Like why don't you buy a dustpan?"

"I hate dustpans," she said, following him off the ferry. Actually she bought them often, but threw them out by mistake.

They stood outside on the way back, leaning on the salty rail, not touching.

"I wish you were happy," he said. "When Ben went to get you . . . it was the most courageous thing I ever saw a man do. He forgave you. It saddens me to see it made so little difference."

She wanted to be seasick, to tell him how ever since she'd been in New York she talked to him all day long, saved his letters to read at dusk on the roof, where the sky seemed like New Mexico.

He ran his hands through his pale hair. "I missed you, Lisa. I have really missed you."

She nodded, her head bent, tears misting the water and foam like frosted glass. Her teeth chattered.

She pointed to the WORLD sign from the *World-Telegram* building glowing neon through the fog.

"That's the first thing I see when I open my eyes every morning. WORLD. Except backwards, of course."

Clearer now, they could see her laundry on the roof above the loft on Greenwich Street. The sooty brilliant clothes flapped against the rain-black buildings around City Hall.

"Look at Diana!" She laughed.

The bronze statue of Diana rose just above her laundry, as if she were going to hurl it all into the Hudson.

"But it was you who forgave me, Paul," she said. As the ferry approached the landing the engines shut off. Even when the ferries are crowded this is a moment of terrible silence. The water slapping against the wooden hull until the boat docks with a sullen thud and a shatter of frightened gulls.

"Paul . . ." Lisa said, but she was alone. Paul had turned. He was walking in long western strides toward the metal gate at the bow, anxious now to be getting back.

CHERRY BLOSSOM TIME

There he was again, the postman. After she first noticed him Cassandra began seeing him everywhere. Like when you learn what *exacerbate* means and then everyone begins to say it and it's even in the morning paper.

He was marching down Sixth Avenue, his shiny shoes lifting high above the ground. One/two. One/two. At Thirteenth Street he turned his head to the right, pivoted, and disappeared. He was delivering mail.

Cassandra and her two-year-old son Matt were on their own morning route. The deli, the A&P, the bakery, the firehouse, the pet shop. Sometimes the laundry. Home for milk and cookies, then back down, to Washington Square. Home for lunch and a nap.

When she had first noticed the postman, how their paths crossed and recrossed, she wondered why she hadn't seen him before. Had her whole life been altered by five minutes? What would happen if it altered by an hour?

Then she noticed that his route was timed so perfectly that for blocks at a time he would step onto the far curb exactly as the light turned red. He never deviated along the way, even the rare pleasantries were accounted for and predictable. Then she noticed that hers and Matt's were too. At nine, for example, a fireman would lift Matt onto the truck or put his hat on Matt's head. At ten fifteen the baker would ask Matt how was his big man today and give him an oatmeal cookie. Or the other baker would say, Hello, beautiful, to Cassandra and give her the cookie. When they got out the door on Greenwich Street there the postman would be, stepping off the curb.

It's understandable, she told herself. Children need rhythm, a routine. Matt was so young, he liked their walks, their time at the park, but by one on the dot he'd be cranky, need lunch and a nap. Nevertheless she began to try to vary their schedule. Matt reacted badly. He wasn't ready for the sandpile or for drowsy swinging until after their walk. If they went home early he was too keyed up for a nap. If they went to the store after the park he'd whine, writhe to get out of the basket. So they went back to their usual routine, right in the postman's footsteps sometimes, across the street at others. No one stood in his way or stepped out in front of him. One/two. One/two, he cut a straight swathe down the center of the sidewalk.

One morning they might have missed him, if, as usual, they had browsed awhile in the pet shop. But in the middle of the shop there was a new cage. Waltzing mice. Dozens of little gray mice running around in berserk circles. They had been bred with defective tympanums so they would run around and around. Cassandra took Matt out of the store and they almost collided with the postman. Across the street a lesbian called up to her lover in the women's prison. She was there every morning at ten thirty.

On Sixth Avenue they stopped at the deli for chicken liver, then next door to pick up the laundry. Matt carried the groceries, she pushed the laundry in a cart. The postman skipped one step to avoid the wheels of the cart.

Cassandra's husband, David, came home at 5:45. He rang

the buzzer three times and she rang him back. She and Matt waited at the bannister, watching him climb one two three four flights of stairs. Hello! Hello! Hello! They would hug and he would come in. He'd sit at the kitchen table with Matt on his lap, pulling off his tie.

"How was it?" she would ask.

"The same," he would say, or "worse." He was a writer, had almost finished his first novel. He hated his job at a publishing company, there was no time or energy left for his book.

"I'm sorry, David," she would say and fix them drinks.

"How was your day?"

"Fine. We walked, went to the park."

"Great."

"Matt napped. I read Gide." (She tried to read Gide; usually she read Thomas Hardy.) "There's this postman—"

"Mailman."

"Mailman," she corrected herself. "He's got me so depressed. He's like a robot. Day in day out the same schedule—he even has the lights timed. Makes me sad about my own life."

David was angry. "Yeah, you've really got it rough. Look, we all do things we don't want to do. Do you think I like the textbook division?"

"I didn't mean that. I love what I do. I just don't want to have to do it at ten twenty-two. Do you see?"

"I guess. Hey, wench—draw me a bath."

He always said that, a joke. Then she'd draw a bath and prepare dinner while he bathed. They would eat when he came out, his hair shining black. After dinner he'd write or think. She'd wash the dishes, give Matt a bath and read to him, sing to him. "Texarkana Baby" and "Candy Kisses" until he fell asleep, a ribbon of drool bobbing from his pink lips. Then she would read or sew until David said, "Let's turn in," and they would. They would make love, or they wouldn't, and fall asleep.

•

The next morning she lay awake in bed, her head aching. She waited for him to say "Good morning, merry sunshine," and he did. When he left she waited for him to kiss her and say, "Don't do anything I wouldn't do," and he did.

On the way to Washington Square she thought to herself that some kid would probably fall off the slide and cut his lip. Later, in the park, Matt fell from the swing and cut his lip. Cassandra held a Kleenex to the cut, fought back her own tears. What's the matter with me? What more do I want? God, let me just see the good things. She forced herself to look around, out of herself, and, in fact, the cherry blossoms were in bloom. They had been coming out little by little, but it was that day they were lovely. Then, as if because she saw the trees, the fountain turned on. Look, Mama! Matt cried and began to run. All the children and their mothers ran to the sparkling fountain. The postman walked right by it as usual. He seemed not to notice that it was on, got wet by the spray. One/two. One/two.

Cassandra took Matt home for his nap. Sometimes she slept too, but usually sewed or worked in the kitchen. She loved this drowsy time of day when the cat yawned and buses cruised outside, when telephones went on ringing and ringing. The sewing machine made a summer sound of flies.

But that afternoon sun flashed from the chrome on the stove, the needle broke on the machine. From the streets came sounds of braking, scrapings. Silver clattered on the drain board, a knife screeched against the enamel. Cassandra chopped parsley. One/two. One/two.

Matt woke up. She washed his face, careful of the lip. They drank milkshakes, waited with chocolate mustaches for David to come home, to ring the buzzer three times.

She wished she could tell him how bad she felt but he was

the one who had it hard, working at that job, no time for his book. So when he asked her how her day had been she said,

"It was a wonderful day. The cherry blossoms are out and they turned the fountain on. It's spring!"

"Great." David smiled.

"The postman got wet," she added.

"Mailman."

"Mailman."

"We're not going to the store today," Cassandra told Matt. They baked peanut butter cookies and he pressed the fork down on each one. There. She made sandwiches and milk, put blankets and a pillow in the laundry cart. They went an entirely new way, down Fifth Avenue, to Washington Square. It was nice to come upon the arch, framing the trees and the fountain.

She and Matt played ball, he played on the slide, in the sandpile. At one she spread the blanket out for a picnic. They ate sandwiches, offered their cookies to people passing by. After lunch, at first, he didn't want to go to sleep, even with his own blanket and pillow. But she sang to him. "She's my Texarkana baby and I love her like a doll, her ma she came from Texas and her pa from Arkansas." Over and over until at last Matt fell asleep and so did she. They slept a long time. When she woke she was afraid at first because she opened her eyes into the pink blossoms against the blue sky.

They sang on the way home, stopping at the laundry to pick up their bundle. Coming out, pushing the heavy cart, Cassandra was surprised to see the postman. They hadn't seen him all day. Lazily she followed in his wake toward the curb. Then she let go of the cart, let it sail down the sidewalk heavy into his heels. It caught one foot in such a way that the shoe came off. He looked around at her with hatred, stooped to untie and put back on his shoe. She retrieved the cart and he started to cross the street. But he was too late, the light turned red when he was halfway across. A Gristedes delivery truck veered around the corner, just missed hitting the postman, its brakes screeching. The postman froze, terrified, then continued to the curb and down Thirteenth Street, running now.

Cassandra and Matt went straight up to Fourteenth Street and around back to their apartment house. It was a whole new different way to go home.

David rang the buzzer at 5:45. Hello! Hello! Hello!

"How was your day?"

"The same. And yours?"

Matt and Cassandra interrupted each other, telling him about their day, their picnic.

"It was beautiful. We slept under the cherry blossoms."

"Great." David smiled.

She smiled too. "On the way home I murdered the postman."

"Mailman," David said, taking off his tie.

"David. Please talk to me."

EVENING IN PARADISE

Sometimes years later you look back and say that was the beginning of . . . or we were so happy then . . . before . . . after . . . Or you think I'll be happy when . . . once I get . . . if we . . . Hernán knew he was happy now. The Oceano hotel was full, his three waiters were working at top speed.

He wasn't the kind of man who worried about the future or dwelt on the past. He shooed the chicle-selling kids out of his bar with no thought of his own orphaned childhood on the streets. Raking the beach, shining shoes.

When he was twelve they had started construction on the Oceano. Hernán ran errands for the owner. He idolized Señor Morales, who wore a white suit and a panama hat. Jowls that matched the bags under his eyes. After Hernán's mother died Señor Morales was the only person to call him by his name. Hernán. Not hey kid, *ándale hijo, vete callejero. Buenos días,* Hernán. As the building progressed Señor Morales had given him a steady job cleaning up after the workers. When the hotel was finished he hired him to work in the kitchen. A room on the roof to live in.

Other men would have hired experienced employees from other hotels. The chefs and desk clerk at the new Oceano were from Acapulco but all of the other workers were illiterate street urchins like Hernán. They were all proud to have a room, their own real room on the roof. Showers and toilets for the men and women workers. Thirty years later every one of the men still worked at the hotel. The laundresses and maids had all come from mountain towns like Chacala or El Tuito. The women stayed until they married or until they got too homesick. New ones were always fresh young girls from the hills.

Socorro was from Chacala. The first day Hernán had seen her she was standing in her doorway in a white dress, her braids plaited with pink satin ribbon. She hadn't put down her rope-tied bundle of belongings. She was turning the light on and off. He was amazed by her sweetness. They smiled at each other. They were both fifteen and they both fell in love that very moment.

The next day Señor Morales saw Hernán watching Socorro in the kitchen.

"She's a little beauty, no?"

"Yes," Hernán said. "I'm going to marry her."

He worked double shifts for two years until they could marry and move into a little house near the hotel. By the time their first daughter, Claudia, was born he was an apprentice bartender. After Amalia was born he was a regular bartender and Socorro stopped working. Their second daughter, Amalia, was having her *quinceañera* party in two weeks. Señor Morales was godfather to both girls and was giving the party in the hotel. A bachelor, he seemed to love Socorro and the girls almost as much as Hernán, never tired of describing them to people.

"They are so fine, so beautiful. Delicate and pure and proud and . . ."

"Smart, strong, hardworking," Hernán would add.

"*Dios mío* . . . those women have hair . . . *tan, pero tan brilloso*."

•

John Apple was at the bar as usual, looking out at the *malecón* above the beach. Trucks and buses rumbled by on the cobblestones outside. John nursed his beer, muttering.

"Smell those nasty fumes? What a racket. It's all over now, Hernán. No more paradise. The end of our fishy little sleeping village."

Hernán's English was very good but he missed things like John's remark. All he knew was that he had been hearing it over and over for years. He ignored the sigh as John pretended again to drain his empty glass. Somebody else could buy him his next drink.

"Not the end," Hernán said. "A new Puerto Vallarta."

Dozens of luxury resorts were going up, the new highway was finished, the big airport just opened. Instead of one flight a week there were five or six international flights a day. Hernán had no regrets about how peaceful the town used to be, when this was the only good bar and he was the only one working in it. He liked having so many waiters to help. He was not even tired now when he got home, could have dinner with Socorro, read the paper, talk awhile.

More and more people were coming in. Hernán sent Memo to the kitchen to get busboys to help out, to bring some extra chairs. Most of the guests at the hotel were reporters or cast and crew of *The Night of the Iguana*. Most of them were in the bar mingling with the "in" people from town, local Mexicans and Americans. Tourists and honeymooners looked for Ava and Burton and Liz.

In those days one Mexican movie a week was shown on the plaza. There was no television so the town wasn't impressed by the cast of *The Night of the Iguana*. Everybody knew who Elizabeth Taylor was, though. Her husband, Richard Burton, was in the movie.

Hernán liked them and he liked the director, John Huston.

The old man was always respectful to Socorro and to his daughters. He spoke Spanish to them and lifted his hat when he saw them in town. Socorro had her brother bring in *raicilla* from the mountains near Chacala, moonshine mescal for Señor Huston. Hernán kept it in a huge mayonnaise jar under the bar, tried to dole it out slowly, and to cut it as often as possible without Señor Huston noticing.

Mexican lawyers and bankers were trying out their English on the blond ingénue, Sue Lyons. Ruby and Alma, two American divorcées, were flirting with cameramen. Both women were very wealthy, owned houses on cliffs above the water. They kept on thinking they'd find romance at the Oceano bar. Usually they met married men on fishing trips or, now, newsmen or cameramen. No man that would ever want to stay around.

Alma was sweet and beautiful until late in the evening when her eyes and mouth turned into bruises and her voice became a sob, like she just wished you'd hit her and leave. Ruby was close to fifty, lifted and dyed and patched together. She was funny and fun but after she drank a lot she got mean and then limp and then Hernán had someone take her home. John Apple went over to sit with them. Alma ordered him a double margarita.

Luis and Victor stood at the entrance long enough to be noticed by everyone. They slid into the bar and sat down where they would be visible. Dark and handsome, they both wore tight white pants, open white shirts. Barefoot, with a bright bracelet on one ankle. White smiles, wet black hair. "*Ratoncitos tiernos.*" Tender little rats, whores call the sexy young ones.

Hernán was already working in the Oceano kitchen when he had first known them as children. Begging from tourists, rolling drunks. They had originally come from Culiacán, called each other *Compa*, for *compadre.*

For years Luis and Victor had slept under *petates* in boats at night, hustled all day. Hernán understood them and didn't judge them, not even for stealing. The way they treated women didn't shock him. He judged the women though. One day he had seen Victor approach Amalia on the *malecón*. She was wearing the plaid skirt and white blouse from school, holding her books tightly against her new breasts. Hernán ran out from the bar and raced across the street. "Go home!" he said to Amalia. To Victor he said, "If you speak to either of my daughters again I will kill you."

Hernán poured martinis into chilled glasses, put them on Memo's tray. He left the bar and went over to the young men.

"*Quibo.* Why does it make me so nervous, seeing you two in my bar?"

"*Cálmate, viejo.* We've come to witness two historic events."

"Two? One must be Tony and the other Beto. What's with Beto?"

"He's coming to celebrate with the movie people. He got a part in *The Night of the Iguana*. Real money. *Lana*."

"*¡No me digas!* Good for him. So now he's not just a beach boy. What's the part?"

"Playing a beach boy!"

"Watch him mess it up. I already know the other event. Tony's doing it to Ava Gardner."

"That's no event. *Fíjate*. There's the event!"

A magnificent new Chris-Craft sprayed into the harbor, rocking the sunset-lit magenta water. Tony stood and waved, let go of the anchor of *La Ava*. A small boy in a rowboat went out to get him.

"*Híjola*. She actually bought it for him?"

"Title's in his name. She was waiting for him last night, naked in a hammock, had it taped to her tit. Guess what he did first."

"Went to see the boat."

The three of them laughed as the beautiful, unsteady Ava came down the stairs, smiling at everyone. She sat alone in a booth, waiting for Tony. Hernán was pleased that although everyone was looking at her and admiring her, nobody bothered her. My customers have manners, he thought.

Hernán went back to the bar, worked quickly to catch up. *Pobrecita*. She is shy. Lonely. He hummed a tune from a Pedro Infante movie. "Rich people cry too."

Hernán watched like everyone else when the lovers kissed hello. Flashbulbs flickered like sparklers throughout the room. The Americans all knew her, the whole town loved Tony. He was about nineteen now. He had streaks of blond in his long hair, amber eyes, and an angelic smile. He had always worked on the boats unloading, loading, cadging rides, saving money for his own boat, someday, to take tourists waterskiing.

The stories differed. Some people said it happened in a dice game, others said he paid Diego cash to let him take the boat of movie stars to the set in Mismaloya every day. After about three days of his golden eyes gazing into her green ones she started taking boat rides with him on her breaks, until, Tony said, fortune had smiled upon him. Memo said that Tony was the lowest, a gigolo.

"Look at him," Hernán said. "He's in love. He won't hurt her."

Across the room Luis called out to an older American woman passing by the bar.

"Madam, please join us. I am Luis and this is Victor. Help us celebrate my birthday," he said.

"Why, I'd love to." She smiled, surprised. She ordered drinks, paid the waiter with a fistful of bills. She was laughing, pleased by their attention, took out all her purchases to show them.

Luis had grown out of beach-boying. He had a tiny dress shop that was the current rage. He sold colonial paintings and pre-Columbian art. No one knew where he got them or who made them. He taught yoga to American women, the same ones who bought all his dresses in every color. It was hard to tell if Luis loved women or hated them. He made them feel good. He got money from all of them one way or another.

Memo asked Hernán if the women paid him to have sex with them. *¿Quién sabe?* He suspected that Luis took them out, brought them home, and robbed them when they passed out. The women would be too embarrassed to tell. Hernán felt no compassion for the women. They asked for it. Traveling alone, drinking, giving themselves to the first *callejeros* they met.

Beto came in with Audrey, a hippy girl of about fifteen. Silken blond hair, the face of a goddess. Newsmen were popping flashes and the blond actress grew sullen. Audrey moved like honey. She had the blind eyes of a statue.

Victor came up to the bar to talk to someone. Hernán asked him what Audrey was on.

"Seconal, Tuinal, something like that."

"You don't sell to her, do you?"

"No. Anybody can get sleepers at the pharmacy. They keep her nice and quiet."

Beto was sitting with the crew. They were toasting him, trying to speak Spanish. He smiled and drank. Beto always wore the stupid expression of someone on a bus that just got woken up.

Señor Huston motioned to Hernán for a *raicilla*. Hernán took the drink over himself, curious to know why the director was talking to Audrey so angrily. Señor Huston thanked Hernán, sent regards to his family. Then he told Hernán that Audrey was the daughter of a dear friend, a great stage actress. Audrey had run away from home last year.

"Imagine how her mother feels. Audrey was younger than both your daughters when she disappeared."

Audrey pleaded with Señor Huston not to tell where she was.

"Beto loves me. Finally somebody loves just me. And now Beto has a job. We can get an apartment."

"What drug are you on?"

"I'm sleepy, you silly. We're having a baby!"

She rose, kissed the old man. "Please," she said and went to sit a little behind Beto, singing softly to herself. Señor Huston stood, stiffly, knocking over his chair. He stood over Beto, began to speak, then shook his head and strode out of the bar. He crossed the street to the *malecón*, where he sat smoking, looking at the water.

Hernán noticed that the newsmen and women and the movie crew all knew Victor; many stopped to talk with him. Victor went to the men's room often, before or after an American went in. He was the main marijuana connection in town, and had a few discreet heroin customers. This was different. No one went out afterward for a stroll down the beach.

Hernán had heard that it had come to Acapulco. Well, now Puerto Vallarta has its own cocaine, he thought.

Sam Newman pulled up in a taxi, waved to Hernán as he went through the courtyard to register and have his bags sent up. He went over to Tony and Ava Gardner, hugged Tony and kissed Ava's hand. He stopped at tables along his way to the bar, shaking hands, kissing the women he knew, checking out the new ones, who all visibly cheered up. He was a handsome, easygoing American, married to a wealthy older woman who kept him on a loose rein. They lived down the coast in Yelapa. Sam came to town every few weeks for supplies and a rest. Living in paradise wore him out, he said. Grinning, he sat on a bar stool, handed Hernán a bag of Juan Cruz's coffee.

"Thanks, Sam. Socorro was missing her coffee." Hernán mixed him a double Bacardi and Tehuacán. "You come over on the *Paladín*?"

"Yes, unfortunately. Packed with tourists. And John Langley. Guess what he said."

"We're all in the same boat."

"He always says that. He's got a new one. We passed the movie set and this lady grabbed his arm. 'Sir, is that Mismaloya?' Langley removed her hand from his arm and said in that English snob way of his: 'Mr. Maloya to you, madam.' So, besides Tony's boat, what's happening?"

Hernán told him about Beto's movie career and about Audrey being a runaway and pregnant and on drugs. He invited Sam to Amalia's *quinceañera* party. Of course Sam would be there, he said. Hernán was pleased.

"Señor Huston is coming too. He is a great man, a man of dignity."

"It's cool that you know that. I mean without knowing that he really *is* a great man. A famous man."

Alma came up, kissed Sam on the lips. John Apple moved back to the bar and Sam bought him a double margarita.

Luis and the American woman were leaving in a cab. Victor was sitting with some reporters. Hernán didn't know what to do about Victor. He would never have him arrested, but he didn't want him dealing in the Oceano. He would ask Socorro tonight. She always knew exactly what to do.

"Sam, take me over to meet Ava Gardner, please," Alma said. "I want to invite her to stay at my house." She and Sam went and joined the enamored couple. On the way over Sam stopped to talk to Victor. They nodded to one another, looking down while they spoke.

Señor Huston came back inside and sat in "his" large booth. Richard and Liz arrived. Wherever they went it was as if a grenade had been thrown through the window. Flashes exploded, people moaned and screamed, cried out, "Aah! Aah!" Chairs scraped and fell over, glass shattered. Running footsteps, running.

The couple smiled all around and waved, like for a curtain call, then sat with Señor Huston in the booth. Liz blew a kiss to Hernán. He was already fixing a tray with a double margarita for her, *agua de Tehuacán* for Burton, who wasn't drinking. A *raicilla* cut with plain tequila for the director. Some guacamole and salsa, the way she liked it with plenty of garlic. She was cussing away. Hernán liked her; she was warm and bawdy. She and Burton had big booming laughs, were simply in it, each other, the place, life.

Little by little the bar emptied as people went to dress for dinner. They left walking or in one of the dozens of cabs outside the hotel. Victor went on foot with five or six men, heading north, to the "bad" part of town. Sam and Alma took off in her Jeep with Tony and Ava.

Ruby, Beto, and Audrey were all fast asleep. John Apple offered to take them home in Ruby's car. Hernán knew John was thinking of her liquor cabinet and refrigerator. At least he was still in shape to drive. Memo and Raúl helped them out to the car.

Left in the bar were two old men, drinking Madero brandy in big snifters. They set up a chessboard and began to play. A young honeymoon couple came in from a walk on the *malecón*, asked for wine coolers.

Hernán wiped down his bar, straightened and replaced bottles. Memo was already asleep, sitting up, as if at attention, on a chair by the kitchen. Hernán looked out at the sea and the palm trees, listening to Liz and Burton and John Huston. They were arguing, laughing, quoting lines from the movie, or other movies, maybe. When he took them fresh drinks Liz asked him if they were making too much noise.

"No, no," Hernán said. "It is wonderful to hear people talk about their work when they love what they do. You are very fortunate."

He sat down behind the bar with his feet up on a stool. Raúl brought him *café con leche* and *pan dulces*. He dunked the pastries in the coffee while he read the paper. There would be some nice quiet hours now. Maybe later some people would have nightcaps before they went to bed. Then he'd walk home, not far, where Socorro would be waiting for him. They would have dinner together and talk about their days and their nights, their daughters. He'd tell her all the gossip. They would argue. She always defended the women. She felt sorry for Alma and Ruby with no one to protect them. He would tell her about Victor and the drugs. Even Sam had seemed to be talking about drugs with him. Socorro would rub Hernán's back when they got into bed. They would laugh about something.

"God, I am fortunate." He said it out loud. He was embarrassed, looked around. Nobody had heard him. He smiled and said, "I am very fortunate!"

"Hernán, are you lonesome? Over there talking to yourself?" Elizabeth Taylor called to him.

"I miss my wife. It's four more hours until I see her!" They asked him to recommend a restaurant. He told them to go to the Italian place behind the church. Tourists never go, they think it's crazy to eat Italian food in Mexico. It is quiet and good.

They left and then the honeymooners and chess players went upstairs. Raúl slept opposite Memo outside the kitchen door. They looked like decorations, giant tourist puppets, in their black *boleros* and red sashes and mustaches.

Hernán was just about to fall asleep himself when a taxi door slammed. Luis got out with the American woman. She was falling-down drunk. Pancho went to help him get her upstairs and to her room. Luis didn't come back down.

Several minutes later there was the slam of another taxi door, a woman yelling "You dickhead!" and then Ava Gardner came in wearing only one high-heeled shoe so her walk made a hiccup sound through the courtyard and up the stairs. The same taxi door slammed again and Hernán was surprised to see Sam, with no shoes and no shirt. He had an enormous black eye, a cut and swollen lip.

"Which is her room?"

"Top of stairs, second, ocean side."

Sam went upstairs, changed his mind and came back down, his hand out for the drink Hernán held out for him. He spoke as if he had novocaine in his mouth, his lip was so swollen.

"Hernán. You can't tell a soul. My reputation will be in shreds. You see a disgraced man before you. Totally humiliated. I insulted her! Oh, God."

Another taxi, another slam. Tony came running in, tears streaming down his cheeks. He flew up the stairs and banged on her door. "*¡Mi vida! ¡Mi sueño!*" Other doors opened all around. "Hush up, you fool! Shaddup! Shaddup!"

Tony came downstairs. He embraced Sam, apologized and shook his hand. He cried in little gasps, like a child.

"Sam, go talk to her. You can explain. I don't speak English. Tell her how it was too dark. Explain to her, please!"

"I don't know, Tony. She's really mad at me. Come on. You just go on in there and kiss her, let her see those alligator tears."

Hernán interrupted. "I don't know what went on. But I'll bet the lady won't even remember tomorrow what terrible thing happened tonight. Don't remind her!"

"Good thinking. Our man, Hernán." Sam went upstairs with Tony, opened Ava's door with a credit card, and gently pushed Tony into the room. He waited a little while but Tony didn't come out.

Sam stood in the cobblestone courtyard, holding up his card, talking to an invisible camera: "Hi, there! I'm Sam Newman . . . world traveler, bon vivant, man-about-town. I wouldn't go anywhere without my American Express card."

"Sam, *¿qué haces?*"

"Nothing. Look, Hernán . . . You have to swear."

"On my mother's grave. Come on, tell me all about it."

"Well . . . Oh, God. So we get to Alma's and she tells the cook to make us dinner. We're out on her terrace, drinking more. Music playing. Tony doesn't have a head for alcohol, usually he never drinks. And I had barely started. But those two women were wasted. It was dark and we were all sort of lying around on those waterbed couches she has when Alma takes Tony by the hand and, well, she drags him into her bedroom. Ava is just looking at the stars, I'm panicking and then she notices they are gone, sits up like a shot, hauls me off with her to find them. Well, they're on Alma's bed, naked, balling away. I thought Ava might hit them with a blunt instrument but no she just smiles and leads me back to the terrace. Oh Lord, how have I failed? I am a disgrace. Sick. Right there in front of God and everybody Ava Gardner herself steps out of her dress and lies back on the sofa. Oh Lord, help me. My friend, that woman is magnificent. She is the color of butterscotch pudding, all over. Her breasts are heaven here on earth. Her legs, man she is the fuckin' Duchess of Alba! No. She is the Barefoot Contessa! So I tear off my clothes and lie down with her. And there she is. Ava, warm, in the flesh, looking into my eyes with those green ones I KNOW. My dick disappeared. It went to Tijuana, my balls took off for Ohio. And this Countess, this Goddess, she did everything possible. It was hopeless. I was dying of shame. I apologized and oh fuck like an IDIOT I said, 'Gee, I'm sorry. It's that I've been madly in love with you ever since I was a little kid!' She's the one who hit me in the lip. Then Tony shows up and really starts beating the shit out of me. Just then the damn cook comes in, turns on the light, and says, 'Dinner is served.' I gave the cook some money and asked her to go find me a taxi, put my pants on, and ran outside. The cook came back with a cab. I got in, then Ava got in after me. Tony was running down the street behind us, but she wouldn't let the guy stop. Ava Gardner. I could shoot myself."

Tony ran lightly down the steps and up to the bar.

"She forgives me, she loves me. She is sleeping now."

"Shall we go back for dinner?" Sam grinned. Tony was offended. Then after a while he said he was, in fact, dying of hunger. Memo had been awake, taking everything in. He said he was hungry too, they should go in the kitchen and fix breakfast.

Victor arrived alone, sat at a far table in the now dim light. Raúl took him hot chocolate and *pan dulces.* Victor never drank or took drugs. Hernán believed he must be very rich by now. Raúl told Victor that Luis was still upstairs. "I'll wait," he said.

Memo came out of the kitchen just as a few people came in for after-dinner drinks. Tony went over to wait for Luis with Victor. Tony had chocolate too and Hernán sent him over some aspirins. Tony didn't mention the evening to Victor, just talked about his new boat.

Sam came to the bar and ordered a Kahlua with brandy. He held his head between his hands. Hernán handed him the drink and said, "You need aspirin, too."

Luis came downstairs, carrying one of the woman's shopping bags. The three friends spoke in whispers, laughing like teenaged boys. They left, loped effortlessly past the open windows of the bar, their laughter trailing back with the sound of the waves, easy and innocent.

"What was that clicking sound. Maracas?"

LA BARCA DE LA ILUSIÓN

The floor of the house was fine white sand. In the morning Maya and Pilla, the maid, raked and swept the sand, checking for scorpions, sweeping it smooth. For the first hour Maya would yell at the boys "Don't walk on my floor!" as if it were newly waxed linoleum. Every six months one-eyed Luis would come in with his mule and carry out saddlebags of sand, make countless trips to the beach for fresh white sparkling sand washed up by the sea.

The house was a *palapa*, the roof made of thatched palm. Three roofs, for there was a tall rectangular structure met on each end by a semicircle. The house had the majesty of an old Victorian ferryboat, that's how it got the name *la barca de la ilusión*. Inside, cool, the ceiling was vast, tall tall posts of ironwood, crossbars lashed together with *guacamote* vine. The house was like a cathedral, especially at night when stars or moonlight glowed through the skylights where the *palapas* joined. Except for an adobe room beneath the *tapanco* there were no walls.

Buzz and Maya slept on a mattress in the *tapanco*, a large loft made of the veins of palm trees. Ben and Keith and Nathan slept in bunks in the adobe room when it was very cold. Usually they slept in hammocks in the large living room, or outside by the datura. The datura that bloomed in a profusion of white flowers that hung heavy clumsily until night when the moonlight or starlight gave the petals an opalescent shimmer of silver and the intoxicating scent wafted everywhere in the house, out to the lagoon.

Most of the other flowers had no perfume and were safe from ants. Bougainvillea and hibiscus, canna lilies, four o'clocks, impatiens and zinnia. The stock and the gardenias and roses were giddy with perfume, alive with butterflies of every color.

At night Maya and her neighbor Teodora patrolled the gardens and the coconut grove with their lanterns, killing the swift columns of cutter ants, pouring kerosene into the nests of these ants that ate their tomatoes and green beans, lettuce and flowers. Teodora had taught Maya to plant during the new moon and to prune when it was full, to tie jugs of water to the lower branches of a mango tree if it wasn't bearing fruit. Juanito, Teodora's seven-year-old son, came to Maya's school in the mornings except when the coffee beans were ripe in the hills and he had to work every day.

Ben and Keith, seven and six, ranged between first and fourth grades in arithmetic and spelling. Keith loved fractions and decimals, a mystery to Ben and Maya. Ben read everything from children's books to adult books like *The White Nile*. Every morning the boys had classes at the big wooden table. Scratching, sighing, erasing, giggling, the boys leaned their bare brown backs over their marbled copybooks. Reading and writing and arithmetic. Geography. Reading and writing in Spanish, with Juanito.

The house was built at the edge of a coconut grove on the bank of the river. Across the river was the beach and the perfect bay of Yelapa. Up the rocks from the beach and over the hill was the village, above a small cove. High mountains surrounded the bay, so there were no roads into Yelapa. Horse trails through the jungle to Tuito, to Chacala, hours away.

The river changed all year long. Sometimes deep and green, sometimes just a stream. Sometimes, depending on the tides, the beach would close up and the river turned into a lagoon. This was the best time, with blue herons and egrets. The boys would spend hours playing pirates in their dugouts, catching crawfish, tossing nets for fish, ferrying passengers across from the beach. Even Nathan could handle a canoe well, and he was barely four. In the dry season there would be no water at all. The children would play soccer with boys from the village, have races on scrawny horses. After the rains began the water would come, sometimes in wild torrents, carrying boughs of flowers, branches of oranges, dead chickens, a cow once, and the swirling muddy water would break through the beach with an enormous gasp and suck of sand, swirling out into the turquoise ocean. And as days passed the river water grew clean and sweet and the warm rock pools filled with the water for baths and washing.

In the evening Teodora strolled past their house to the river with a huge rattling tin tub of dishes on her head. Donasiano followed her, a few paces behind, carrying a machete, wearing a straw hat with ACAPULCO on it. Teodora was a widow, Donasiano her lover, although he had a wife and family in town. They would return after dark, the dishes clattering, slower now. In the morning before he went to the hills to pick coffee Donasiano would squat on the other side of the river, in the shadow of the strangler fig or yellow-blossomed papelillo, waiting for deer to come to the water to drink. Only once had Maya actually seen him kill a deer, although he did often, sharing the meat with the village. He had sprung out from behind the tree and beheaded the doe with one glittering blow of his machete. The head fell into the sand, blood flowed in the current, the fawns fled.

Buzz and Maya worked to keep the fence mended against the donkeys and pigs, to keep the garden watered and weeded.

Pilla and Luis carried endless buckets of water, from upriver, or from the well in the village during the dry season. Luis and Pablo and Buzz gathered and chopped wood for the fire that burned all day.

"It's tough, this living in paradise," Buzz said.

Maya wondered how long they could stand living in paradise. At night while she read at the table Buzz would lie in the hammock smoking weed, staring out to sea.

"Are you okay, Buzz?"

"I'm bored," he said.

Maybe if they had a farm, a real one, or started a real school. The problem was Buzz didn't have to do anything. He never had. His father had been a wealthy Boston physician. Handsome and bright, Buzz had been an honors student at Andover and Harvard, Harvard graduate school. In his second year of medical school he had begun to play saxophone, to go hear Dizzy and Bird, Jaki Byard, Bud Powell. He had become addicted to heroin, was expelled from medical school for morphine. He had married Circe, a Boston heiress, got off drugs. They went around the world. They settled in New Mexico, where he played saxophone and raced Porsches, in the U.S. and Europe. For something to do he started a business. He bought the first Volkswagen franchise west of the Mississippi, almost instantly became close to a millionaire. He stopped racing cars, he stopped playing saxophone. He and Circe were divorced. He and Maya fell in love, had an affair.

"Give me something to live for—you and the boys" was how he had proposed to her. Maya had actually thought that was romantic. They were married. He adopted Ben and Keith and they had Nathan. She had not known he was back on heroin until a month after they were married. Heroin is easy to hide if you are rich, because you always have it.

When he was off drugs their life was wonderful. They loved

each other, they had beautiful children. They were wealthy and free, traveled in their little plane all over the United States and Mexico.

But finally drugs became Buzz's only reason for living. Soon the children would be old enough to be aware of it. The only people they saw were connections and dealers, the narcs that followed them. Heroin was the focus of every day, all day, for both of them. The move to Yelapa was their only chance.

Little by little it began to seem all right. That Yelapa could be home. Buzz started to fish from the boat inside the bay, catching sierra or red snapper. He did free dives near the rocks, coming back with oysters and lobster. More and more Ben and Keith went with him. Illogically, since she was so afraid of coconuts falling on their heads, Maya didn't worry about the children, out to sea in the tiny open boat. True, sometimes there were dangerous swells, sharks, manta rays that played with the boat. Underwater there were stingrays, moray eels. But they returned with fish and clams and lobster, tales of dolphins and humpback whales, giant sawfish. Maya loved to hear Buzz and the boys telling about their trip, arguing, exaggerating. Keith was the best fisherman, patient and determined; Ben was the finder, of fine conches or the tip of blue lobster feeler hidden in the rocks.

After a year Buzz got a generator that he set up on the point. They filled scuba tanks and hunted for fish underwater, with spear guns. Little by little more village boys learned to dive and get fish, began to make their living this way. Sefarino and Pablo bought their own boats and tanks and sold fish in town. A little restaurant opened in town. Ronco and Buzz bought a motor and a fiberglass boat. They went farther out to dive, as far as the islands. When they anchored in the late afternoon their calls and laughter floated across the ocean.

Days and months passed in an easy rocking rhythm. Just

before dawn the roosters crowed and at the first light a thousand laughing gulls flew past the house upriver. Flocks of parrots flashed green dazzling against the cool gray coconuts. A different Nile, green iguanas sunned on the river rocks. Pigs grunted in the mud and horses from Chacala snorted on the trail. Spurs. The gentle surf whispered day and night and the palms rustled with the same beat as the sea. At noon every day the *Paladín* would dock in the bay and twelve tourists would ford the gentle surf to the beach. They would wade in the river, or let Nathan ferry them if it was too deep. Some rode horseback upriver or through the village and up to the waterfall. Sometimes Ben and Keith, like the village children, would act as guides. The tourists would often ask Nathan directions but he didn't speak English. If they wanted to cross the river he would simply point into his dugout and say, "Sit!" They would sit, holding tight; he stood imperiously at the back, poling or rowing, his pale blue eyes serious in his brown face, curly blond hair shining.

At three the *Paladín* would be gone and only the six or seven gringo houses and the two hundred people of the village remained. Dogs barking, chopping wood. When it got dark the pulsating sound of crickets and peepers, and later the cry of owls.

Liz and Jay often came down from their house on the rise. They were old friends, from New Mexico. The couples would drink jamaica juice or manzanilla tea, smoke marijuana and watch the sun set pink on the bay. Maya would grill fish or chicken, with beans and rice, fresh greens from the garden. During the rainy season, especially, they would stay up late playing Scrabble or Monopoly or gin. Sometimes Ben and Keith spent the night up at Liz and Jay's, cooking fudge, sleeping on a waterbed under the stars. Liz and Jay were weavers; the boys made a hundred God's eyes from scraps of wool.

They had to renew their tourist cards every six months. Maya, the children, Liz, and Jay just made a quick trip to the border and back, but Buzz usually had several weeks of business in New Mexico. Talks with his business partner, tax papers, leases to sign. In the beginning, each time he went he scored heroin, but it was less each time. A week of staying high, a week of being sick. He has the "dengue," Maya told Pilla and Teodora. Once Teodora brought him a tea to cure him, and it did, overnight, all the withdrawal symptoms gone, even though it was a cure for dengue, a kind of malaria. A tea of papaya leaves, chamomile, and a horse turd. Finally, the second year, when Buzz made his trip he came back clean, with no drugs. That was the time he came back with the scuba tanks. And as the days and months went by that world began to seem far in the past. Connections and dealers and police, fear seemed far in the past.

Everyone was strong and healthy. There was no candy or sodas. No one fell from trees or rocks. The rare times anyone was sick Maya and Liz consulted the Merck manual and a *PDR*, if necessary gave antibiotics.

Keith got a bad sore throat that didn't get better even with injections of ampicillin. Maya took him in the *Paladín* to Puerto Vallarta, flew with him to a clinic in Guadalajara. The doctor there took his tonsils out and kept him for a few days. After he was better he and Maya had a three-day holiday. They took taxis and buses all over town, spent hours in the market and shops buying presents and supplies. Keith loved the telephone and the television. They called room service for hamburgers and ice cream, went to a movie and to a bullfight. El Cordobés himself was staying in their hotel, signed his autograph for Keith.

And then getting out of the elevator she saw Victor, a drug dealer, in the lobby. She tried to shoo Keith back in but the doors closed and there Victor was. Out of prison. For years he had always found Buzz, in New Mexico, in Chiapas. Several times he had burned Buzz for thousands of dollars. But there is no recourse when that happens. It was because Maya had gone to buy the heroin, and didn't test it. Maya's fault, Buzz had slapped her so hard she fell, cracked her head. In Guatemala Buzz had been strung out and sick. Victor made him crawl across the floor to get a fix.

Close, always he stood so close you could smell him. Dark, almost black, lean, feral. He was an orphan, from Mexico City streets. They had first met him in Acapulco. He had been a gigolo then, too, a handsome beach boy with a throaty laugh, shiny white teeth. One night he had stolen all of an old woman's money and jewels and had also taken her false teeth.

In front of the elevator Victor gripped Maya's arm. "Where's Buzz?"

"Ajijic," she said. "We live in Ajijic." She in turn gripped Keith's wrist, praying that he wouldn't speak. "Don't come, Victor. He's clean now."

"Oh, I'll stop by sometime . . . Give me some money, Maya, so I won't join you for dinner. I only have a . . . Give me some money, Maya."

She gave him what was in her purse. Fifty thousand pesos. "Ciao."

The next morning Maya and Keith flew to Vallarta, arrived in time to catch the *Paladín*. The radio on the *Paladín* blared the Rolling Stones and the tourists were drinking rum, laughing and talking, necking, throwing up. The sea was rough. Keith cheered when they finally reached the white rocks and saw the bay of Yelapa. Pelicans dove all around them; dolphins raced the boat. Buzz and Ben and Nathan waved from the beach.

Maya and Keith talked at once while they unpacked presents. Butterfly nets, games, a periscope, a telescope, a globe of the world. Peanut butter! Chocolate bars! They had brought a knife for Juanito and a canary in a wooden cage. Cans and cans of flowers and vegetables for Maya and Teodora, who insisted they had to be planted this very moment as tonight was the new moon.

Buzz helped them plant, starting the holes with a pick, carrying buckets from the river. When they were through they sat outside. Ben was in his hammock, insisted he could read perfectly by the light of the stars. Keith stood at the fence with the telescope, cried out when he spotted a school of phosphorescent fish in the bay. "Quick let's go swimming!"

Later Buzz told her that it was dangerous to swim around the phosphorescent fish, because sharks are attracted by the light. But that night they dove among them with masks and flippers, treaded water and watched the patterns on the tapestries made by the fish. Skinny, shivering, Ben and Keith lay with the telescope on the beach, taking turns looking at the stars. Out in the rocking of the sea Buzz and Maya embraced, salty and intertwined, laughing wet into the warm night sky. They lay on the sand later, by the boys, and passed the telescope back and forth. Buzz stroked Maya's arm, laid his hand gently on her belly.

"It must be a girl," he said. "You're still so small."

Maya sat up on her elbow, kissed Buzz's salty lips.

"I'm glad about the baby now. What a lucky baby!"

At that moment, then, she believed that their baby would be coming into a sweet safe world.

Keith reminded them that they had brought marshmallows from Guadalajara for cocoa. Buzz built a fire in the huge copper pot on the living room floor; Maya cooked hot chocolate on the Coleman stove, beat it frothy with a wooden whisk. It was one in the morning, but they got Nathan up out of bed to join them.

For the next few days, instead of school, Buzz and the boys and Juanito caught butterflies that fluttered undulating in the killing jar and were mounted on cotton batting under glass. What they hadn't bought, what they really needed, was a butterfly book.

Early one morning Buzz and the boys packed sandwiches and jamaica juice and went up river, looking for the neon-green-and-black butterflies they had seen in the lavender lantana on the trail to Chacala. Nathan had begged to go too, so after Pilla built the fire and brought water Maya told her she could have the rest of the day off. Sulking, Pilla left. She wanted to be with Nathan or to stay in the beautiful garden.

Maya raked the floor, lay in a hammock to watch the gulls go upriver. From time to time she got up to check the beans, lay back down in a lazy reverie. A hawk soared high above the strangler fig and on the far bank *zopilotes* flapped around the carcass of a deer.

It was pleasant to have the house alone. She lay in the scent of the datura until she heard the whistle of the *Paladín*. She got up then and put more wood on the fire. With a long fork she toasted green chilies, peeled them with a paring knife. They were pungent and hot. Tears came to her eyes and she wiped them with the back of her hand.

Victor had appeared without a sound, without warning. The river was too high to cross. He must have walked across the beach and over the trail. His expensive shoes were dusty from the path. Maya smelled his sweat and cologne. She didn't speak or think. She stabbed him in the stomach with the paring knife. Blood gushed down his white sharkskin pants. He laughed at her, grabbed a rag.

"Get me a bandage."

She didn't move. With a thief's instinct he went straight for the basket where the first-aid kit was. He put alcohol on the still bleeding cut, bound it tightly. Blood seeped red against the white gauze, his black hard skin.

He went up the *tapanco*, came down wearing a pair of Buzz's pants, a T-shirt that said SUPPORT MENTAL HEALTH. It had been a present, a joke. He poured himself a glass of *raicilla* and stretched out in a hammock near her, rocked himself with one foot, bare now.

"Don't worry," he said, "it was only a flesh wound."

"Go away, Victor. Buzz is clean. I'm having a baby. Leave us alone."

"I can't wait to see old Buzz."

"He'll be back late. You'll miss the boat."

"I'll wait."

They waited; Victor in the hammock, Maya still standing at the stove, still holding the knife. The *Paladín* whistled and set out to sea.

They came back, laughing on the trail. Oh what wonderful butterflies. But Ben and Keith had wood ticks, in their hair, on their legs. They knelt in the grass while Maya got them out; some had to be burned out with a cigarette. The boys took soap then and went running to the river to bathe.

Buzz and Victor sat at the table, talking softly, sharing a joint.

"Were you surprised to see Victor?" Buzz asked. Maya didn't answer; she chopped meat and onions for tacos.

"She was surprised," Victor said. "Gave me a swell welcome."

She sent the boys up to Liz and Jay's with some green chili and a note asking if they could spend the night. They were pleased, took the telescope, and the butterfly nets for morning.

Dusk began to fall. Teodora and Donasiano passed by the gate with her dishes. Her chickens squawked as they settled in the bushes and trees for the night. After dinner Maya cleared the table and took Nathan into the adobe room. She lit a lantern, checked the bed for scorpions. Nathan's eyes were closing;

he was tired after going upriver, but she continued to sing to him and stroke his hair even after he was asleep. "Swing Low, Sweet Chariot." "The Red River Valley," she sang to herself, tears soaking the pillow.

Buzz had built a big fire in the copper pot; the men sat cross-legged by it, drinking coffee, smoking marijuana. Maya sat at the table with a glass of *raicilla*. She left, obediently, when Buzz said she must be tired, ready to hit the sack. "*Duerme con los angelitos*," Victor said.

The surf crashed on the far beach, the river lapped at the bank just outside. Somewhere someone was chopping wood, someone else was playing a guitar. She tried not to hear their voices beneath those sounds, but couldn't keep from listening.

"I figure you owe me five thousand. Dollars," Buzz said.

"Jesus that was a raw deal, *ese*. What a scam . . . I lost ten thousand on it myself. That's why I've been looking for you. I can make it up to you, wait till you see what I got."

"What, some of that *caca*-colored Mexican shit?"

"No way. This is a sealed box. Sealed. Glass vials inside. Pure medicinal morphine. Ten milligrams a pop. Check it out, man. Sealed. We're talking unadulterated high. This is my apology to you, brother."

Silence. She didn't want to hear, to look. She drank more *raicilla*, covered her head with a pillow, but she couldn't keep herself from crawling to the edge of the *tapanco* and looking down, like people stare spellbound by a fire, a fatal accident. She watched, even though she was sickened by that look on their faces, both gaunt, skull-like in the firelight. The look of the addict about to fix, intensely sexual, a look of greed, desperate need. Close to each other they tied up each other's arm. Victor heated the spoon in the fire. "Go easy, man, this shit ain't cut like we're used to." Buzz filled the needle first, tried and tried until he finally found a vein. The needle filled with blood and he jammed in the plunger. The tie fell from his arm. His face turned to stone, his eyes euphoric, hooded. His body too seemed to turn to stone, but he rocked slowly, smiling, the erotic smile of a figure on an Etruscan tomb. He was moaning, softly, like a chant. Victor watched him, grinning, and then he filled the needle and fixed. The minute Victor got a hit he fell forward into the flames. Maya screamed but Buzz didn't move. She leapt down, far, landed on her knees. Her knees were scraped; tears stung her eyes, a child with skinned knees. There was a nauseating stench of burning hair and skin. She grabbed Victor and beat his head into the sand. He was dead. Buzz was lying down now. He was breathing shallowly, his pulse was slow. Maya couldn't wake him. She covered him with a Navajo blanket. She blew out the lantern and sat in the dark. Shaking, Maya sat at the table for a long time, utterly alone.

She checked on Nathan. He slept soundly. She kissed his damp salty hair. Back in the living room she hid the needle and the box of morphine in a canister. She emptied Victor's pockets, burned his wallet and ID in the remaining coals. She rolled his glasses up in the SUPPORT MENTAL HEALTH shirt and put it in the *tapanco.*

She dragged his body by the feet, out of the house, over the grass and out the gate. She rested then in the moonlight. There was a swiftly moving line of cutter ants in the path. Maya began to giggle, hysterically, but then was quiet, hauling him over the rushes to the riverbank, where she finally heaved his body into the boat. He stank of burned skin and shit. She gagged and vomited. She shoved at the *panga* but it didn't move; at last she got down on her hands and knees and pushed it with her shoulder until it slipped slowly into the water. Splashing in the cold water she chased the boat and jumped in, tugging at his arms and legs to get at the oars. The dugout glided smoothly as she paddled, a breeze blew in her sweat-soaked hair. She pulled the oars in when she reached the *boca*, praying to hit the incoming surf just right. A wave sent the boat high into the air. It landed with a whap, spinning wildly. She rowed furiously then, humming to calm herself, paddling first to one side then the other.

The canoe was in the middle of the bay, skimming smoothly and evenly now out toward sea. A mist had covered the moon and stars so it was dark, but the waves hitting the receding beach shone neon silver. There was only one tiny light on in the village. Her hands were blistering but she kept rowing, past the white rocks, past the point. She rowed until the light in the village disappeared and until she could feel the boat being pulled south by the swift current outside the bay. The little boat spun and teetered as she pulled and shoved at Victor's body. At last she heaved it into the water where it regained its lightness and sank in an instant.

Her lungs were bursting, heart bounding with fear as she rowed, fighting the swift current to get back into the bay. Once inside she had to keep pausing to hear where she was, listening for the gentle whisper of waves breaking on the beach. The mist had turned to clouds. It was so dark, her hands so bloody now she couldn't beach the canoe. It capsized; she lost the oars. She swam then underwater until she was free of the boat. Flailing, choking, she realized that she could stand. Cool white foam swirled around her. She lay in the sand until she could make it across the river. The river water seemed warm, heavy after the ocean. Crabs, a turtle, bumped her leg; schools of minnows tickled her ankles like raindrops.

She reached the path and by force of habit followed the line of cutter ants into the garden. Even in the dark she could see that they had eaten the stock and the roses. Two donkeys were in the vegetable garden; she shooed them out and shut the gate, the barn door. She giggled. Inside, Buzz had moved to a hammock. Nathan slept peacefully. It was still dark, but roosters had begun to crow, donkeys to bray.

Maya was shaking as she bandaged her badly blistered hands. Buzz woke, sat up straight, disoriented.

"Where's the box?"

"It's safe."

"Where's the box."

"In the blue canister."

"Where's Victor?"

"He's dead. He OD'd."

"Where's Victor?"

"He's gone. Go up to bed."

Buzz went out to the far corner of the garden to pee. The sky was turning lavender. Stiff-legged he walked back to the ladder and climbed up to the *tapanco.* He had the box with him.

Maya dragged the copper fire kettle up the trail beyond the house, dumped the still red embers and ashes into the flowing water. She scoured the pot with sand.

Inside she made a fire to boil water, put dry bandages on her hands. Everything was hard, muffled, because of her hands. Raking, sweeping. Awkwardly, determinedly she swept the sand of the living room until it was smooth, as if no one had been there.

Pilla arrived before Nathan woke. Maya had changed and combed her hair, was drinking coffee at the table.

"Doña! Are you ill? And your hands! *¿Qué pasó?*"

"Pilla, it was a terrible night. The señor was very ill, maybe the dengue. I stayed up with him, fell from the ladder onto my hands."

Immediately, when an addiction resumes, the lies resume. Fear comes back.

Suspicion comes. Those gringos must have gotten drunk, Pilla thought. My poor Nathan!

"And the Mexican man?"

"He is gone."

Pilla went out into the garden.

"The boat is gone too," she said drily.

"*No te digo pues* . . . it was a terrible night."

"*¡Aí, y las rosas!* The ants ate them!"

Losing patience, Maya interrupted her.

"Please, dress Nathan and take him for breakfast in the village. Bring him back at dinnertime. I have to rest. I'm worried about my baby."

"You're not spotting or cramping?"

"No, but I'm exhausted. Please, take Nathan for me." Maya thought she might scream, sob, vomit, but she stayed calm, rocked Nathan, awake now, weeping bitterly about the missing boat. Luis came running down the trail, his machete glinting in the sun. Hot already.

"*Fíjase, señora.* Ronco found your canoe smashed up at the point, on the pelican rocks."

"And the man? Maybe he's drowned!" Pilla was cheering up with all this news to tell in the village.

"No. He left on foot," Maya said. "I expect the canoe just came unmoored. The river is high. We'll get a new one, a nicer one, Nathan." For God's sake please go, all of you, she said to herself.

"Didn't like his looks. *Callejero . . . vicioso,*" Pilla whispered to Luis. Vicious, the Spanish word for addict.

Maya lay in the hammock under the mango tree, was falling asleep when Liz appeared, smiling at the gate. Good morning! She was beautiful in a pink shift, her red hair crackling in the strong sunlight.

"Come in, Liz. I'm too tired to get up."

The women embraced; Liz pulled a leather chair out by the hammock. She smelled clean.

"You are so clean!" Tears ran down Maya's face.

"What's wrong, love? Oh, is it the baby? You're not losing the baby?" She held Maya's hand.

"No. It's Buzz. A connection showed up yesterday; Buzz is back on drugs."

"He's been clean a long time, Maya. He'll do it again. Be patient. He loves you and the children. He's a very beautiful man, a man with a beautiful noble soul. And you love him very much . . . be patient."

Maya nodded while Liz spoke, shivering, her teeth chattering.

"I want to go back to the real world," she said.

Liz pointed up to the green palms, to the sky. "This is real, Maya. You're just worn out. Rest all day. Jay took the boys and Juanito up past the waterfall to the orchards."

The women drank tea. Liz stroked Maya's hair, patted her shoulder. "Don't worry," she said. "It will be all right." Maya fell asleep then and Liz left.

Maya was awakened when she heard the *Paladín*'s whistle. Is it coming or going? I don't know if I'm coming or going! Why do I make jokes at the worst of times, like Mama did?

The *Paladín* headed out of the bay toward the ocean. Maya lay back in the hammock in the hot sultry afternoon. No, she thought, it isn't going to be all right. The fear and the desolation felt familiar to her, like coming home. Ashes.

MY LIFE IS AN OPEN BOOK

You know, the only place in Corrales that's not adobe. That three-story white farmhouse, grove of cottonwoods higher than the house. Sits on two acres of land, next to Gus's field with the herd of Black Angus. She's been gone for years now but all anybody ever calls it is the Bellamy house. Before Claire Bellamy moved in it was the Sanchez place, no matter who lived in it. He's the sheep rancher who built it back in 1910.

The whole town was just dying to see what poor fool had bought the place. Couldn't help but feel sorry for her even though it was only a thousand down. Course she'd be rich now if she'd a kept the place. Anybody coulda told her the pump was about to go, about the termites and the wiring. Nobody figured on the roof caving in. That had been a darn good roof.

Claire was divorced, no more'n thirty, with four children. The oldest was around ten, the baby not even walking. She taught Spanish at the university, did some tutoring too. Took the older boys to school every morning and the little ones over to Lupe Vargas's. Painted the whole inside of the house herself, fenced in the corral, planted vegetables, built rabbit hutches. Course they didn't eat the rabbits or ducks, just had them running wild, and a goat and pony too. Two dogs and near to a dozen cats. Come on out back . . . you can see the house plain as day.

You could see better when she was there. She didn't have curtains on any of them tall windows. And I have these here binoculars. For the birds. Pileated woodpecker lives down in that old dead cottonwood. She loved birds too, used to go lean on Gus's fence evenings, when the red-winged blackbirds were all out. Prettiest sight you can ever see, them birds against the green grass, the black cattle.

It was just like a living doll house. Children all over hell and gone, hers and the neighbors'. In trees, in wagons, on trikes and the pony, running in the sprinkler. Cats in every window of the house. Evenings you could see her and the boys at the table, and after she had bathed the little ones she'd put them to bed and read to Ben and Keith. She'd wash up then, feed the animals. Dining room light would go on; she'd be studying for hours. If me or Arnold got up to let the dog out, twelve, one o'clock she'd be up . . . couple of times she fell asleep right there, her head on the typewriter. She'd be up at six though, feeding the animals and then getting the kids ready for school. She was in PTA; Ben and Keith were in Scouts and 4-H. Ben took violin lessons from Miss Handy. The town had been keeping its eye on her, had just about decided she was a worker and a darn good mother.

Then she up and carries on with that Casey boy. A bad one, Mike Casey. Him and his brother, Pete. Always had been. Dropouts, thieves, dope fiends. Smoked that marijuana right there front of God and everybody, outside Earl's grocery. Their folks are two old drunks. I'll tell you it was pitiful. Least Mike helped out at home. Cooked some and cleaned up. Most of the time he just played the guitar or made boats. Models, from scratch, perfect as could be. He was a sight. Long dirty hair and a earring. Motorcycle clothes with a skull on the back, big old knife. I mean to say he was something to see. Just plain scary.

Now we all would have understood if she took up with some nice man, but this was sicko and him barely nineteen, to make things worse. And not that ever she bothered to hide anything. They'd walk to the ditch in broad daylight, her and Casey, the children and dogs and one cat that liked to swim. Weekends they'd load up his pickup truck with bedrolls and a cookstove and take off Lord knows where.

She still studied late as ever only he'd be there writing too or playing his guitar. Then the light in her room would be on, their room I guess. Couple of times in the full moon I saw them out on the roof, in the treetops. A body couldn't help but see them, plain as day.

One night I saw him carry in something heavy in a gunnysack. Finally made out it was that pink marble angel from the cemetery. Real old, people come special to see it. I had a mind to call Jed, he's the State Police, but Arnold said wait and see. Sure enough she had a fit, waving her arms and hollering. He took it back that night; only he put it on the grave backwards, facing the mountains. Still sets that way.

Bessie thought somebody ought to give her a talking-to. That boy had been in Nazareth, and in detention hall twice. He was likely to break any minute and murder all them poor children, or worse. She even left that baby with him. When she was gone he let Ben and Keith drive his pickup in the field and shoot tin cans with his BB gun. We was all worried sick, just sick. Didn't talk to her though but we told Mattie Price and Lupe Vargas not to let their kids play over there.

We have a movie of the afternoon we met Casey. Nathan had learned to swim in the clear ditch the day before and he wanted it documented. It was the second hot summer day. I lay on the blanket watching the kids, listening to the crows, looking at dragonflies through the zoom lens. Dozens of them, startling neon blue, sunlight paler blue through the tracery of their wings, darting, hovering, lapis lazuli skimming the green water.

Then a Spanish galleon in full sail glided right through them. An exquisitely made boat, about eighteen inches long. It belonged to Casey. I had seen his brother, Pete, just that morning out on North Fourth, in a phone booth with a blowtorch. Casey just seemed to look bad, all decked out and bizarre in leather, with a skull studded on his back. He had always seemed magic to me, like a figure from *Black Orpheus*. Or a Harlequin, from afar, against the white sand dunes or the pink tamarisk in the woods, against the red wet sand of the riverbed.

He squatted on the bank of the ditch, let the kids play with his boat, told them how he made it. After a while he politely took it away from them, dried it with a T-shirt and wrapped it in his black jacket. He took off his pants and dove into the water, dragonflies scattering. His body was beautiful. He had a Civil War face, sort of hillbilly and gaunt, sunken shifty eyes, a sullen mouth, bad teeth. He came home with us for dinner and then just stayed. That night he showed me a trapdoor that led to the roof, to a ledge right in the tops of the cottonwoods. You could see the whole little town, look down on the sleeping black cattle. Owl in the tree. We became lovers up there on the roof. In the morning when we woke in my bed he was already known to me, familiar. There was no transition. When I went downstairs he and the boys were cooking flapjacks and after breakfast the three older ones went off with him to the ditch.

I try to remember what we ever talked about, but I can't. And I'm a talker, so are my boys. We did wordless things with Casey. All day on the mesa digging for pot shards, muttering or sighing, letting out a yell whenever we found abalone shell, turquoise, a big piece of pottery. Quiet, our fishing lines in the water. Padding through Canyon de Chelly, climbing Acoma. The baby, Joel, would sit mesmerized, watching his brothers help Casey work on boats. At night when I studied and graded papers Casey drew or played his guitar. When I'd glance up he would glance up too.

We camped out a lot at our cliffs. Not far from town but the road was bad, long hike in. Stark red cliffs, sheer above a valley and looking far to the south, beyond Route 66, beyond Acoma. No sign of Indians ever being there, which was strange; it was such a holy place. Sky all around and in sight of all the sacred places. The Sandias, the Jemez, the Rio Grande. We explored, climbed, watched the hawk against the sunset. Porcupines with the green quills. Nighthawks at dusk and an owl at night. Wild dogs the boys thought were coyotes. We watched the puma kill a deer. That was lovely. Really. No one else ever went to our cliffs except the hunter who killed the puma. We hadn't seen the man but his picture and the puma's were in the paper. We looked for tracks then, found deer tracks and puma tracks and then dog tracks and man tracks. By the stream.

Took eight months before I thought. I had ignored glares from old women at Earl's store and we had all just laughed at Jennie Caldwell watching us with binoculars from her back porch. Casey and I were the town scandal, Betty Boyer told me. Then Keith told me the Price kids weren't allowed to come to our house. I sat on the back porch. The reason I had moved to Corrales was to start a new life, bring my children up right. In a small peaceful town, part of a community. I planned to get my doctorate and teach, just be a good teacher and a good mother. If I had thought of a man in my future he would have been graying, kindly, with tenure. Now look.

Casey was washing dishes. He called out, asking me what I was doing.

"Thinking."

"Jesus, Claire, please don't think." But I had already.

"You have to go, Casey."

He got his guitar, said, "See you around," and was gone. It was as hard on the kids as on me. Worse when we found a Zuni grave without him, and at the deer dance in San Felipe.

Marzie, another graduate student, kept asking me to go out with her. She belonged to the Sierra Club and Swinging Singles, even Parents Without Partners, and she wasn't even a parent.

Casey sort of eased back into our lives. He didn't live there and we weren't lovers, most of the time, but he was there a lot. He and the boys were digging a duck pond. He'd watch the kids while I was at the library. Finals were coming up. Weekends we went swimming in the ditch or out to the cliffs. Joel learned how to walk.

I remember talking to Ben and Keith on the phone, saying it was a red-letter day, whatever that means. My last final and that afternoon I was picking up a new VW camper. I had told Marzie that I would go out with her, to celebrate. To a dance at the German American Club. No intellectuals, no academics. Just swingers, she said.

I drove the new van home. The boys were thrilled with it. It had a built-in bed, a refrigerator, and a stove. Joel got in it right away with his blanket and toys, climbed in and out for hours. Casey took them all for a ride while I cooked dinner and dressed. Miniskirt and long earrings. The kids were so upset about me going out I realized I should have done it long before. I told Casey I'd be at the German American Club. I said I would be home late, would call him later to check in. I remembered to put on perfume, went back upstairs.

The German American Club was pretty bad. Loud disco and then a German polka band wearing lederhosen. Accordions.

We danced with jet pilots from Kirtland and technicians from Sandia. Bomb makers. What was I doing there? I called home four or five times but it was busy. Phone must be off the hook. We had one smart cat who used to knock it off so she could hear the voice say your phone is off the hook. After a while I began to have fun, dancing and drinking beer. Anybody can tell you I have no head for liquor. Marzie looked even sillier than I did, in a silver lamé jumpsuit. She disappeared and I ended up with a pilot named Buck. Handsome in a Nazi way, like old black-and-white Richard Widmark.

I figured that Casey boy had gone berserk for sure, run plumb amok. He was driving that pickup like a bat out of hell up and down the ditch roads, spinning on the bank, dust flying, crows squawking and three of those poor Bellamy children up front in the cab. That settles it, I said, and called the State Police. Jed must have been down to the store talking with Earl; the police car was there in five minutes, lights, sirens, and all. Casey began to speed up and get away but then he stopped and got out of the truck. He looked like a madman. He and Earl climbed up on the bank and looked down in the water, like they was wondering if fish were biting. Earl went and talked on his radio and then Casey and the kids followed him to the Bellamy house. I got my sweater and flashlight and took off across Gus's field.

She had gone out, in the new van, to the Spanish American Club to celebrate the end of school. That's what she taught, Spanish. They'd all been eating dinner and then Casey saw Joel was gone. That baby had just started walking. They called him and looked all over the house and then they looked outside and there were his little red tennis shoes. Saddest thing you ever saw, them little red shoes. Couldn't have gone far barefoot, I said, but Jed said the ditch wasn't far. He said there weren't nothing to do but drain them ditches. He called the volunteer fire department and called in for more police.

The men all went to the ditch. Casey and the boys were searching in the woods. Folks from town were arriving so I had Arnold bring over the church coffee urn, go get some Styrofoam cups and cream over to Earl's. Earl sent a case of Coke, cold. I sent Arnold back home for some tuna-and-macaroni casseroles from the freezer and two berry pies. Bessie never wants to be outdone. She went home and got chicken, a whole ham, and potato salad. Lupe Vargas showed up with a full washtub of tamales. Did your heart good, to see how our town pulls together when folks are in trouble. And those volunteers, the men who were draining the ditches were the very farmers who needed that water for their crops, that time of year more'n any. But not one complaint. Just doing what anybody would of done.

We got to find the mother, I said. I kept thinking about the Casey boy's face, chalk white, so shook he could hardly talk. He said she was out celebrating. Claire Bellamy hadn't gone out once, not in a year since they moved in. Casey looked scared and guilty. That's how he looked, guilty. Where was she? Maybe he had murdered them both and buried their bodies without me seeing, though that wasn't hardly likely. Maybe they were dead in the attic. I looked in the phone book for the Spanish American Club. No such place. Called the university and got hold of the names of her professors. None of them ever heard of the club either, but were all pretty shook about the baby maybe drowned. They gave me numbers of students and friends of hers, but none of them had heard of any celebration so then I really got to worrying.

Where was his gun? What if he felt cornered and shot into the crowd? You read about that all the time. I figured I better tell

Bessie. We left Mabel Strom to keep on calling people from Claire Bellamy's phone book while we searched the house with a fine-tooth comb. We went through all the drawers and closets but didn't find the gun. In her room though, right there in the open were these drawings of her. Stark naked. Not a stitch on. Right there for those poor innocent children to see. And some poems talking about a silk breast and other such trash. Just about broke our hearts, so we ripped all the poems and pictures right up. She keeps a clean house, you must say, Bessie said, and that was the truth.

The helicopter and the bloodhounds came about the same time. Awful racket, clattering and yapping. The Bellamy kids came tearing back from the ditch to watch the helicopter land in their backyard and the dogs sniffing them little red shoes. I told them they should be ashamed, having such a whale of a time, with their baby brother most likely drowned. They got serious for about two minutes, Nathan even cried, and then they took off across the fields after the dogs. There were crowds of people by that time so Bessie and me got busy in the kitchen. Lots of Claire Bellamy's friends. Mabel must of called every name in Claire's phone book. Two nuns from a school where she used to teach. About ten students from Rio Grande High came straight from the prom, in formals and tuxedos. Her professors came and her ex-husband came, in what turned out to be a Lotus. All the kids went out to look at the car. He was with a Frenchwoman who spoke French with the nuns. Then still another ex-husband showed up. That could have knocked us over with a feather. He was with his mother, a real battle-axe. Hate to have her snooping in my house. The first ex-husband had just got back from Italy, had never met the second one. But they were real polite, shook hands and one of them said, well, nothing to do but wait. There was plenty they coulda been doing, but I held my tongue. Two mean-looking Mexkins came. Then two nice ladies who knew the first mother-in-law. Then more professors came. They got really upset when bigmouthed Bessie told them it wasn't just the baby feared drowned, that Claire Bellamy herself may have met foul play.

The men came in tired from the ditch. Casey came back with the children, fed them, and took them upstairs to bed. The men all ate and then went outside to smoke and pass around a bottle, like at a party. Inside folks were eating and chattering away. Jed came up and asked me what was this darn fool talk about foul play. I told him about the romance and the breakup, how Casey had been lurking in the trees. When Casey came downstairs Jed and Wilt, the deputy, took him in the sewing room for about an hour. When they came out Jed said "You got holt of her yet?" and he and Wilt went back to the woods. Casey came at me, furious. I liked to a died. But he just said "You filthy bitch" and went out the back door.

I went home with Buck, to where he lived, weaving through his exercycle and rowing machine and barbells to his waterbed. Later he said, "Wow, that was good. Was that good for you?" "Yes," I said, "I have to call home." The line was still busy. Buck said he was starved. "Aren't you starved?" Why yes, I was. We went to that truck stop on Lomas, ate steak and eggs and laughed. Pleasant. I was getting to like him. It was almost morning. The *Journal* truck came; the driver dropped off a stack of papers. Buck went to get a paper and check out the sports page. I was just glancing over the front page when I saw it at the bottom. CORRALES BABY FEARED DROWNED—DITCHES DRAINED. And then right below that it said Joel Bellamy. That was my son.

Buck dropped me at my van and I raced home, through red blinking lights, yellow blinking lights. I didn't cry, but my chest made a keening sound like wind. Just outside Corrales, at Dead Man's Curve, I heard a noise and a rustle and then Joel said, "Hi, Mama!" He climbed over the seat and onto my lap. I skidded to a stop. I sat there, holding him, smelling him. Finally I stopped shaking and drove us the rest of the way home.

The rest of that night is like a dream, and I don't mean dreamy. Distorted and out of sync. People coming in and out of focus, out of context. Our land had turned into a vast nightmare parking lot. A policeman waved me to a spot with his flashlight. Betty Boyer was drunk on the back porch. "Welcome to *This Is Your Life*!"

First off there was old Jennie Caldwell washing dishes, with Casey drying. He moaned, almost passed out when he saw Joel. Betty and I helped him sit down. He held Joel, rocking him, still moaning. Our house was full of people, strangers. No, they weren't all strangers. People were running around yelling that the baby had been found, was okay. But after the initial relief and joy a bad reaction seemed to set in. As if everyone had been tricked, and here it was, four in the morning. One of the farmers said that leastways both other times they'd drained the ditches there'd been a body in them. In all fairness, everyone was on edge from exhaustion and worry. Still it did seem the only ones simply glad Joel was safe were Casey and Sister Cecilia and Sister Lourdes. Or who didn't imply I was to blame for the whole thing. Even my own children felt that way. They had known I shouldn't be going out anywhere. I don't want to talk about my ex-husbands, Tony and John, or about my ex-mother-in-law. I ignored their malicious comments. The entire Spanish department was there, even Dr. Duncan, the chairman. He had been suspicious of me ever since that incident on First Street, but that's another story. I am a very private person. Well at least I had showered at Buck's and had eaten breakfast. I was refreshed, actually, but even that seemed to annoy people.

The worst was Mr. Oglesby, from the bank. I had never seen him before. He was the person who called me if I had an overdraft. "Say, Claire, this is Oglesby, up to the bank. Better get some money in here, hon." What was Mr. Oglesby doing in my kitchen? Two women I hadn't seen since the baby shower for Keith, nine years before.

The police finally got everyone to leave. They didn't leave, though, sat down with me and Casey at the kitchen table. The goat and the pony put their heads in the window. I'll go feed them, Casey said. You stay right where you are, the policeman told him. It was as if a crime had been committed. Where had Joel been when I left? Were the van doors open? No, I never did say Spanish American. Where had I been from two until four? Buck who? I told them I had called home, about seven times.

"Now then, little lady," Jed said, "if you didn't know there was something mighty wrong down here . . . how come you kept on trying to call?"

"Just to say hello," I said.

"Hello. You call up your babysitter at three in the morning just to say hello?"

"Yes."

Casey smiled. He looked really happy. I smiled back at him.

"Judas Priest," the policeman said. "Come on, Wilt, let's git out of this loony bin, git us some grub."

THE WIVES

Anytime Laura thought about Decca, she saw her as if in a stage set. She had met Decca when she and Max were still married, many years before Laura married him. The house on High Street, in Albuquerque. Beau had taken her. Through the wide-open door into a kitchen with dirty pots and pans, dishes and cats, open jars, plates of runny fudge, uncapped bottles, cartons of takeout Chinese, through a bedroom, bumping into piles of clothes, shoes, stacks of magazines and newspapers, mesh sweater dryers, tires. Dimly lit center stage a bay window with frayed saffron nicotine-stained shades. Decca and Max sat in leather chairs, facing a miniature TV on a stool. The table between them held an enormous ashtray full of cigarette butts, a magazine with a knife and a pile of marijuana, a bottle of rum and Decca's glass. Max wore a black velour bathrobe, Decca a red silk kimono, her dark hair loose and long. They were stunning to look at. Stunning. Their presence hit you physically, like a blow.

Decca didn't speak but Max did. His thick-lashed heavy-lidded stoned dark eyes looked deep into Laura's. He rasped, "Hey, Beau, what's happening?" Laura couldn't remember anything after that. Maybe Beau asked to borrow the car or some money. He was staying with them, on his way to New York. Beau was a saxophone player she had met by chance, walking her baby in his stroller on Elm Street.

Decca. How come aristocratic Englishwomen and upper-class American women all have names like Pookie and Muffin? Have they kept the names their nannies called them? There is a news reporter on NBC called Cokie. No way is Cokie from a nice family in Ohio. She is from a fine old wealthy family. Philadelphia? Virginia? Decca was a B——, one of the best Boston families. She had been a debutante, studied at Wellesley, was partly disinherited when she eloped with Max, who was Jewish. Years later, Laura too had been disinherited when her family heard of her own elopement with Max, but they relented when they realized how wealthy he was.

Decca called around eleven that night. Laura's sons were asleep. She left them a note and Decca's number in case one of them woke up, said she'd be back soon.

The reason it always seems like a stage set, she told herself, is because Decca never locks her doors and never gets up to answer the doorbell or a knock. So you just go in and find her in situ, stage right, in a dim light. At some point, before she sat down and started drinking, she had lit a piñon fire, candles in niches and kerosene lanterns whose soft lights catch now in her cascading silken hair. She wears an elaborately embroidered green kimono over a still lovely body. Only close up can you see that she is over forty, that drink has made her skin puffy, her eyes red.

It is a large room in an old adobe house. The fire reflects in the red tile floor. On the white walls are Howard Schleeter paintings, a Diebenkorn, a Franz Kline, some fine old carved Santos. Underwear dangles from a John Chamberlain sculpture. Over the baby's crib in a corner hangs a real Calder mobile. If you looked you could see fine Santo Domingo and Acoma pots.

Old Navajo rugs are hidden beneath stacks of *Nations*, *New Republics*, *I. F. Stone's Weeklys*, *New York Times*, *Le Monde*, *Art News*, *Mad* magazines, pizza cartons, Baca's takeout cartons. The mink-covered bed is piled with clothes, toys, diapers, cats. Empty straw-covered jugs of Bacardi lie on their sides around the room, occasionally spinning when cats bat at them. A row of full jugs stands next to Decca's chair, another by the bed.

Decca was the only female alcoholic Laura knew that didn't hide her liquor. Laura didn't admit to herself yet that she drank, but she hid her bottles. So her sons wouldn't pour them out, so she wouldn't see them, face them.

If Decca was always set onstage, in that great chair, her hair in the lamplight shining, Laura was particularly good at entrances. She stands, elegant and casual in the doorway, wearing a floor-length Italian suede coat, in profile as she surveys the room. She is in her early thirties, her prettiness deceptively fresh and young.

"What the fuck are you doing here?" Decca says.

"You called me. Three times, actually. Come quick, you said."

"I did?" Decca pours some more rum. She feels around under her chair and comes up with another glass, wipes it out with her kimono.

"I called you?" She pours a big drink for Laura, who sits in a chair on the other side of the table. Laura lights one of Decca's Delicados, coughs, takes a drink.

"I know it was you, Decca. Nobody else calls me 'Bucket Butt' or 'Fat-Assed Sap.'"

"Must have been me." Decca laughs.

"You said to come right away. That it was urgent."

"How come you took so long, then? Christ, I'm operating in total blackout now. You still on the sauce? Well, yeah, that's obvious."

She pours them both more rum. Each of them drinks. Decca laughs.

"Well, you learned how to drink, anyway. I remember when you two were first married. I offered you a martini and you said, 'No thanks. Alcohol gives me vertigo.'"

"It still does."

"Weird how both his wives ended up lushes."

"Weirder still we didn't end up junkies."

"I did," Decca says. "For six months. I got into drinking trying to get off of heroin."

"Did using make you closer to him?"

"No. But it made me not care." Decca reaches over to an elaborate stereo system, changes the Coltrane tape to Miles Davis. *Kind of Blue.* "So our Max is in jail. Max won't handle jail in Mexico."

"I know. He likes his pillowcases ironed."

"God, you're a ditz. Is that your assessment of the situation?"

"Yeah. I mean if he's like that about pillowcases, imagine how hard everything else will be. Anyway, I came to tell you that Art is taking care of it. He's sending down money to get him out."

Decca groans. "Christ, it's all coming back to me. Guess how the money is getting there? With Camille! Beau was on the plane with her to Mexico City. He called me from the airport. That's why I called you. Max is going to marry Camille!"

"Oh, dear."

Decca pours them both more rum.

"Oh, dear? You're so ladylike it makes me sick. You'll probably send them crystal. You're smoking two cigarettes."

"You sent *us* crystal. Baccarat glasses."

"I did? Must have been a joke. Anyway, Camille told Max they're going to Acapulco for their honeymoon. Just like you did."

"Acapulco?" Laura stands up, takes off her coat and throws it on the bed. Two cats jump off. Laura is wearing black silk pajamas and slippers. She is weaving, either from emotion or so much rum. She sits.

"Acapulco?" She says this sadly.

"I knew that would get you. Probably to the same suite at the Mirador. The scent of bougainvillea and hibiscus wafting into their room."

"Those flowers don't smell. Nardos would be wafting." Laura holds her head in her hands, thinking.

"Stripes. Stripes from the sun through the wooden shutters."

Decca laughs, opens a new jug of rum and pours.

"No, Mirador is too quiet and old for Camille. He'll take her to some jive beach motel with a bar in the swimming pool, the stools underwater, umbrellas in the coconut drink. They'll drive around town in a pink Jeep with fringe on it. Admit it, Laura. This pisses you off. A dumb file clerk. Tawdry little tart!"

"Come on, Decca. She's not so bad. She's young. The same age as each of us were when we married him. She's not exactly dumb."

This fool is genuinely kind, Decca thought. She must have been so kind to him.

"Camille *is* dumb. God, but so were you. I knew you loved him, though, and would give him sons. They are beautiful, Laura."

"Aren't they?"

I am dumb, Laura thought, and Decca is brilliant. He must have missed Decca a lot.

"I wanted a baby so badly," Decca says. "We tried for years. Years. And fought over it, because I was so obsessed, each of us blaming the other. I could have killed that OB/GYN Rita when she had his baby."

"You know she researched all over town and picked him. She didn't want a lover, just a baby. Sappho. What a name, no?"

"Weird. Weirder is years after we're divorced and I'm forty years old, I get pregnant. One night, one damn night, no maybe ten blooming minutes in mosquito-infested San Blas I fuck an Australian plumber. Bingo."

"Is that why you named your baby Melbourne? Poor kid. Why not Perth? Perth is pretty." Unsteadily, Laura gets up and goes to look at the child. She smiles and covers him.

"He's so big. Wonderful ginger hair. How is he doing?"

"He's great. He's a pretty damn great kid. Starting to talk."

Decca stands, stumbles slightly as she crosses the room to check on the child and then goes to the bathroom. Laura finishes her drink, starts to stand and go home.

"I'll be going now," she says to Decca when she comes back.

"Sit down. Have another drink." She pours. They are drinking from ludicrously small teacups considering how often they are refilled.

"You don't seem to grasp the seriousness of this situation. Now, I'm fine, set for life. I got a huge divorce settlement plus I have family money. What about any inheritance for your children? This woman will wipe him out. You were a fool not to get child support. Blithering fool."

"Yeah. I thought I could support us. I had never had a job before. His habit was eight hundred dollars a day and he was always wrecking cars. So I just got money for their college funds. You want to know the honest truth? I didn't think he could possibly live much longer."

Decca laughs, slapping her knee. "I knew you didn't! What's her name, she didn't want any child support either. Old lawyer Trebb called me after your divorce came through. He wanted to know why it was that all three of us women had gigantic life insurance policies from Max."

Decca sighs, lights up a fat joint that had been lying on the table. It sputters and crackles; little flames make three big holes in her lovely kimono. One right in the middle of the Italy-shaped rum stain. She beats on them, coughing, until the fires are out, passes the joint to Laura. When Laura inhales, she too creates a little shower of sparks that burn holes in her silk top.

"At least he taught me how to deseed weed," she says, talking funny through the smoke.

"So," Decca continues. "He'll be clean when he gets out. Alive and well in Acapulco. I gave him the best years of my life and now look. He's alive and well in Acapulco with a carhop." Decca's speech is slurred now, her nose running as she wails, "The best years of my life!"

"Hell, Decca, I gave him the *worst* years of my life!" The two women find this hysterically funny, slap at each other, hold their sides, stomp their feet and knock over the ashtray, laughing so hard. Laura starts to take a drink but spills it down the front of her pajamas.

"Seriously, Decca," Laura says. "This may be a really good thing. I hope they're happy. He can show her the world. She will adore him, take care of him."

"Take him to the cleaners. Is she a floozy or what? Tacky carhop."

"You're dating yourself. She's more of a Clinique salesgirl, I'd say. You know she was once Miss Redondo Beach?"

"You have style, B.B. A subtle, ladylike bitch. You'll act simply delighted for the nuptial pair. Probably throw rice at them. So tell me now, how does it *really* feel, thinking of them in Acapulco? Imagine. Sunset now. The sun is making a green dot and vanishing. "Cuando Calienta el Sol" is playing. Lots of throbbing saxophone, maracas. No, the music is playing "Piel Canela" now but they're still in bed. She's asleep, tired after sun and waterskiing. Steamy sweaty sex. He lies full against her back. He grazes the back of her neck with his lips, leans, chews on her ear, breathing."

Laura spills some of a freshly poured drink down her shirt-front. "He did that to you?" Decca passes her a towel to dry herself with.

"Bucket-Butt, you think you've got the only earlobe in the world?" She grins, enjoying this now. "Then he'd brush your breast with the palm of his hand, right? You'd groan and turn toward him. Then he'd catch your head in . . ."

"Stop it!"

They're both depressed now. They smoke and drink with the elaborately careful slow motion of the very drunk. Cats come near them, weaving, but they both absentmindedly kick them away.

"At least there weren't any before me," Decca said.

"Elinor. She still calls him, middle of the night. Cries a lot."

"She doesn't count. She was his student at Brandeis. One rainy intense weekend at Truro. Her family called the dean. End of romance and teaching career."

"Sarah?"

"You mean Sarah? His sister Sarah? You're not so dumb, B.B. Sarah is our biggest rival of all. I never said it out loud though. Do you think they ever actually made love?"

"No, of course not. But they are so close. Fiercely close. I don't think anybody could adore him like she does."

"I was jealous of her. God, I was jealous of her."

"Decca. Listen! Oh, wait a minute. I've got to pee." Laura stands, totters, reels across the room into the bathroom. Decca hears her fall, the crack of head against porcelain.

"You okay?"

"Yeah."

Laura returns, crawling on all fours to her chair.

"Life is fraught with peril." She giggles. There is already a big blue goose bump on her forehead.

"Listen, Decca. There is nothing to worry about. He'll never marry Camille. Maybe he said that to get her down there. But he won't. I'll bet you a billion dollars. And you know why?"

"Yep. I've got it. Sister Sarah! She'll never get past old Sarah."

Decca had been tying her hair up with an elastic, high on top of her head so it looked like a crooked palm tree. Laura's hair had come loose from her chignon, so a hunk just flops out of one side of her head. They sit smiling stupidly at one another in their burned wet clothes.

"That's right. Sarah really likes you and me. You know why?"

"Because we are well-bred."

"Because we are ladies." They toast each other with a fresh drink, laughing uproariously, kicking the floor.

"It's true," Decca says. "Although perhaps at this moment we're not quite at our best. So, tell me, were you jealous of Sarah too?"

"No," Laura says. "I never had a real family. She helped me feel part of one. Still does, and she loves the boys. No, I was jealous of the dope dealers. Juni, Beto, Willy, Nacho."

"Yeah, all the pretty punks."

"They always found us. A year and a half clean. Beto found us in Chiapas, at the foot of the church on the hill. San Cristóbal. Streaks of rain on his mirror sunglasses."

"You ever know Frankie?"

"I knew Frankie. He was the sickest."

"I saw his dog die, once when he got busted. He even had his toy poodle strung out on junk."

"I once stabbed a connection, in Yelapa. I didn't even hurt him, really. But I felt the blade go in, saw him bleed."

Decca is crying now. Sad sobs, like a child's. She puts on *Charlie Parker with Strings*. "April in Paris."

"Max and I were in Paris in April. Rained the whole damn time. We were both pretty lucky, Laura, and drugs ruined it all. I mean for a short time we had everything a woman could want. Well, I knew him in his golden years. Italy and France and Spain. Mallorca. Everything he did turned to gold. He could write, play saxophone, fight bulls, race cars." She pours them more rum.

Laura can't express herself. "I knew him when, when he was . . ."

"You almost said happy, didn't you? He was never happy."

"Yes, he was. We were. No one ever was so happy as we were."

Decca sighs. "That might be true. I thought it, seeing you all together. But it wasn't enough for him."

"Once we were in Harlem. Max and a musician friend went into the bathroom to fix. The man's wife looked at me, across the kitchen table, and she said, 'There our men go, to the lady in the lake.' Maybe we were wrong, Decca. Hubris or something, wanting to mean too much to him. Maybe this girl, what's her name? Maybe she'll just be there."

Decca had been talking to herself. Aloud she said, "No one could ever ever mean so much to me. Have you met any man who can touch him? His mind? His wit?"

"No. And none of them are so kind or sweet, like how he cries at music, kisses his sons good night."

Both women are sobbing now, blowing their noses. "I get really lonesome. I try to meet men," Laura says. "I even joined the ACLU."

"You what?"

"I even went to the Sundowner for Happy Hour. But all the men just got on my nerves."

"That's it. Other men *jar* after Max. They say 'you know' too much or repeat the same stories, laugh too loud. Max never bored, Max never jarred."

"I went out with this pediatrician. A sweet guy who wears bow ties, flies kites. The perfect man. Loves children, healthy, handsome, rich. He jogs, drinks rosé wine coolers."

The women roll their eyes. "Okay, so I have it all set up. The children are asleep. I'm in white chiffon. We're at the table on the terrace. Candles. Stan Getz and Astrud Gilberto bossa nova. Lobster. Stars. Then Max shows up, drives up on the lawn in a Lamborghini. Wearing a white suit. He gives us a little wave, goes in to see the kids, says something idiotic like he loves to look at them when they're sleeping. I lost it. Smashed the rosé wine cooler pitcher on the bricks, threw the plates of lobster, smash, smash, salad plates, smash. Told the guy to hit the road."

"Which he did, right?"

"Right."

"See, Laura, Max would never have left. He'd have said something like, 'Honey, you need some loving,' or he'd start throwing plates and dishes too until you were both laughing."

"Yeah. Actually he sort of did when he came out. He smashed some glasses and a vase of freesia but he rescued the lobster and we ate it. Sandy. He just grinned and said, 'That pediatrician is hardly an improvement.'"

"There's never been a man like him. He never farted or belched."

"Yes, he did, Decca. A lot."

"Well, it never got on my nerves. You just came over to upset me. Go home!"

"Last time you told me to go home you were in my house."

"I did? Hell, I'll go home, then."

Laura gets up to leave. She lurches toward the bed to get her coat, stands there, getting her bearings. Decca comes up behind her, embraces her, touches her neck with her lips. Laura holds her breath, doesn't move. Sonny Rollins is playing "In Your Own Sweet Way." Decca leans, kisses Laura on the ear.

"Then he brushes your nipple with the palm of his hand."

She does this to Laura. "Then you turn to him and he holds your head in both hands and kisses you on the mouth." But Laura doesn't move.

"Lie down, Laura."

Laura stumbles, slides down onto the mink-covered bed. Decca blows out the lantern and lies down too. But the women are facing away from each other. Each is waiting for the other to touch her the way Max did. There is a long silence. Laura weeps, softly, but Decca laughs out loud, whacks Laura on the buttock.

"Good night, you fat-assed sap."

In just a short time, Decca is asleep. Laura leaves quietly, arrives home and showers, dresses before her children wake up.

NOËL, 1974

> Dear Dearest Zelda, I'm sorry your vacation comes at such a bad time for us. Christmas, school, etc. I'm a teacher now—will be grading term papers and working on a Christmas play. We have a very small house. The landlord thinks I only have two sons, for the two small bedrooms, so when he comes one of them has to disappear. Ben (he's 19 now!) sleeps in the garage. Keith (17) sleeps on the couch in the living room. Joel has a small bedroom, a closet really, and I have the other one. I know you say you'll be happy to sleep on the floor, but a friend of Ben's, from New Mexico (Jesse), is already sleeping on the living room floor. I'd love to see you but present circumstances would make it uncomfortable for everyone. I'm happy to hear about your new life. Love, Maggie

"Now is that an assertive letter or not?" Maggie recopied it, put it in an envelope and outside for the mailman.

"Who is Aunt Zelda anyway?" Joel asked.

"Your father's big sister. Really big. I only met her once, at a bar mitzvah in Rhode Island. Her daughter Mabel is at Cal but her commune has a rule about no parents. I run into Mabel sometimes and she's great, but she's gay now and dreads telling her mother. Well, Zelda can't come here and that's it."

But Zelda came anyway, six days later, with a schefflera plant and three pounds of lox. Mabel met her at the airport and dropped her off, said she'd see her later. Maggie greeted Zelda stiffly, introduced her to Joel, who carried the bags up to Maggie's room. Zelda followed him up, to unpack.

Ben, Keith, and Jesse were playing poker in the garage. "Jumpin' Jack Flash" on the stereo.

"What will I do with her? What if she stays for Christmas?"

Jesse stretched his boots out on the bed. "Want me to leave, Maggie? Early, I mean—I'll be going before Christmas."

"No, of course not. We told you you were welcome. It's that I told her she wasn't. Ballsy bitch."

Joel knocked on the door and came in.

"Cheer up, Ma, guess what Aunt Zelda is doing?"

"God knows."

"Washing dishes. We got us a nice Jewish mama."

"But I want a Japanese houseboy." Maggie laughed though and followed him inside.

Zelda was a new woman. She had lost seventy pounds since her divorce, had had her ears pierced and a tubal ligation. "I'm prepped for adventure!" she said and Maggie giggled, envisioning shaved private parts. Zelda was determinedly cheerful, hugging everybody and repeating things like "Far out!" and "Outta sight!"

Keith moved upstairs into Joel's room and Joel moved downstairs to the couch above Jesse's sleeping bag. Maggie slept in the hammock in the dining room. She didn't have the time nor the energy to entertain Zelda. Mabel didn't either, busy in school and rebuilding a VW engine. But Zelda was determined to have a good time and she did. She went to Gump's and

I. Magnin and Cost Plus. She took the Sausalito ferry, rode cable cars, lunched at Jack London Square. The rest of the time she washed dishes, not just the dirty dishes but all of the dishes and pots and pans in the cupboards, relining the shelves. She defrosted the refrigerator, ironed. Jesse wouldn't let her clean the living room while he was there, writing music, playing the guitar. She wouldn't let him walk on her waxed kitchen floor. Keith called them the Odd Couple. But it was working out okay, Maggie admitted. Stuffed cabbage would be simmering when she got home exhausted from school. Zelda prepared hors d'oeuvres, bought cheese and wine for Fun Time, which was every night. (Her husband had sold Fun Time party mixes.)

Ben made jewelry that he sold on Telegraph after school. Afterward he would come home with four or five street artists. Greg the glassmaker, always. Keith's girl, Lauren, came every night, usually with other girls, to meet Jesse the handsome, lanky longhair from New Mexico. Lee was always there, a Chicano biker whose leather clothes had zippers that rang like Russian sleighs. Lee played harmonica and bongos, flirted with Mabel. He didn't realize she was gay as she encouraged him, for Zelda's sake, while she rubbed thighs under the spool coffee table with her lover, frizzy-haired Big Mac. Big Mac sang; Mabel and Jesse played guitars.

Aunt Zelda laughed, glowed, choked on marijuana. Keith and Lauren sat at the dining room table, doing homework, playing chess while Maggie graded papers, read for the next day's classes, sipping Jim Beam which she kept separate from the Fun Time beer and wine.

Joel and his friends went up and down stairs. Stereos and radios, televisions and guitars and bongos and harmonicas and electric football. The washing machine and the dryer and the pachinko machine. Maggie wrote notes in the margins, worried about money and the landlord. She had spent all her salary on

Christmas presents, sold the last of her Zuni jewelry for the rent. She was tense and tired and she missed her bed, was afraid it would forever smell of Estée Lauder.

"Too much!" Zelda said when Maggie joined her by the fire. Zelda was flushed and teary, listening to Mabel and Big Mac doing "Lay, Lady, Lay." She blew her nose. "I don't ever want to go home!" she said. Jesse grinned at Maggie, who crossed her eyes at him. He asked her to hand him the keys to the truck, on the mantel. When he opened the front door the air was cool, the rain quiet. The pickup truck double-clutched, backed out of the driveway. Maggie went outside too. She and Chata, the dog, walked in the empty BART parking lot, neither one avoiding puddles. Chata heard the truck first, shifting down.

"Going my way, lady?"

"Hi, Jesse. Sure. I just came out for some air."

"You knew I'd pick you up. Get in. No, not you, Chata. Dawg, get out of here." Took two blocks to lose the dog.

Miles of deserted streets in southwest Oakland. It was good to get away from the house and she liked the way he never spoke. She started to say something about Zelda, but he interrupted her.

"I don't want to hear about Zelda, or your kids or your school."

"That doesn't leave me anything to talk about."

"Right." He reached behind the seat for a Jim Beam bottle, took a sip, and handed it to her.

"Your drinking scares me, Jesse. Seventeen is too young to be an alcoholic."

"I'm old for my age. Thirty-five is young to be a burnout."

They ended up in the U.S. Mail depot in West Oakland. Blocks of parked trailer trucks, each labeled for a different state of the union.

"Howdja get in here?" the man in Louisiana asked, but went

back to sorting mail. Jesse and Maggie strolled from state to state. She wanted to find New York; he went to Wyoming, Mississippi. The first word she had learned to spell. Uncle John taught her. The wind blew around the New Mexico trailer but there was no sound, just the bird flutter of letters. They watched the man sorting, silent, as if they were on the other side of a window. "Better get out of here," the New Mexico man said. They hadn't seen the DO NOT ENTER sign when they came in. As they were driving out a little guard came out of a booth signaling them to stop.

"Get down out of the truck," he said, but when they did they were both so tall he stammered, "Get back in the truck!" He began talking on his radio, groping for his gun. Jesse shifted and drove away, fast. Zing, a bullet hit the bumper. "Hot damn!" Maggie laughed. An adventure.

When they got home everyone had gone to bed. Jesse got right into his sleeping bag by the fire, coals now. Maggie still had stacks of papers to grade, sipped Jim Beam to stay awake.

Christmas busy. Jesse and Ben sold jewelry on Telegraph, doing well in spite of the rain. Maggie and Joel stayed late at their schools, both practicing for Christmas programs. Maggie had written a parody of *A Christmas Carol*. Scrooge had a used-car lot in Hayward; Tiny Tim was a militant paraplegic. It was fun, hectic.

Aunt Zelda shopped. In the evenings she helped Maggie bake and wrap presents, chattering on about her new self-image, about finding a new relationship. Maggie was silent. Zelda assumed that Maggie simply suffered from a broken heart, but that everything would turn out all right.

"Any day now my brother will come to his senses. You were a gorgeous couple. I'll never forget the two of you at Marvin's bar mitzvah. So happy! And you in that suit. Norell?"

"B. H. Wragge." That was a good suit.

"And the way he used to always light two cigarettes at a time and hand you yours."

Maggie laughed. "He got that from John Garfield." Only Shelley Berman did it better—he'd forget to give the woman hers, just nervously smoked both of them. Come to his senses? One's senses. Taste smell hearing touch.

"I've taken leave of my senses," Maggie said.

Zelda smiled, "Far out" as usual. Only occasionally did a natural response burst out. None of you have slippers? You drink in the morning? You have no toilet brush?

They all went to the Christmas pageant at Joel's school. Zelda and Maggie got teary right from the first Hark the Herald Angel. Jesse and Ben went outside a few times to smoke a joint. Keith and Lauren kept getting up to talk to old teachers, talk with friends.

The showstopper was when the fourth-grade girls came out in miniskirts and reindeer headdresses, did bumps and grinds to Marvin Gaye's "Let's Get It On." Shocked gasps from the audience. Then the fifth grade did "Partridge in a Pear Tree." Ben started them all off, giggling, as they envisioned the mess all those presents would make in their house on Russell Street. French hens, geese, lords a-leaping.

Joel's class had the last skit and the nicest one. It was very simple, like a ballet. He and two other boys were turned into statues while they were having a snowball fight. They stayed perfectly frozen while the snowman, really Darryl, began to melt, smaller and smaller until the Spirit of Christmas transformed them all again. Joel didn't even blink as a statue, after the first brown-eyed flickering until he found his family.

When the program was over Santa Claus and the principal, Mrs. Beck, came out onstage to much applause. "Joy to the

World" played loudly as they started to hand out presents. Tonka trucks. Barbie dolls. Heavy government poverty-program money. Within seconds the stage was mobbed, mostly teenaged kids but many adults. It was like Altamont. Joel was shoved to the ground, his lip cut, bleeding. Ben and Jesse jumped onto the stage. Ben picked up Joel. Jesse knocked his truck away from the kid who had grabbed it. Mrs. Beck's frosted wig was tilted. She screamed into the mike.

"These presents are just for our kids! Just for the kids! Get back, motherfuckers!"

"Let's get out of here." Maggie led the way. Jesse had Joel by the hand.

"How about an ice cream, Maggie? You buy and I'll fly."

"Jesse—did I look frozen?"

"Yeah—for so *long*. Give me five." Slap, slap.

Aunt Zelda's last night. Jesse and Joel had gone to Martinez to cut down the tree. It was fragrant, beautiful. Maggie was relaxed. She had sold the Navajo rug from her bedroom, bought more presents, had money enough not to worry for a while. She and Zelda chatted, stuffing dates, a family tradition that no one ever ate, like the pickled watermelon rind at Christmas dinner.

Keith and Lauren were at the dining room table stringing cranberries; the others were decorating the tree, arguing. Ben and Joel always wanted everything on the tree; Keith and Maggie liked it simple. Jesse couldn't understand why they didn't have icicles. Because Ben and Joel got them last year.

"I can't wait to get home," Jesse said. He was leaving in two days for New Mexico, hitchhiking home for Christmas. Squawk as he stepped on a cat under the tree. Chata the dog just hung around, wet, getting in the way. Three street artists dried off by the fire, passed decorations and bulbs up to the others. In the kitchen Mabel and Big Mac were making fudge and divinity. Cost Plus candles glowed like Aunt Zelda.

"I can't wait to tell my analyst about my vacation," Zelda said. Maggie wondered what she would say. Zelda had made no comments about Mabel.

Knocking at the door. It was Linda, their next-door neighbor, asking to use the shower. She hated to take baths when she had her period. She sure gets her period a lot, Jesse said. No, I think she just likes to come over, especially if something is going on. Well, hell, Maggie, why not just ask her to come over?

More knocking. It was John and Ian, two teachers from the school where Maggie taught. As she was taking their coats Lee roared up the walk on his Harley, black leathers dripping like a wetsuit. Maggie introduced everyone, sat the two teachers at the table.

"You're just in time to say good-bye to Zelda." Zelda came in with a tray of piroshki, cookies, candies, stuffed dates. One of the street artists passed Ian a joint in a scrimshaw holder.

"Good God, Maggie, do you smoke dope in front of your children?"

"I don't smoke it. Wish I did. No hangover, not fattening. I'm glad none of my sons drink."

"Didn't mean to crash a party." John talked funny because he had just smoked. He had eggnog on his mustache.

"Oh, you're welcome to stay," Zelda said. "Have some more eggnog."

Ian and John sipped, clearing their throats.

"We had wanted to talk to you, Maggie," John said. Linda came downstairs from the shower, wearing a coral chenille bathrobe, her wet hair in a braid.

"Dates! I love your stuffed dates, Maggie."

"Have some. Take some home."

"Please," Keith said. Zelda and Linda went into the living room.

Ian spoke, in his low grown-up voice that always irritated Maggie, the oldest teacher at the school.

"It's about Dave Woods."

"Christ," Maggie said. She was the only teacher at Horizon who required attendance, who gave grades, not just pass-fail.

"I gave him every possible break I could. He failed both English and Spanish. I won't reconsider, if that's why you came."

"That's cold, Maggie. How can you have such a loose lifestyle and be so rigid a teacher? We're supposed to be geared to the individual student."

"Well, that individual failed both my classes."

"It's like you don't believe in the philosophy of our school."

"Philosophy? Three thousand a year, beautiful campus, good dope, no homework?" Keith kicked Maggie under the table.

"No need to get hostile. We came here in good faith," Ian said.

"Have some divinity." Mabel passed the tray, gliding around. John's eyes focused on her fine braless breasts. Maggie wished there wasn't so much food and drink and general largesse. Linda lounged, radiant, between two artists, her robe gaping over Rubenesque thighs.

"What is this called again?" John asked Mabel, the candy sticking to his fingers.

"Divinity—with nuts," Mabel drawled.

"Sounds like a Lutheran bishop to me," Zelda guffawed, poking Maggie. The two of them collapsed into teary giggles. Ian took one of Maggie's cigarettes.

She wished he would start smoking again and buy his own. At least the two teachers had lost interest in Dave Woods's Fs, were listening to Mabel and Big Mac. "Lay, Lady, Lay" again. Maggie went into the kitchen, poured Jim Beam into her eggnog. Ben and Lee were watching Lauren cut more squares of candy.

"Don't worry—I'll torch the school tomorrow." Lee smiled. Another knock on the door.

"Sounds like a bust," Jesse said. Close. It was the landlord. Ben and Keith eased people out into the garage but the damage was done. He had seen that someone was living in the garage, that hippies were smoking dope.

"We have friends here for the holidays," she said, but he was talking about the ruined garden.

"Ruined? I planted most of it, have worked on it for two years. The rain has ruined it."

"I'm selling the house. Only four white houses left on the block."

"Why didn't you say so—you don't need jive reasons to blame me."

"I certainly have more than 'jive' reasons to break the lease."

Maggie exhaled. "Please leave now," she said and she opened the door for him. She drank, poured more whiskey into her eggnog, and went back into the dining room. She sat down by Ian and John.

"I'm sorry I was so rude. Dave is the brightest kid we have . . . I wish you had flunked him in math and science too. As it is he'll fail any college entrance exams. He knows he can do better than Fs and I think he will."

"More eggnog?" Zelda asked.

"No thanks. School tomorrow. Is the Christmas play ready, Maggie?"

"No, but it's going to be great."

Everyone had left or moved out to Ben's room in the garage. Joel was on the couch, Jesse in his sleeping bag. The lights were out but the two of them were talking. Zelda and Mabel were arguing upstairs, then Mabel came stomping down the stairs.

"Well, I told her," she said and left, slamming the door. Maggie washed dishes, put food away, and swept the floor until the crying stopped, then tiptoed upstairs to the bathroom.

"Maggie!"

Zelda sat up in bed, streams of tears superimposed upon the glisten of Elizabeth Arden.

Maggie hugged her. "You must be so tired. I'm tired. Come on—" But Zelda clung to her, her slick cheek sliding into Maggie's hair.

"Mabel! My *child.* What do I do now?"

Maggie broke away, went to the bathroom where she wiped the cream off her face, dampened two washcloths with witch hazel.

"Here, let me put this over your eyes. Stop crying." She sat on the edge of the bed, holding the other rag over her own eyes.

"My daughter," Zelda said. "You can't possibly understand."

"Maybe I don't. Seems like I wouldn't care if any of my sons were gay. On the other hand if one of them became a cop or a Hare Krishna I might blow my brains out."

Zelda started to cry again. "I'm just so—"

"You're hurting. Mabel's fine. You got any sleeping pills?"

"Valium." Zelda pointed to her makeup box.

Maggie handed her the pills and some water, took one herself. She fixed Zelda pillows, turned out the light. In the light from the Bekins sign Zelda looked old and afraid.

"You okay?"

"No. I feel old and afraid."

Maggie held her, kissed her slippery forehead. "I'm glad you came, though."

•

Downstairs, Maggie realized she had forgotten to take off her clothes or wash her face. Too tired. She took blankets from the closet, poured a glass of bourbon, climbed into the hammock, remembered cigarettes, got back out, back in, arranged the blankets around her, the glass and ashtray on the floor, settled down for her own good cry.

"Sweet Jesus," Jesse said from the living room. He got up, threw his sleeping bag over his shoulder.

"Where are you going?"

"Sleep in the truck. Never saw you sorry for yourself before."

When he had gone she stopped crying, smoked a cigarette, drank what was left in the glass. Racine's *Phèdre*, Act II. He's gone! She laughed at herself, got up and washed her face at the kitchen sink, hid the bottle of Jim Beam in the washing machine for morning.

Damn, it is morning. Two more days of school. The play. Christmas. I can't make it. I can make it, got to stop drinking. Messed up again so fast. Taper off tomorrow. Jesse will be gone in a few days. That will make it easier. Not really. I'll get the radio for Joel tomorrow after school, the book for Lauren too. Zelda's leaving—Praise the Lord! My bed! I haven't even talked with Joel for weeks. I'm a rotten mother. Got to get well for my sons. God, I'm a wreck. This house is a wreck.

She filled her glass with wine, moved the glass and the bottle with her as she dusted and polished furniture. She swept, mopped, and waxed the floors. Joel slept on, even when she moved the couch. She emptied garbage in the rain, picked a huge bunch of Linda's pink poinsettias. Linda's bedroom window flew up. "What in hell's name are you doing? It's four in the morning!" The window crashed down again. Damn, some people just aren't themselves until they've had that first cup of coffee. Inside, Maggie arranged the flowers in a brass vase.

There. Things are looking better. She straightened paintings, turned on the Christmas tree lights. Grate some cheese, make macaroni and cheese now, buy the radio and book after school.

"What are you doing washing windows? It's five in the morning, Ma." Keith was dressed, sleepy-eyed.

"Hi. Couldn't sleep. They're all sooty from the fireplace. How come you're up so early?"

"Field trip. Let me put the wine bottle away. You won't be able to go to school. Stop, Ma, have some breakfast with me."

He took the bottle upstairs. She knew it was to the crawl-space behind the bathroom wall. She put water on for coffee, made orange juice, cooked sausages and French toast. She and Keith didn't talk, read the paper. Zelda came down, pale, with her luggage. Maggie cooked her breakfast. Keith left after hugging them both good-bye, just as Mabel was arriving to take her mother to the airport. The three women drank coffee without any pleasantries.

It was still dark when Zelda and Mabel left. Maggie shivered outside, waving to the SISTERHOOD IS POWERFUL bumper, went inside to make more French toast for Joel and Ben. While they were eating she remembered the bottle in the washing machine. Jesse came in from outside. "I'll get my own breakfast," he said.

It was so foggy on the freeway she was afraid Zelda's plane wouldn't take off. She was afraid that she was going to run into other cars and then she became afraid that she wasn't on the freeway at all. Exit. Up a hill and around. The Mormon Temple glowed magically like the castle in *The Wizard of Oz*. Monolith telephone booth, white light. She called Horizon School, told them her car had broken down. Probably should cancel her afternoon classes also. No, not the rehearsal—that could go fine without her. No, thanks. Triple A was coming any minute. She drove down the hill to MacArthur where there wasn't any fog but she was still afraid. She followed a 53 bus all the way to downtown Oakland, waiting every other block for passengers to get on and off. Downtown she got behind a 43 bus on Telegraph and followed it home. She was too drunk to see straight.

She dropped her coat and book bag inside the front door, climbed the stairs to her room. It was dark, the curtains closed. Jesse was asleep in her bed. "Hey, what's the big idea?" she asked but he didn't move. She climbed over him and fell instantly asleep but he woke up and turned toward her, kicking off his boots. "Hello, Maggie."

THE PONY BAR, OAKLAND

There are certain perfect particular sounds. A tennis ball, a golf ball hit just right. A fly ball in a leather glove. Lingering thud of a knockout. I get dizzy at the sound of a perfect pool break, a crisp bank shot followed by three or four muffled slides and consecutive clicks. The caressing twist twist of chalk on the cue. Pool is erotic any way you look at it. Usually in a dim pulsating jukebox light.

Cricket in Santiago. Red parasols, green grass, white Andes. Red-and-white-striped canvas chairs at the Prince of Wales Country Club. I signed chits for lemonade, tipped the tuxedoed waiters, applauded John Wells. Perfect crack of the cricket bat. I wore white, was careful of the grass stains, flirted with boys who wore Grange School gray flannels, blue blazers in summertime. Cucumber sandwiches for tea, plans for Sunday at Viña del Mar.

At the Pony Bar I remembered feeling as alien on the green grass as I did on the bar stool next to the biker. He had hinges tattooed on his wrists, at the bend of his elbow, behind his knees.

"You need a hinge on your neck," I said.

"You need a screw up your ass."

DAUGHTERS

The courage of my own convictions? I can't even hold a perception for longer than five minutes. Just like the radio in a pickup truck. I'll be barreling along . . . Waylon Jennings, Stevie Wonder . . . hit a cattle guard and bang it's a preacher from Clint, Texas. Your laff is trash. Laugh? Life? From one day to the next the 40 bus alters. Some days there will be people on it from Chaucer, Damon Runyon. A Brueghel feast. I feel close to them all, at one with them. We are a vivid tapestry of riders, then there is an epidemic of Gilles de la Tourette syndrome and we're all victims, trapped in a steamy capsule, forever. Sometimes everyone is tired. Whole bus plumb wore out. Heavy shopping bags. Cumbersome carts, strollers. Panting up the steps, sleeping past their stops, the people slump, they sway limp from the poles like languorous seaweed. Or everyone has growth on their heads. Row after row, and standing, packed, they all have hair growing out of their heads. Not green willow or eucalyptus or moss but a billion strands, filaments of hair. Punk hair, blue lady hair, wet afro hair. Ach, the man in front of me has no hair at all. He doesn't even have any tiny little holes in his head for it to come out of. I feel faint. A little girl gets on the bus, wearing a Saint Ignatius uniform. Someone, a grandmother *hold still now child* has plaited her hair into braids so tight her eyes slant. The braids are tied with white bows, real satin ribbons. She sits behind the driver. The morning sun gleams on her perfect part, makes a halo behind her head. I love the child's hair. I touch my own, pat my own hair, which is short and rough, like a Samoyed's or a Chow's. Good boy. Kill, White Fang.

I should have taken that job stringing graduated pearls. Working for a doctor, well, it's life or death all day long. I glide around, a real angel of mercy. Or a ghoul. Mmmm, Dr. B. . . . interesting, these bone marrow results on Mr. Morbido. That's his name, honest. Truth is weirder than my imagination, which really goes berserk with the dialysis machines. Breakthroughs in modern medicine. Lifesavers that by late afternoon turn into headless plastic vampires, draining blood away. The patients get paler and paler. The machines make a humming sucking sound with an occasional slurp that sounds like a laugh.

By late afternoon I'm ready to strangle Riva Chirenko's daughter. I don't know her name. Nobody calls her Mrs. Tomanovich. She's Mr. Tomanovich's wife. Riva's daughter. Irena Tomanovich's mother. She's what's wrong with all us women, that schleppe from the steppe. But at other times it is this same woman, Riva Chirenko's daughter, that I respect, revere. If I could only accept as she has done, just accept. Acceptance is faith, Henry Miller said. I could strangle him, too.

Yesterday was the Christmas party at the dialysis center. No matter how I look at it, it was a lovely party, a celebration. All the patients and their families. Rocky Robinson came. Nobody had seen him since he got a cadaver transplant, and he was looking good. There is a bond between dialysis patients, like with people in AA or earthquake survivors. They are conscious of a reprieve, treat one another with more tenderness and respect than ordinary people do.

I was busy with the buffet and the punch. It was good, tons of food. No added salt. Mr. Tomanovich, Riva Chirenko's son-in-law, was a help, standing at the head of the table hailing all the guests. Food good! Drink good!

It was a lot healthier when I used to see people as animals. Mr. Tomanovich a sweaty manatee. Now they are all diseases. Shingles or toxic shock. Mr. Tomanovich is hypertensive, for sure, with his red face and sweaty sickles around his powder-blue underarms. Potential glomerulosclerosis and renal failure. His wife, Riva Chirenko's daughter, the yak . . . a hysterectomy in store for her, her pain is of the womb.

Riva Chirenko herself is beyond disease. You always hear about little old ladies. The big old ladies all die, that's why, except for Riva, who is 280 pounds and eighty years old. Folds of red velvet spill over the plastic of her gurney. Red blood hums away. IVs drip steadily into the mesas on her arms. She looks like Father Christmas. White hair and eyebrows, rosy cheeks, white hair sprouting from her chin. She barks in Russian at her daughter, who fans her, soothes her brow with a cool cloth, sings to her in Russian in a mournful voice. Back and forth from the dining room, filling her red plate each time with morsels for her mother. Swedish meatballs, croissants with ham, roast beef, deviled eggs, asparagus, quiche, Brie, olives, onion dip, pumpkin pie, champagne, cranberry juice, coffee. It all just quietly disappears into Riva Chirenko's amazingly tiny and pretty mouth.

"Where's Dr. B.?" Mr. Tomanovich keeps asking. I have worked for him for two years and I never know where he is. Is he in fact declotting a Scribner's shunt? Taking a nap? Sitting shiva? "He's in surgery," I say.

Riva Chirenko's daughter, each time she fills her mother's plate, touches Irena's, her own daughter's, hair and encourages her to eat. She says, in Russian, "*Kushai, dochka.*" Irena's father, too, comes over from time to time and says,

"*Tebe ne khorosho?*"

They are saying, "Shape up, you little slut!" No, of course not. They are saying, "Eat, my little princess."

The daughter, Irena, sits on the only chair in the dining room. An ugly plastic chair, all wrong. I want to throw it out, go rent her another one, buy one, quick. Her profile, with a long neck, is curved like an albino dinosaur, a marble cobra, an anorexic whippet. See, I'm sick. I make her sound grotesque. She is the most lovely creature I have ever seen. Pale green eyes, hair like white honey, like the inside of a pear. She is fourteen, in white, wearing the now-fashionable lace gloves with no fingers. Her bony hands lie in her lap like the little white birds you eat whole in Guadalajara . . . too much cinnamon. She wears white lace stockings with no feet. Pulsating blue traceries on her ankles. Her mother touches her pale hair. Irena flinches, does not acknowledge her mother at all. When her father does the same thing she doesn't speak to him, but she bares her exquisite white teeth.

Dr. B. finally arrives. There is an uproar. Patients and their families flock around him. They adore him. He looks tired. Mr. Tomanovich gets his wife to translate. He has been waiting to show Dr. B. photographs of Irena in Hawaii. Irena had won the Skagg's Drugstore Father's Day Contest. An essay: "My Dad Is the Greatest!" A trip to Hawaii for her and her parents. Of course her mother couldn't leave Riva Chirenko. Irena had entered the Skagg's Mother's Day essay contest too but she had only won honorable mention and the Polaroid that took all the pictures. Irena by a bird-of-paradise. Irena wearing a lei, in a sugarcane field, on the terrace. No beach. She hates the sun.

Dr. B. smiles. "You are fortunate to have such a talented and pretty child."

"God is good!" Riva Chirenko's daughter is always saying that. God brought them from Russia. God gave her mother the dialysis machine.

Dr. B. looks at Irena, sitting there, head high, scornful. Snowflakes flutter down. She raises her tiny white hand, for him to shake, kiss? It curves in the air, poised, curved. She turns into an Egyptian frieze. Dr. B. stares at her. He is transfixed.

"Have you eaten?" he asks. For God's sake. That kid hasn't eaten for years. Dr. B. goes to greet patients and guests. Irena turns her extended hand into a point toward the cloakroom. Mr. Tomanovich rushes to get her fur-trimmed coat, puts it on her. Her mother comes, buttons up the coat, frees her hair from the fur, strokes Irena's hair. Irena doesn't flinch, doesn't speak. She turns to leave. Her father touches the small of her back. She freezes and stops. He removes his hand and opens the door, following her out.

I clean up the dining room. Most of the guests have left, were leaving. The dialysis patients still have another hour on their run. Some are vomiting, some are asleep. The tape plays "Away in a manger, no crib for His bed." My own grandmother's favorite carol, but it used to scare me because she always told me not to be a dog in the manger. I thought the dog had eaten baby Jesus.

The food had been just right. Nothing is left except two large Tupperware bowls that Anna Ferraza brought. A real flop. Strawberry Jell-O and cranberries, bitter as a bog. I leave it there. The color is pretty by the red plates, the poinsettia.

There are only a few nurses and techs left. Dr. B. is on the phone in his office. The Christmas tree in the middle of the big room has hundreds of bubble lights that gurgle and flow louder than the COBE II machines and it's as if they are transfusing the tree. You can smell the green pine of the tree. Riva Chirenko's daughter still fans Riva even though she is asleep. Finally she stops, stands. She is stiff and sore. Osteoporosis. Postmenopausal bone loss. She covers Riva with a soft shawl, comes into the dining room just as I'm leaving with a bag full of garbage. I realize that Riva Chirenko's daughter has not

RAINY DAY

Man, this detox gets full when it rains. I'm sick of being on the street, you know? My old lady and me went over to the bleachers . . . it's nice—real quiet and lots of room. Then it started to rain and she started to cry. I kept on asking her, What's the matter, hon? What's the matter? You know what she finally said? "All the cigarette butts are getting wet." Shit, so I hit her. She went nuts, cops took her to jail and brought me here. I can stand a drying out. Trouble is when I sober up I start to think. Alcoholics think more than most people and that's the truth. I drink just to shut off the words. Shit, what if I was a drummer? Last time I was in here there was a *Psychology Today*, talking about skid-row drunks. It proved alkies thought more. Said they scored higher on tests than normal people and higher on retention. There was just one thing they scored bad on, couldn't do worth a damn, but I can't remember what it was.

OUR BROTHER'S KEEPER

When some people die they just vanish, like pebbles into a pool. Everyday life just smooths back together and goes on as it did before. Other people die but stay around for a long time, either because they have captured the public's imagination, like James Dean, or because their spirit just won't let go, like our friend Sara's.

Sara died ten years ago, but still, anytime her grandchildren say something bright or imperious, everyone will say, "She's just like Sara!" Whenever I see two women driving along and laughing together, really laughing, I always think it's Sara. And of course each spring when I plant I remember the fig tree we got in the garbage bin at PayLess, the bad fight we had over the miniature coral rosebush at East Bay.

Our country has just gone to war, which is why I'm thinking about her now. She could get madder at our politicians, and be more vocal about it, than anybody I know. I want to call her up; she always gave you something to do, made you feel you could do something.

Even though all of us continue to reminisce about her, we stopped talking about the way she died very soon after it happened. She was murdered, brutally, her head bashed in with a "blunt instrument." A lover she had been going with had repeatedly threatened to kill her. She had called the police each time but they said there was nothing they could do. The man was a dentist, an alcoholic, some fifteen years younger than she was. In spite of the threats, and of other times that he had hit her, no weapon was found, no evidence placed him at the scene of the crime. He was never charged.

You know how it is when a friend is in love. Well, I guess I'm talking to women, strong women, older women. (Sara was sixty.) We say it's great being our own person, that our lives are full. But we still want it, recognize it. Romance. When Sara spun around my kitchen laughing, "I'm in love. Can you believe it?" I was glad for her. We all were. Leon was attractive. Well-educated, sexy, articulate. He made her happy. Later, as she did, we forgave him. Missed appointments, unkind words, thoughtlessness, a slap. We wanted everything to be okay. We all still wanted to believe in love.

After Sara's death her son Eddie moved into her house. I cleaned his house every Tuesday, so it turned out I was cleaning at Sara's. It was hard, at first, to be in her sunny kitchen with all the plants gone but the memories still there. Gossip, talks about God, our children. The living room was full of Eddie's CDs, radios and computers, two TVs, three telephones. (So much electronic equipment that once when the phone rang I answered it with the TV remote control.) His junky mismatched furniture replaced the huge linen couch where Sara and I would lie facing each other, covered with a quilt, talking, talking. Once one rainy Sunday we were both so low we watched bowling and *Lassie*.

The first time I cleaned the bedroom was terrible. The wall near where her bed used to be was still splattered and caked with her blood. I was sickened. After I cleaned it I went outside into the garden. I smiled to see the azaleas and daffodils and ranunculus we had planted together. We didn't know which end of the ranunculus to plant, so we decided to put in half of them with the point facing down and the other half with the point up. So we still don't know which are the ones that grew.

I went back in to vacuum and make the bed, saw that under Eddie's bed was a revolver and a shotgun. I froze. What if Leon came back? He was crazy. He could kill me too. I took out each of the guns. Hands trembling, I tried to figure out what you did with them. I wanted Leon to come, so I could blow him away.

I vacuumed under the bed and put the weapons back. I was disgusted by my feelings and tried hard to think about something else.

I pretended that I was a TV show. A cleaning lady detective, sort of a female Columbo. Half-witted, gum chewing . . . but while she's feather dusting she's really looking for clues. She always just happens to be cleaning houses where a murder happens. Invisible, she mops the kitchen floor while suspects say incriminating things on the phone a few feet away. She eavesdrops, finds bloody knives in the linen cupboard, is careful not to dust the poker, saving prints . . .

Leon probably killed her with a golf club. That's how they met, at the Claremont Golf Club. I was scrubbing the bathtub when I heard the creak of the garden gate, a chair scraping on the wooden deck. Someone was in the backyard. Leon! My heart pounded. I couldn't see through the stained-glass window. I crawled into the bedroom and grabbed the revolver, crawled to the French doors that led to the garden. I peeked out, gun ready, although my hand was shaking so bad I couldn't have shot it.

It was Alexander. Christ. Old Alexander, sitting in an Adirondack chair. Hi, Al! I called out, and went to put the gun away.

He was holding a clay pot of pink freesia that he kept meaning to bring to Sara. He had just felt like coming over to sit in her garden. I went in and poured him a cup of coffee. Sara had coffee going day and night. And good things to eat. Soups or gumbos, good bread and cheese and pastries. Not like the Winchell's doughnuts and frozen macaroni dinners Eddie kept around.

Alexander was an English professor. He could drone on for hours, Gerard Manley Hopkins gashing gold vermilion. He and Sara had known each other for forty years, had been young idealistic socialists way back when. He had always been in love with her, would plead with her to marry him. Lorena and I used to beg her to do it. "Come on, Sara . . . let him take care of you." He was good. Noble and dependable. But, if a woman says a man is nice it usually means she finds him boring. And, like my mother used to say, "Ever tried being married to a saint?"

And that's just what Alexander was talking about . . .

"I was too boring for her, too predictable. I knew this chap was bad news. I only hoped that I would be around when he left, to help pick up the pieces."

Tears came into his eyes then. "I feel responsible for her death. I knew he had hurt her, would hurt her. I should have interfered some way. All I cared about was my own resentment and jealousy. I am guilty."

I held his hand and tried to cheer him up, and we talked for a while, remembering Sara.

After he had gone I went in to clean the kitchen. Hey, what if Alexander really was guilty? What if he had come over that night, with the pot of freesia, or to see if she wanted to play Scrabble? Maybe he had looked through the curtains on the French doors, seen Sara and Leon making love. He had waited until after Leon left, out the front door, and had gone in, wild with jealousy, and killed her. He was a suspect, for sure.

The next Tuesday the house wasn't as messy as usual so I spent the last hour weeding and replanting in the garden. I was in the potting shed when I heard the bells and tambourine. Hare Hare Hare. Sara's youngest daughter, Rebecca, was dancing and chanting around the swimming pool.

Sara had been upset at first, when she had become a Krishna, but one day we were driving down Telegraph and saw her among a group of them. She looked so beautiful, singing, bobbing around, in her saffron robes. Sara pulled the car over to the curb, just to sit and watch her. She lit a cigarette and smiled. "You know what? She's safe."

I tried to talk to Rebecca, get her to sit down and have some herbal tea or something, but she was spinning, spinning like a dervish, moaning away. Then she was jumping and twirling on the diving board, interrupting her chants with violent outbursts. "Evil begets evil!" She raved on about her mother's smoking and coffee drinking, about her eating red meat, and cheese with retin or something in it. And fornication. She was at the very tip of the diving board now, and every time she hollered "Fornication!" she'd bounce about three feet up into the air.

Suspect number two.

I only cleaned Eddie's once a week, but invariably at least one person came into the backyard. I'm sure people came in every other day as well. Because that's how she was, Sara, her heart and doors open to everyone. She helped in big ways, politically, in the community, but in little ways too, anyone who needed her. She always answered her phone, she never locked her doors. She had always been there for me.

One Tuesday, out of the blue, the biggest, worst suspect of all showed up in the backyard. Clarissa. Eddie's ex-girlfriend. Wow. I don't think she had ever been near Sara's house before, she hated her so much. She had tried to get Eddie to leave his mother's law firm, come live with her in Mendocino and be a full-time writer. She wrote letters to Sara, accusing her of being domineering and possessive, and fought with Eddie all the time about his law career and his mother. Clarissa and I had been friends until finally it came down to choosing between the two women. But not before I heard her say a hundred times, "Oh, how I'd love to murder Sara." And there she was, standing under the lavender wisteria that covered the gate, chewing on the stem of her dark glasses.

"Hi, Clarissa," I said.

She was startled. "Hi. I didn't expect to see anyone. What are you doing here?" (Typical of her . . . when in doubt, attack.)

"I'm cleaning Eddie's house."

"Are you still cleaning houses? That's sick."

"I sure hope you don't talk to your patients like that." (Clarissa's a psychiatrist, for Lord's sake . . .) I tried hard to think of what questions my cleaning lady detective would ask her. I was at a loss, she was too intimidating. She really was *capable de tout*. How could I prove it though?

"Where were you the night Sara was killed?" I blurted.

Clarissa laughed. "My dear . . . are you implying that I am guilty of the crime? No. Too late," she said as she turned and walked out the gate.

As the weeks went by my list of suspects continued to grow, everyone from judges to policemen to window washers.

The only thing about the window washer was the weapon, the pole he carries around with him, along with his bucket. It was scary, seeing his silhouette through the curtains. A big man, carrying a pole. I had wondered about him for years. He is a homeless young black man who sleeps at night on Oakland buses and sometimes in the lobby of Alta Bates Emergency. During the day he goes from door to door asking people if they want their windows washed. He always has a book with him. Nathaniel Hawthorne. Jim Thompson. Karl Marx. He has a nice voice and dresses very well, tennis sweaters, Ralph Lauren T-shirts.

After Sara paid him for washing windows she'd always give him some god-awful old clothes of Eddie's. He'd say, Thank you, ma'am, real polite, but I used to be sure he threw them in the garbage on his way out. Maybe she was a symbol or something. A jumpsuit with a broken zipper the last straw?

"Hello, Emory, how are you?"

"Just fine, and you? I saw that Miss Sara's son was living here now . . . wondered if he needed his windows washed."

"No. I'm cleaning for him now, and do the windows too. Why don't you try at his office, on Prince Street?"

"Good idea. Thanks," he said. He smiled and left.

Okay, I said to myself. Pull yourself together and cut this suspect business out right now.

I went in and got some coffee, went back to sit in the garden. Oh. The Japanese iris were in bloom. Sara, if only you could see them.

She had called me several times that day, telling me about his threats to her. I was impatient with her about Leon by then . . . why didn't she just break up with him? I listened to her and I said things like, "Call the police. Don't answer your phone."

When she called why didn't I say, "Come right on over to my house"? Why didn't I say, "Sara, pack your bag . . . Let's get out of town."

I have no alibi for the night of the crime.

LOST IN THE LOUVRE

As a child I would try to capture the exact moment that I passed from awake to asleep. I lay very still and waited, but the next thing I knew, it was morning. I did this off and on as I grew older. Sometimes I ask people if they have ever tried this, but they never understand what I mean. I was over forty when it first happened, and I wasn't even trying. A hot summer night. Arcs from car headlights swept across the ceiling. The whirr of a neighbor's sprinklers. I caught sleep. Just as it came quiet as a cool sheet to cover me, a light caress on my eyelids. I felt sleep as it took me. In the morning I woke up happy and I never needed to try it again.

It certainly had never occurred to me to catch death, although it was in Paris that I did. That I saw how it comes upon you.

I'm sure this sounds melodramatic. I was very happy in Paris, but sad too. My lover and my father had died the year before. My mother had quite recently died. I thought about them as I walked the streets or sat in cafés. Especially Bruno, talking to him in my head, laughing with him. My childhood friends, girls lying around on the grass, on the beach, talking about going to Paris someday. They were dead too. So was Andres, who had given me *Remembrance of Things Past*.

The first few weeks I explored every tourist destination in the city. L'Orangerie, the lovely Sainte Chapelle on a sunny day. Balzac's house, Hugo's museum. I sat upstairs at the Deux Magots, where everyone looked like a Californian or Camus. I went to Baudelaire's grave in Montmartre and thought it was funny for feminist Simone de Beauvoir to be buried with Sartre. I even went to a museum for medical instruments and a stamp museum. I loitered on the rue de Courcelles and walked the Champs Elysées. Napoleon's tomb, the Sunday bird market. La Serpente. Some days I took random combinations of Metros and walked and walked in each new quarter. I sat in the square beneath Colette's apartment and walked in the Luxembourg Gardens with everybody from Flaubert to Gertrude Stein. I went to Boulevard Haussmann and to the Bois de Boulogne with Albertine. Everything I saw seemed vividly *déjà vu*, but I was seeing what I had read.

I took the train to Illiers, to see the aunt's house and the village Proust used for much of Combray. I took a very early train and got off at Chartres. It was a stormy day, so dark no light came through the stained-glass windows. An old woman prayed at a side chapel and a boy was playing the organ. No one else was there. It was too dark to see the stone floor but it was worn smooth as satin. A dim light that came through the dirty clear-glass windows showed the intricate carvings in sharp relief. The exquisite stone figures seemed especially striking with no color anywhere, the way black-and-white films seem true.

The little train to Illiers was exactly as I had imagined. The dull relentless landscape, the workers and countrywomen, the cane seats. The spire of the church! The train stopped long enough for me to get off. Eerily, there were no cars to be seen, only a bicycle leaning against the wall of the train station. I knew where to go, down the avenue de la Gare under the lime trees, almost bare now in October, the wet leaves muffling my footsteps. Right at rue de Chartres, Florent d'Illiers to the town square. I saw no one at all.

I walked around the village, waiting for the tour of the house, which began at ten. I did finally see some people, dressed in such an old-fashioned way that I could have been back in time.

At the gate to Aunt Amiot's house was an elderly German couple. They rang the bell and smiled and I rang it and smiled too. It sounded just as it was supposed to. Muttering at us through his cigarette, an old man came to let us in. He spoke too quickly for me or the Germans to understand, but it didn't matter. We followed him through the tiny house. So few stairs for Marcel's mother to climb! A begonia on the landing seemed out of place. The moldy windowless kitchen not at all "a miniature temple of Venus."

The three of us stayed for a long time in Marcel's bedroom, silent. We smiled at one another, but I could tell they too felt a deep sadness. The pitcher, the magic lantern, the little bed.

I stood in the cemented garden. I tried to see the house as a drab, tacky little place, and the town as a typical village, but they kept turning into the garden, the house, the village of Combray and were dear to me.

The dining room was truly ugly. Flocked green wallpaper and massive furniture. It was now a museum, with postcards and books. In a glass-covered stand was a page of original manuscript written in a spidery hand, the ink sepia now, the paper amber. The "page" was several inches thick because each sentence had additional sentences pasted on, like ruffles, with still more clauses pasted on top of those and here and there a word pasted onto a phrase. These appendages were neatly folded down like an accordion, but so dense they fanned apart. The case was sealed but the pasted papers opened and closed, slightly, as if the page were breathing.

"*Finis*," the old man said, and showed us to the door. I understood that the German woman was inviting me to walk with them to the "Méréglise way." I thanked them and said that there wasn't that much time before the train, which they didn't understand, but when I said the church of Saint Jacques, they nodded. We shook hands, warmly, in the freezing drizzle, and later we turned back to wave.

It was raining hard by the time I got to the church and I was disappointed to find that it was locked. I had started to look for a café when an arthritic, ancient woman called out to me, waving her stick. "*J'arrive!*" She unlocked a creaking side door and let me into the church. It was dark, lit only by votive candles. She crossed herself and took a feather duster from behind the communion rail, flicked it everywhere as she led me around, talking softly without teeth. I understood that she was Matilde and eighty-nine. She was the caretaker of the church, swept it and dusted it and put flowers on the altar. Her pale gray eyes could barely see me and fortunately didn't see the cobwebs on the cross or the dead Michaelmas daisies. She told me about the church as we walked around. I caught "Eleventh century, rebuilt in the fifteenth." I put some money in the alms box and lit three candles. Then I lit another one, for me or for her. I knelt on the cold wood and said a Hail Mary. I was exhausted and hungry now. But there it was, the pew of the Duchesse of Guermantes. I wanted to sit there quietly. To be, well, *perdu*, but instead I got lost with Matilde. She crossed herself again, genuflected before the altar, and knelt next to me. Suddenly she grabbed my arm and cawed, "*Berenice! Petite Berenice!*" She embraced me then and kissed both my cheeks, happy to see me again and how was my mother, Antoinette. She hadn't seen us for many years. She thought I lived in Tansonville, where she was born. She kept telling me about people in Illiers (my mother was from Illiers), asking me about my family, not waiting for answers. She heard so poorly that she didn't notice my poor French. She asked if I had married. "*Oui. Mais il est mort!*" She was so sorry to hear this, her eyes swam with tears. When I told her I had to leave for the train, that I lived in Paris now, she kissed my cheeks again. She didn't cry, stated matter-of-factly that she would never see me again, that she would be dead soon, probably.

I cried unreasonably on the way to the train station. I had a very bad lunch at the town's only inn.

On the train to Paris I tried to remember any bed from my own childhood, but I couldn't. I couldn't really remember my own children's beds. So many bassinets and cribs and bunk beds, trundle beds, hide-a-beds, waterbeds. None seemed as real to me as the little bed in Illiers.

The next day I went to see Proust's grave at Père Lachaise. It was a beautiful clear day and the old tombs clustered together like Nevelson sculptures. Old women knitted on benches and there were cats everywhere. Perhaps it was because it was so early I saw few people, only caretakers and the knitters, a stocky man in a blue windbreaker. I had a map, and it was fun searching for Chopin and Sarah Bernhardt, Victor Hugo and Artaud, Oscar Wilde. Proust was buried with his parents and his brother. Poor brother, imagine. There were many bouquets of Parma violets on Proust's black grave. His shiny black tomb seemed vulgar against the pale worn stone throughout the cemetery. It must take about a hundred years to look aged and beautiful, like Eloise and Abelard's or the man whose tomb said IL A FROID.

I started walking quickly down the tree-lined paths, partly because it was getting cold and windy but also because the man in the windbreaker was always about half a block behind me. The wind blew my map away just as rain began pouring down. I ran toward where I thought the exit was, but finally had to jump a railing and find shelter inside a mossy crypt. Except for being cold it was wonderful watching the yellow and red leaves blowing in whirlwinds from the trees, the silver sheets of rain darkening the stones. But it kept getting darker and colder, and I heard not just the wind howling but moans, anguished cries. Mournful dirge-like songs, diabolical laughter. I told myself I was crazy, but I was very frightened and I became convinced that the man in the windbreaker was death, come for me. Then the band of Jim Morrison fans ran past, their boombox playing, "This is the end, my friend!" I felt pretty ridiculous. I left the crypt and tried to follow the sound of their voices since now I was hopelessly lost. It would seem logical to catch death, that hour in Père Lachaise as I ran and ran and there was no way out. I could hear traffic and horns from afar, but there was not a soul to be seen, not any cats or birds, not even the man in the windbreaker.

No, it wasn't where I caught death, although when I sat down to rest I did wonder. What if I died there of exposure? I had no papers, no ID at all. Should I write my name down and add, "Please bury me here in Père Lachaise?" But I had no pen. I decided to walk in a completely straight line on one path. I would at last come to a wall and would luckily choose the direction which led outside. I was faint with hunger, my beautiful Italian shoes had stretched in the rain and were making blisters. I came in sight of a wall just as I also saw a familiar sad and unkempt grave in the middle of the well-tended ones with fresh flowers. This had been close to Colette, who was near the gate and the flower vendors. Dear Colette, she was still there. The gates were locked and death crossed my mind again, but a man came out of a booth and let me out. The flowers were gone, but a taxi was at the curb.

I ate in a Greek restaurant near my hotel, then had espresso and a pastry, two espressos and pastries. I smoked and watched people passing by and that's when I first wondered if I could catch death, the way I had caught sleep. When people died, were they aware of it, the moment it came for them? As he was dying, Stephen Crane told his friend Robert Barr, "It isn't bad. You feel sleepy—and you don't care. Just a little dreamy anxiety about which world you're really in, that's all."

Croissant and café crème the next morning and then I went to the Louvre. They were building the pyramid so it was as hard to get into the museum as it was to get out of the cemetery. At last I have seen the Louvre. Just walking miles trying to get in was thrilling. It is monumental. I never knew anything so vast. Maybe the first time I crossed the Mississippi.

The inside of the Louvre was as elegant and grand as I had ever imagined. I had seen beautiful photographs of the Victory of Samothrace. And of course I love her because of Mrs. Bridge. But nothing had prepared me for the enormity of the hall. For the way she stands, so regal, so, well, victorious, above the crowds in that space.

The first day I went very slowly, reverently. Not because of the art, although the Victory and Ingres made me shiver, many things did, but because of the grandeur of the place, the history of it. Although there were mummies and Anubi and caskets, I wasn't preoccupied with death. In fact, an embracing couple on an Etruscan sarcophagus was so beautiful I felt better about Jean-Paul and Simone.

I walked from room to room, upstairs and downstairs and back upstairs again, walking with my hands clasped behind my back as I imagined Henry James might. I thought of Baudelaire, who had seen Delacroix himself here, showing an old lady around the museum. I loved everything. Saint Sebastian. Rembrandts. I never saw the *Mona Lisa.* There was always a line in front of her and she was behind a window just like they have in liquor stores in Oakland.

I sat outside at a café in the Tuileries. The waiter brought me a croque monsieur and a café crème. He said he would be inside if I needed him; it was too cold to stay out there. I sat there wishing I could talk to somebody about everything I had seen. It was hard not being able to have a real conversation in French. I missed my sons. I felt sad about Bruno and my parents. Not sad because I missed them, but because I really didn't. And when I died it would be the same. Dying is like shattering mercury. So soon it all just flows back together into the quivering mass of life. I told myself to lighten up, I'd been alone too long. But still I sat there, looking back on my life, a life filled with beauty and love actually. It seemed I had passed through it as I had the Louvre, watching and invisible.

I went inside and paid the waiter, told him he was right, it was too cold out there. On my way back to the hotel, I stopped at a beauty salon and had my hair washed. I asked the hairdresser to rinse it still another time, so desperately I wanted to be touched.

The second day at the Louvre I enjoyed going back to the works I had really liked. Bronzino's sculptor. Géricault's horses! *Derby at Epsom.* To think he died falling from a horse, only thirty-three years old. I turned into a Flemish room and then somehow I was back with Rembrandt, and when I took the stairs down I was in the mummy room. Then I got really lost, like in the cemetery, even though there were thousands of people around me. I took some stairs I had not seen before. I sat on the landing to rest. The strange thing is that I knew that outside there were some people in the streets. Maybe five or six tables with coffee drinkers at the café in the Tuileries. But inside the Louvre there were hordes of people. Thousands and thousands, going upstairs, downstairs, streaming past the pharaohs and the Apollos and Napoleon's salon.

Perhaps we were all caught inside a microcosm. What a laughable word to use about the Louvre. Perhaps we were all part of a performance piece that had been lovingly placed in someone's tomb, along with the jewelry and slaves, all of us mummified but moving cleverly upstairs and downstairs past all the works of art whose creators were long dead. Past the Rembrandts and Fragonard's *The Bolt*, whose poor lovers were long dead too. Probably they were only models, having to earn their wages for hours and days in that uncomfortable position. Stuck that way for eternity! I had no idea where the staircase was going to lead me. Oh, good, Etruscans. Since no one spoke to me or even looked at me, it added to the illusion that we were all performers for eternity in the Immortality piece, so I ignored them also as I took my random turns and stairways until I was in a near hypnotic trance and, it felt, at one with the goddess of Hathor, with the Odalisque.

At last I would force myself to leave, have oysters and pâté at the Apollinaire and go fall into bed and sleep without reading or thinking. I went back to the Louvre three or four more times, each time seeing new sculptures or tapestries or jewelry, but also losing myself until I felt as if I were flying out of time.

An interesting phenomenon was that if I took a wrong turn and came upon the Nike herself I was immediately restored to reality. The last day I was in the Louvre, I suspected that a staircase would lead me to her, so to avoid that I crossed the room and went through a narrow hall, down some unfamiliar stairs.

My heart was beating. I was excited, but wasn't sure why. I came upon a new hall. A wing entirely unknown to me. I had read nothing about it, seen no photographs. It was an odd and charming assortment of everyday artifacts from different periods. Tapestries and tea sets, knives and forks. Chamber pots and dishes! Snuffboxes and clocks and writing desks and candelabras. Each little room contained lovely mundane objects. A footstool. A watch. Scissors. Like death, this section was not extraordinary. It was so unexpected.

SOMBRA

The waiter retrieved her napkin from the floor, slid it onto her lap, his other hand swirled a plate of pastel fruit onto the table before her. Music came from everywhere, not transistors walking down city streets, but faraway mariachis, a *bolero* on a radio in the kitchen, the whistle of the knife sharpener, an organ grinder, workmen singing from a scaffold.

Jane was a retired teacher, divorced, her children grown. She hadn't been in Mexico for twenty years, not since she had lived there with Sebastian and their sons, in Oaxaca.

She had always liked traveling alone. But yesterday, at Teotihuacan, it was so magnificent she had wanted to say it out loud, to confirm the color of the *maguey.*

She had liked being alone in France, being able to wander anywhere, talk to people. Mexico was hard. The warmth of the Mexicans accentuated her loneliness, the lost past.

This morning she had stopped at the Majestic desk and joined a guided group to the Sunday bullfights. The immense plaza, the fans, were daunting to face alone. *Fanático,* Spanish for "fan." Imagine fifty thousand Mexicans arriving on time, long before four o'clock, when the gates were locked. Out of respect for the bulls, her cab driver said.

The bullfight group assembled in the lobby at two thirty. There were two American couples. The Jordans and the McIntyres. The men were surgeons, at a convention in Mexico City. They were tennis-fit and tanned. Their wives were expensively dressed, but in that time warp doctors' wives have, wearing pantsuits fashionable back when they put their husbands through medical school. The women wore cheap black felt Spanish hats, with a red rose, that were sold on the streets as souvenirs. They thought they were "fun hats," not realizing how coquettish and pretty they looked in them.

There were four Japanese tourists. The Yamatos, an old couple in black traditional clothes. Their son, Jerry, a tall, handsome man in his forties, with a young Japanese bride, Deedee, dressed in American jeans and a sweatshirt. She and Jerry spoke English to each other, Japanese to his parents. She blushed when he kissed her neck or caught her fingers between his teeth.

It turned out that Jerry too was a Californian, an architect, Deedee a chemistry student in San Francisco. They would be in Mexico City for two more days. His parents had come from Tokyo to join them. No, they had never seen a bullfight, but Jerry thought it would seem very Japanese, combining what Mishima called Japanese qualities of elegance and brutality.

Jane was pleased that he should say something like that to her, almost a stranger, liked him immediately.

The three spoke about Mishima, and Mexico, as they all sat on leather sofas, waiting for the guide. Jane told the couple that she had spent her own honeymoon in Mexico City, too.

"It was wonderful," she said. "Magic. You could see the volcanoes then." Why do I keep thinking about Sebastian, anyway? I'll call him tonight, and tell him I went to the Plaza Mexico.

Señor Errazuriz looked like an old bullfighter himself, lean, regal. His too-long greasy hair curled in a perhaps unintentional *colita*. He introduced himself, asked them to relax, have a sangria while he told them a little about the *corridas*, gave a concise history and an explanation of what they were to expect. "The form of each *corrida* as timeless and precise as a musical score. But with each bull, the element of surprise."

He told them to take something warm, even though now it was a hot day. Obediently they all went for sweaters, got into an already crowded elevator. *Buenas tardes*. It is a custom in Mexico to greet people you join in an elevator, in line at the post office, in a waiting room. It makes waiting easier, actually, and in an elevator you don't have to stare straight ahead because now you have acknowledged one another.

They all got into a hotel van. The two women continued a conversation about a manic-depressive called Sabrina, begun back in Petaluma or Sausalito. The American doctors seemed ill at ease. The older Yamatos spoke softly in Japanese, looked down at their laps. Jerry and Deedee looked at each other, or smiled for photographs they had Jane take of them, in the hotel, in the van, in front of the fountain. The two doctors braked and cringed as the van sped down Insurgentes toward the plaza.

Jane sat in the front with Señor Errazuriz. They spoke in Spanish. He told her they were lucky to see Jorge Gutierrez today, the best matador in Mexico. There would also be a fine Spaniard, Roberto Dominguez, and a young Mexican making his debut, his *alternativa*, in the plaza, Alberto Giglio. Those aren't very romantic names, Jane commented, Gutierrez and Dominguez.

"They haven't earned an *apodo* like 'El Litri,'" he said.

Jerry caught Jane looking at him and his wife as they kissed. He smiled at her.

"Forgive me, I didn't mean to be rude," she said, but she was blushing too, like the girl.

"You must be thinking of your own honeymoon!" He grinned.

They parked the van near the stadium and a boy with a rag began washing the windows. Years ago there were parking meters in Mexico, but nobody collected the money or enforced the tickets. People used slugs or simply smashed the meters, as they did with the pay phones. So now the pay phones are free and there are no parking meters. But it seems as if each parking spot has its own private valet, who will watch your car, a boy appearing from nowhere.

Electric, exhilarating, the excitement of the crowd outside the plaza. "Feels like the World Series!" said one of the doctors. Stands sold tacos, posters, bulls' horns, capes, photographs of Dominguín, Juan Belmonte, Manolete. A huge bronze statue of El Armillita stood outside the arena. Some fans laid carnations at his feet. They had to bend down to do this, so it seemed as if they were genuflecting before him.

The groups' bags were searched by heavily armed security guards. All women, as were most of the guards all over Mexico. The entire Cuernavaca police force is female, Señor Errazuriz told Jane. Narcs, motorcycle cops, chief of police. Women are not so susceptible to bribery and corruption. Jerry said he had noticed how many women there were in public office, more than in the U.S.

"Of course. Our whole country is protected by the Virgin of Guadalupe!"

"Not that many female bullfighters, though?"

"A few. Good ones. But, really, it is for men to fight against the bulls."

Below in the plaza *monosabios* in red-and-white uniforms raked the sand. Pointillist whirls of color as the spectators climbed far up in the tiers to the blue circle of sky. Vendors carrying heavy buckets of beer and Coke scampered along the metal rims above the cement seats, ran up and down stairs as narrow as on the pyramid of Teotihuacan. The group looked at their programs, the photographs and statistics of the toreros, of the bulls from the Santiago herd.

Men in black leather suits, smoking cigars, *charros* in big hats and silver-decorated coats gathered around the *barrera*. Except for the two Spanish hats, their group was definitely underdressed. They had all come as for a ball game. Most of the Mexican and Spanish women were dressed casually, but as elegantly as possible, with heavy makeup and jewelry.

Their seats were in the shade. The plaza was perfectly divided into *sol y sombra*. The sun was bright.

At five minutes to four, six *monosabios* walked around the plaza bearing aloft a cloth banner painted with the message, "If anyone is surprised throwing cushions they will be fined."

At four o'clock the trumpets played the opening thrilling *paso doble*. "Carmen!" Mrs. Jordan cried. The gate opened and the procession began. First the *alguaciles*, two black-bearded men on Arabian horses, dressed in black, starched white ruffs, plumed hats. Their fine horses pranced and strutted and reared as they crossed the plaza. Just behind them were the three matadors in glittering suits of light, embroidered capes over their left shoulders. Dominguez in black, Gutierrez in turquoise, and Giglio in white. Behind each matador followed his *cuadrilla* of three men, also carrying elaborate capes. Then the fat picadors on padded, blindfolded horses, then the *monosabios* and *areneros*, in red and white. The men who actually removed the dead bulls were dressed in blue. In the last century in Madrid there was a popular group of trained monkeys performing in a theater, whose costumes were the same as the men who worked in the bullrings. They were called the Wise Monkeys—*monosabios*. The name stuck for the men in the *corridas*.

The toreros all wore salmon-colored stockings, ballet slippers which seemed incongruously flimsy. No, they have to feel the sand. Their feet are the most important part, Señor Errazuriz said. He noticed how Jane liked the colors and the clothes, the quilted, tufted upholsteries covering the picadors' horses. He told her that in Spain the matadors were starting to wear white stockings, but most true aficionados were against this.

A *monosabio* came out of the *torillo* gate and held up a wooden sign painted with CHIRUSIN 499 KILOS. The trumpet sounded and the bull burst into the ring.

The first *tercio* was beautiful. Giglio made graceful swirling *faenas*. His *traje de luces* sparkled and shimmered in the late sun, turning into an aura of light around him. Except for a rhythmic *olé* during the passes, the plaza was silent. You could hear Chirusín's hooves, his breath, the rustle of the pink cape. "*¡Torero!*" the crowd yelled, and the young bullfighter smiled, a guileless smile of pure joy. This was his debut and he was welcomed wildly by the fans. There were many whistles though, too, because the bull wasn't brave, Señor Errazuriz said. The trumpet sounded for the entrance of the picadors, and the *peones* danced the bull to the horse. It was undeniably lovely.

The Americans were lulled by the ballet-like grace of the bullfight, surprised and sickened when the picador began jabbing the long hook into the back of the bull's *morrillo*, again and again. Blood spurted thick and glistening red. The fans whistled, the entire arena was whistling. They always do, Señor Errazuriz said, but he doesn't stop until the matador says so. Giglio nodded and the trumpets played, signaling the next *tercio*. Giglio placed the three pairs of white *banderillas* himself, running lightly toward Chirusín, dancing, whirling in the center of the ring, just missing the horns as he stabbed them perfectly, symmetrically each time until there were six white banners above the flowing red blood. The Yamatos smiled.

Giglio was so graceful, so happy that everyone who watched felt delight. Still, it's a bad bull, dangerous, Señor Errazuriz said. The crowd gave the young man all their encouragement, he had such *trapío*, style. But he could not kill the bull. Once, twice, then again and again. Chirusín hemorrhaged from his mouth but would not fall. The *banderilleros* ran the bull in circles to hasten its death as Giglio plunged the sword still once more.

"Barbaric," Dr. McIntyre said. The two American surgeons rose as one, and took their wives away with them. The women in their pretty hats kept pausing on the steep stairway to look back. Señor Errazuriz said he would see them to a cab, and pay it of course. He would be right back.

The old Yamatos politely watched Chirusín die. The young couple was thrilled. The *corrida* was powerful, majestic to them. At last the bull lay down and died and Giglio withdrew the bloody sword. Mules dragged away the bull, to whistles and jeers from the crowd. They blamed the bad kill on the bull, not on the young matador. Jorge Gutierrez, his *padrino*, embraced Giglio.

There was a frenzy of activity before the next *corrida*. People ran up and down visiting, smoking, drinking beer, squirting wine into their mouths. Vendors sold *alegrías* and bright green oval pastries, pistachio nuts, pig skins, Domino's pizzas.

There was a warm breeze and Jane shuddered. A wave of the deepest fear came over her, a sense of impermanence. The entire plaza might disappear.

"You are cold," Jerry said. "Here, put on your sweater."

"Thanks," she said.

Deedee reached across Jerry's lap and touched Jane's arm. "We'll take you outside, if you want to leave."

"No, thank you. I think it must be the altitude."

"It gets to Jerry, too. He has a pacemaker; sometimes it's hard to breathe."

"You're still trembling," Jerry said. "Sure you're okay?"

The couple smiled at her with kindness. She smiled back,

but was still shaken by an awareness of our insignificance. Nobody even knew where she was.

"Oh, good, you're in time," she said when Señor Errazuriz returned.

"I don't understand it," he said. "I, myself, I can't watch American films. *Goodfellas*, *Miami Blues*. That is cruelty to me." He shrugged. To the Yamatos he apologized for the bulls from Santiago, as if they were a national embarrassment. The Japanese man was equally polite in his reassurances that on the contrary, they were grateful to be here. Bullfighting was a fine art, exquisite. It is a rite, Jane thought as the trumpet sounded. Not a performance, a sacrament to death.

The coliseum pulsated, throbbed with cries of Jorge, Jorge. Whistles and angry jeers at the judge. *Culero!* Asshole! Because he didn't get rid of the bull, Platero. *No se presta*, he doesn't lend himself, Señor Errazuriz said. In the second *tercio* the bull stumbled and fell, and then just sat there, as if he just didn't feel like getting up. "*¡La Golondrina! ¡La Golondrina!*" a group in the sunny section chanted.

Señor Errazuriz said that was a song about swallows leaving, a farewell song. "They're saying, 'Good-bye with this *pinche* bull!'" Jorge was obviously disgusted, and decided to kill Platero as soon as possible. But he couldn't. Like Giglio before him he bounced the sword off the bull, jabbed it too high, too far back. Finally the animal died. The bullfighter left the ring downcast, humiliated. The continued chants of "*torero*" from his loyal fans must have felt like mockery. The *monosabios* and mules came for Platero, who was dragged away to whistles and curses, thousands of flying cushions.

Whereas Giglio had been lyrical and Gutierrez formal, authoritative, the young Spaniard, Dominguez, was fiery and defiant, sweeping the bull Centenario after him across the sand, flaring his cape like a peacock. He stood with pelvis arched inches from the bull. *Olé, olé.* The matador and bull swirled like water plants. The picadors entered the ring, the *banderilleros* took turns. Capes swaying, they lured the bull toward the horse. The bull attacked the belly of the horse. Again and again the picador thrust the spear into the bull. Furious, then, the bull pawed the sand, his head lowered, then thundered toward the nearest *banderillero.*

At that moment a man leaped into the field. He was young, dressed in jeans and a white shirt, carrying a red shawl. He raced past the subalterns, faced the bull, and executed a lovely pass. *Olé.* The entire plaza was in an uproar, cheering and whistling, throwing hats. "*¡Un espontáneo!*" Two policemen in gray flannel suits jumped into the arena and chased after the man, running clumsily in the sand in their high-heeled boots. Dominguez gracefully fought the bull whenever it came his way. Centenario thought it was a party, jumped up and down like a playful labrador, charged first a *subalterno,* then a guard, then a horse, then the man's red shawl. Wham—he tried to knock over a picador, then raced to get the two policemen, knocking them both down, wounding one, crushing his foot. All three subalterns were chasing the man, but stopped and waited each time the man fought the bull.

"*¡El Espontáneo! ¡El Espontáneo!*" cried the crowd, but more police entered and tossed him over the *barrera* to waiting handcuffs. He was taken into custody. There was a stiff sentence and fine for "spontaneous ones," Señor Errazuriz said, otherwise people would do it all the time. But the crowds kept cheering for him as the wounded guard was carried away and the picadors left, to the music.

Dominguez was going to dedicate the bull. He asked the judge permission to dedicate it to the *espontáneo,* and for him to be set free. It was granted. The man was taken out of handcuffs. He leapt the *barrera* again, this time to accept the bullfighter's *montera*, and to embrace him. Hats and jackets sailed from the stands to his feet. He bowed, with the grace of a torero, jumped the fence, and climbed way, way up into the sunny stands, up by the clock. Meanwhile the *banderilleros* were distracting the bull, who was totally ruined now, like a hyperactive child, careening around the ring, ramming his horns into the wooden fence and the *burladeros* where the *cuadrilla* hid. Still everyone merrily sang "*¡El Espontáneo!*" Even the old Japanese were shouting it! The young couple were laughing, hugging each other. What a glorious, dazzling confusion.

Dominguez was denied a change of bull, but managed to fight the nervous animal with spirit and much daring, since Centenario had become erratic and angry. Whenever he tried to kill the bull, it shied and jumped. Catch me if you can! So again there were repeated bloody stabbings in the wrong places.

Jane thought that Jerry was yelling at the matador, but he had simply cried out, tried to stand. He fell onto the cement stairs. His head had cracked against the cement, was bleeding red into his black hair. Deedee knelt on the stairs next to him.

"It's too soon," she said.

Jane sent a guard for a doctor. Jerry's parents knelt side by side on the step above him while vendors scurried up and down past them. With a hysterical giggle Jane noticed that whereas in the States a crowd would have gathered, no one in the plaza took their eyes from the ring, where Giglio fought a new bull, Navegante.

The doctor arrived as just below them the picador was stabbing the bull, to fierce whistles and protests. Sweating, the little man waited until the noise abated, abstractedly holding Jerry's hand. When the picadors left he said to Deedee, "He is dead." But she knew that, his parents knew. The old man held his wife as they looked down on him. They looked at their son with sorrow. Deedee had turned him over. His face had an amused expression, his eyes were half-open. Deedee smiled down at him. A raincoat vendor covered him with blue plastic. "Thank you," Deedee said.

"Five thousand pesos, please."

Olé, olé. Giglio whirled in the ring, the *banderillas* poised above his head. With an undulating zigzag he danced toward the bull. Two women guards came. They couldn't get a gurney down the steps, one of them told Jane. They would have to wait until the *corrida* was over to bring one to the *callejón*, then his body could be lifted over the *barrera*. No problem. They would come as soon as they could get through. Another guard told Jerry's parents they had to return to their seats, they might be hurt. Obediently the elderly couple sat down. They waited, whispering. Señor Errazuriz spoke to them gently and they nodded, although they didn't understand. Deedee held her husband's head in her lap. She gripped Jane's hand, stared unseeing into the ring where Giglio was exchanging swords for the kill. Jane spoke with the ambulance driver, translated for Deedee, took the American Express card from Jerry's wallet.

"Has he been very ill?" Jane asked Deedee.

"Yes," she whispered. "But we thought there was more time."

Jane and Deedee embraced, the armrest between them pressing into their bodies like sadness.

"Too soon," Deedee said again.

The plaza was on its feet. Jorge had given Giglio an extra bull, Genovés, as a present for his *alternativa.* Before the next *corrida*, *areneros* in blue, with wheelbarrows, came to cover up the blood in the sand, others raked it smooth. The plaza was empty when the gurney wheeled up below the *barrera.* Meet us in front, the medics said, but Deedee refused to leave him. It took a long time to move Jerry's body, and to get him down through the now frenzied crowd and onto the gurney. Once in the *callejón* outside of the ring they kept having to wait, move out of the way of running *banderilleros*, of the man with water bottles to wet the red cape, the *mozo de las espadas*, the man who carried the swords. Indignant shouts at Deedee, because she was a woman, a taboo in the *callejón*.

Señor Errazuriz and Jane accompanied the old couple on the far, far climb to the top of the plaza. Giglio had killed Genovés with one perfect thrust. He was awarded two ears and a tail. The brave bull was being dragged triumphantly around the place to cries of "*¡Toro! ¡Toro!*" People spilled onto the narrow steps, many drunk, all ecstatic. The *alguacil* was walking across the sand to Giglio, carrying the ears and the tail.

Jane walked behind the Yamatos. Señor Errazuriz and a guard led the way to the blare of trumpets, deafening shouts of "*Torero, torero.*" Roses and carnations and hats flew through the air, darkening the sky.

LUNA NUEVA

The sun set with a hiss as the wave hit the beach. The woman continued up the checkered black and gold tiles of the *malecón* to the cliffs on the hill. Other people resumed walking too, once the sun had set, like spectators leaving a play. It isn't just the beauty of the tropical sunset, she thought, the importance of it. In Oakland the sun set into the Pacific each evening and it was the end of another day. When you travel you step back from your own days, from the fragmented imperfect linearity of your time. As when reading a novel, the events and people become allegorical and eternal. The boy whistles on a wall in Mexico. Tess leans her head against a cow. They will keep doing that forever; the sun will just keep on falling into the sea.

She walked onto a platform above the cliffs. The magenta sky reflected iridescent in the water. Below the cliffs a vast swimming pool had been built of stones into the jagged rock. Waves shattered against the far walls and spilled into the pool, scattering crabs. A few boys swam in the deeper water, but most people waded or sat on the mossy rocks.

The woman climbed down the rocks to the water. She took off the shift covering her bathing suit and sat on the slippery wall with the others. They watched as the sky faded and a new orange moon appeared in the mauve sky. *¡La luna!* people cried. *¡Luna nueva!* The evening grew dark and the orange moon turned to gold. The foam cascading into the pool was a sharp metallic white; the clothes of the bathers flowed eerie white as if under a strobe light.

Most of the bathers in the silver pool were fully clothed. Many of them had come from the mountains or ranchos far away; their baskets lay in piles on the rocks.

And they couldn't swim, so it was nice to lie suspended in the pool, for the waves to rock them and swirl them back and forth. When the breakers covered the wall it didn't seem that they were in a pool at all, but in their own calm eddy in the middle of the ocean.

Streetlights came on above them against the palms on the *malecón*. The lights glowed like amber lanterns on their intricate wrought-iron poles. The water in the pool reflected the lights over and over, first whole, then into dazzling fragments, then whole again like full moons under the tiny moon in the sky.

The woman dove into the water. The air was cool, the water warm and salty. Crabs raced over her feet, the stones underfoot were velvety and jagged. She remembered only then being in that pool many years ago, before her children could swim. A sharp memory of her husband's eyes looking at her across the pool. He held one of their sons as she swam with the other in her arms. No pain accompanied the sweetness of this recollection. No loss or regret or foretaste of death. Gabriel's eyes. Her sons' laughter, echoing from the cliffs into the water.

The bathers' voices ricocheted too, from the stone. Ah! they cried, as at fireworks, when the young boys dove into the water. They swayed in their white clothes. It was festive, with the clothes swirling, as if they were waltzing at a ball. Beneath them, the sea made delicate traceries on the sand. A young couple knelt in the water. They didn't touch, but were so in love it seemed to the woman that tiny darts and arrows shot out into the water from them, like fireflies or phosphorescent fish. They wore white clothes, but seemed naked against the dark sky. Their clothes clung to their black bodies, to his strong shoulders and loins, her breasts and belly. When the waves flowed in and ebbed out, her long hair floated up and covered them in tendrils of black fog and then subsided black and inky into the water.

A man wearing a straw hat asked the woman if she would take his babies out into the water. He handed her the smallest one, who was frightened. It slipped up through the woman's arms like a skittish baboon and climbed onto her head, tearing at her hair, coiling its legs and tail around her neck. She untangled herself from the screaming baby. "Take the other one, the tame one," the man said, and that child did lie placidly while she swam with it in the water. So quiet she thought it must be asleep, but no, it was humming. Other people sang and hummed in the cool night. The sliver of moon turned white like the foam as more people came down the stairs into the water. After a while the man took the baby from her and left then, with his children.

On the rocks a girl tried to coax her grandmother into the pool. "No! No! I'll fall!"

"Come in," the woman said, "I'll take you swimming all around the pool."

"You see I broke my leg and I'm afraid I'll break it again."

"When did it happen?" the woman asked.

"Ten years ago. It was a terrible time. I couldn't chop firewood. I couldn't work in the fields. We had no food."

"Come in. I'll be careful of your leg."

At last the old lady let her lift her down from the rock and into the water. She laughed, clasping her frail arms around the woman's neck. She was light, like a bag of shells. Her hair smelled of charcoal fires. "*¡Qué maravilla!*" she whispered into the woman's throat. Her silver braid wafted out behind them in the water.

She was seventy-eight and had never seen the ocean before. She lived on a rancho near Chalchihuites. She had ridden on the back of a truck to the seaport with her granddaughter.

"My husband died last month."

"*Lo siento.*"

She swam with the old lady to the far wall where the cool waves spilled over them.

"God finally took him, finally answered my prayers. Eight years he lay in bed. Eight years he couldn't talk, couldn't get up or feed himself. Lay like a baby. I would ache from being tired, my eyes would burn. At last, when I thought he was asleep I would try to steal away. He would whisper my name, a horrid croaking sound. *¡Consuelo! ¡Consuelo!* And his skeleton hands, dead lizard hands would claw out to me. It was a terrible, terrible time."

"*Lo siento,*" the woman said again.

"Eight years. I could go nowhere. Not even to the corner. *¡Ni hasta la esquina!* Every night I prayed to the Virgin to take him, to give me some time, some days without him."

The woman clasped the old lady and swam out again into the pool, holding the frail body close to her.

"My mother died only six months ago. It was the same for me. A terrible, terrible time. I was tied to her day and night. She didn't know me and said ugly things to me, year after year, clawing at me."

Why am I telling this old lady such a lie? she wondered. But it wasn't such a lie, the bloody grasp.

"They're gone now," Consuelo said. "We are liberated."

The woman laughed; *liberated* was such an American word. The old lady thought she laughed because she was happy. She hugged the woman tightly and kissed her cheek. She had no teeth so the kiss was soft as mangos.

"The Virgin answered my prayers!" she said. "It pleases God, to see that you and I are free."

Back and forth the two women flowed in the dark water, the clothes of the bathers swirling around them like a ballet. Near them the young couple kissed, and for a moment there was a sprinkle of stars overhead, then a mist covered them and the moon and dimmed the opal lamplight from the street.

"*¡Vamos a comer, abuelita!*" the granddaughter called. She shivered, her dress dripping on the stones. A man lifted the old woman from the water, carried her up the winding rocks to the *malecón.* Mariachis played, far away.

"*¡Adiós!*" The old woman waved from the parapet.

"*¡Adiós!*"

The woman waved back. She floated at the far edge in the silken warm water. The breeze was inexpressibly gentle.

THE WRITING

Lucia Berlin (1936–2004; pronunciation: Lu-see-a) published seventy-six short stories during her lifetime. Most, but not all, were collected in three volumes from Black Sparrow Press: *Homesick* (1991), *So Long* (1993), and *Where I Live Now* (1999). These gathered from previous collections of 1980, 1984, and 1987, and presented newer work.

Publication commenced when she was twenty-four, in Saul Bellow's journal *The Noble Savage* and in *The New Strand*. Later stories appeared in *Atlantic Monthly*, *New American Writing*, and countless smaller magazines. *Homesick* won an American Book Award.

Berlin worked brilliantly but sporadically throughout the 1960s, 1970s, and most of the 1980s. By the late '80s, her four sons were grown and she had overcome a long-term problem with alcoholism (her accounts of its horrors, its drunk tanks and DTs and occasional hilarity, occupy a particular corner of her work). Thereafter she remained productive up to the time of her early death.

THE LIFE

Berlin was born Lucia Brown in Alaska in 1936. Her father was in the mining industry and her earliest years were spent in the mining camps and towns of Idaho, Kentucky, and Montana.

In 1942, Berlin's father went off to the war, and her mother moved Lucia and her younger sister to El Paso, where their grandfather was a prominent, but besotted, dentist.

Soon after the war, Berlin's father moved the family to Santiago, Chile, and she embarked on what would become twenty-five years of a rather flamboyant existence. In Santiago, she attended cotillions and balls, had her first cigarette lit by Prince Aly Khan, finished school, and served as the default hostess for her father's society gatherings. Most evenings, her mother retired early with a bottle.

By the age of ten, Lucia had scoliosis, a painful spinal condition that became lifelong and often necessitated a steel brace.

In 1954 she enrolled at the University of New Mexico. By now fluent in Spanish, she studied with the novelist Ramón Sender. She soon married and had two sons. By the birth of the second, her sculptor husband was gone. Berlin completed her degree and, still in Albuquerque, met the poet Edward Dorn, a key figure in her life. She also met Dorn's teacher from Black Mountain College, the writer Robert Creeley, and two of his Harvard classmates, Race Newton and Buddy Berlin, both jazz musicians. And she began to write.

Newton, a pianist, married Berlin in 1958. (Her earliest stories appeared under the name Lucia Newton.) The next year, they and the children moved to a loft in New York. Race worked steadily and the couple became friends with their neighbors Denise Levertov and Mitchell Goodman, as well as other poets and artists including John Altoon, Diane di Prima, and Amiri Baraka (then LeRoi Jones).

In 1961, Berlin and her sons left Newton and New York, and traveled with their friend Buddy Berlin to Mexico, where he became her third husband. Buddy was charismatic and affluent, but he also proved to be an addict. During the years 1961–68, two more sons were born.

By 1968, the Berlins were divorced and Lucia was working on a master's degree at the University of New Mexico. She was employed as a substitute teacher. She never remarried.

The years 1971–94 were spent in Berkeley and Oakland, California. Berlin worked as a high school teacher, cleaning woman, switchboard operator, and physician's assistant, while writing, raising her four sons, drinking, and finally, prevailing over her alcoholism. She spent much of 1991 and 1992 in Mexico City, where her sister was dying of cancer. Her mother had died in 1986, a probable suicide.

In 1994, Edward Dorn brought Berlin to the University of Colorado, and she spent the next six years in Boulder as a visiting writer and, ultimately, associate professor. She became a remarkably popular and beloved teacher, and in just her second year, won the university's award for teaching excellence.

During the Boulder years she thrived in a close community that included Dorn and his wife, Jennifer, Anselm Hollo, and her old pal Bobbie Louise Hawkins. The poet Kenward Elmslie became, like myself, a fast friend.

Her health failing (the scoliosis had led to a punctured lung, and by the mid-1990s she was never without an oxygen tank), she retired in 2000 and the next year moved to Los Angeles to live with her son Dan. She fought a courageous battle against cancer, but died in 2004, in Marina del Rey.

POSTSCRIPT

In 2015, eleven years after Lucia's death, *A Manual for Cleaning Women: Selected Stories* was published. It became a bestseller and was named one of *The New York Times Book Review*'s Ten Best Books of 2015. The Spanish edition, from Alfaguara, was named Book of the Year by *El País* (Madrid). Editions are out or in the works in thirty countries. New readers are discovering her work every day.

—Stephen Emerson*

Connect online:
www.readlucia.com • www.facebook.com/readlucia
twitter.com/readluciaberlin • www.instagram.com/readlucia

* "A Note on Lucia Berlin" reprinted by permission from *A Manual for Cleaning Women.*

ACKNOWLEDGMENTS

Thank you.

Especially to Katherine Fausset, Emily Bell, and Barbara Adamson.

This book wouldn't exist without the publication of *A Manual for Cleaning Women*. Thank you to FSG.

Stephen Emerson, Barry Gifford, and Michael Wolfe, who spearheaded the effort to republish Lucia's work. Extra thanks and deep appreciation go to Stephen Emerson, whose extraordinary work and care made *A Manual for Cleaning Women* the great book that it is.

Lydia Davis, for writing the foreword to *A Manual for Cleaning Women*, the best we've ever read.

Jennifer Dunbar Dorn and Gayle Davies.

At Curtis Brown: Katherine Fausset, Holly Frederick, Sarah Gerton, Olivia D. Simkins, Madeline R. Tavis, and Stuart Waterman.

At FSG: Emily Bell, Stephen Weil, Amber Hoover, Devon Mazzone, Naoise McGee, and Jackson Howard.

Friends (old and new): Keith Abbott, Staci Amend, Karen Auvinen, Fred Buck, Tom Clark, Robert Creeley, Dave Cullen, Steve Dickison, Ed Dorn, Maria Fasce, Joan Frank, Ruth Franklin, Gloria Frym, Marvin Granlund, Anselm Hollo, Elizabeth

Geoghegan, Sidney Goldfarb, Bobbie Louise Hawkins, Laird Hunt, Chris Jackson, Steve Katz, August Kleinzahler, Erika Krouse, Steven Lavoie, Chip Livingston, Kelly Luce, Jonathan Mack, Elizabeth McCracken, Peter Michelson, Dave Mulholland, Jim Nisbet, Ulrike Ostermeyer, Kellie Paluck, Mimi Pond, Joe Safdie, Jenny Shank, Lyndsy Spence, Oscar van Gelderen, David Yoo, and Paula Younger.

The publishers of the previous books: Michael Myers and Holbrook Teter (Zephyrus Image), Eileen and Bob Callahan (Turtle Island), Michael Wolfe (Tombouctou), Alastair Johnston (Poltroon), and John Martin and David Godine (Black Sparrow).

The family: Buddy, Mark, David, Dan, C. J., Nicolas, Truman, Cody, Molly, Monica, Andrea, Patricio, Jill, Jonathan, Josie, Pao, Nacé, Barbara, Paul, Race, and Jill Magruder Gatwood. Much love.

—Jeff Berlin